PHANTOM WARRIORS
BUNDLE 2

JORDAN SUMMERS

PHANTOM WARRIORS: SABER-TOOTH

Katy Manfred is tired of being assigned to wild goose chases. This latest job is no exception. Her boss wants her to go to La Brea Tar Pits to trap a saber-tooth tiger. Talk about an impossible task! They haven't existed for over eleven thousand years.

Kegar knew he shouldn't have shape-shifted and snuck off the spaceship, but he was eager to begin his search for a mate. The last thing he expected was to be shot in the flank by a beautiful blonde bent on making a science project out of him.

Awake and naked in his human form, Kegar finds the woman of his dreams bending over him. What's a feline in heat to do? Why pounce of course. He only has a few hours to convince this sexy tracker that she's his mate. It'll take all of Kegar's sensual skills to bring out the hidden wild cat in Katy. Lucky for her, he's more than *up* to the task.

PHANTOM WARRIORS: TALON

Lynn Regis wasn't looking for anything but her newly released condors, when she hiked into the Grand Canyon National Park. The last thing the plus-sized beauty expected to find was a sexy as sin man, with eyes as sharp as a hawk, bent on seducing her.

Talon knew Lynn was mate material the moment he laid eyes on her. With only three days to convince that they're meant for each other, this determined raptor will have to use every strategy in his well-stocked, sensual arsenal. Good thing Phantom Warriors always come prepared.

PHANTOM WARRIORS: RIOT

Veterinarian Nina Whitetail's world is falling apart. Her beloved grandfather is dying, her best-friend is getting married and plans to move away, and someone is hunting bears out of season. Nina can't do anything about the first two problems, but she's determined to stop the poachers. The encounter doesn't go well and she has to run for her life. In the confusion, Nina stumbles upon the Great Bear from Cherokee mythology…or so she thinks.

Nina knows there's more than magic happening, when the bear speaks and shape-shifts into an alarmingly large man determined to seduce her. Suddenly Nina is torn between love, loyalty, and a future amongst the stars.

Riot has always been different from his Phantom Warrior brethren. His size and strength make finding a mate nearly impossible, especially when they all scream and run away. Nina is the exception. She thinks he's the Great Bear. Riot doesn't have the heart to correct her, until she asks him to save her grandfather. By then, it's too late. Riot's in love. Even with all their power and strength, a Phantom Warrior cannot cheat death. If he admits the truth, it will shatter their fragile bond and he'll lose his only chance at happiness. If Riot doesn't tell her, he'll lose her trust and her love. Either way, he loses.

PHANTOM
WARRIORS
Sabertooth
JORDAN
SUMMERS

"A saber-tooth tiger has been spotted at the famous La Brea Tar Pits," the television announcer said, his voice filled with excitement and more than a little skepticism.

Katy Manfred did a double take at the screen as the news station moved its feed from the studio to a live shot from a hovering helicopter over downtown Los Angeles. She saw a flash of brownish red move across the screen, but it was too fast to catch what it was before it disappeared beneath the thick foliage.

It had to be some kind of joke. A saber-tooth tiger? *Puleaseee.* Those cats lived in the Cenozoic period before the Holocene and had been extinct for over eleven thousand years. Katy snickered. Someone should probably inform the press.

Katy shook her head, sending strawberry blonde hair into her face. She pulled the hair tie off her wrist and swept her shoulder-length bob into a quick ponytail. She didn't bother checking in the mirror to see if it was straight. Katy didn't care.

The camera filming the famous tar pits, where several prehistoric bones had been recovered, swung wildly in an attempt to catch the fleeing animal. So far, other than the flash of movement, which could've been an obese squirrel, they hadn't managed to film anything but trees. The camera swung around again. A crowd of people stood on the sidewalk waving and pointing.

Katy laughed. Everyone in L.A. wanted their fifteen minutes of fame. This had to be a publicity stunt. She tried to recall the upcoming filming schedules she'd read about in the popular movie industry rag, but nothing came to mind. Katy turned away from the television, muting the sound just as the phone rang.

"Manfred here." She paused to listen. "Yes, I saw the news."

"I want you to try to get to the La Brea Tar Pits before animal control arrives," Roger Sylvan said.

"They're already there. I spotted their truck when the cameras tried to capture the cat on film."

"Then I suggest you hurry. You need to catch the animal before they do."

"Are you sure you want me to do that, sir? Animal control doesn't like the private sector stepping on their toes. I'm sure they can handle the situation. I doubt very much that it's a saber-tooth tiger," Katy said.

"I don't pay you to question my orders, Manfred. Get down there now. If there's even a remote chance this thing is real, I want Bio Tech to possess it. Do whatever it takes."

"You're the boss," she said through gritted teeth.

"And don't you forget it," Roger said. Like he'd ever let her. There was a click and the line went dead.

Katy hung up the phone, then strode across the living room of her Santa Monica bungalow. The place wasn't much, but it was all she had left of her parents. Despite the years that had gone by since the boat fire, loneliness still plagued her. The loss was as painful today as it had been when the accident occurred. Katy pushed her pain aside. She had a job to do and couldn't afford the distraction.

She glanced at the television once more. The cameraman was still trying to catch the feline on film. She hit the power button and watched the screen dim. Going to La Brea Tar Pits was a total waste of time. Katy knew it and so did her boss, Roger Sylvan. He'd been sending her out on wild goose chases for the past few months in an attempt to get her to quit. This was what she got for dating her boss.

At first, she'd been was too stubborn to concede, but lately Katy had come to realize her resistance had more to do with the fact that she had nowhere else to go. She punched in a code on her wall and a hatch popped open, displaying her pistol. Strapping on her weapon, she headed for the front door.

Katy grabbed a canvas bag that remained packed at all times, unzipping it to ensure she had extra ammo. The dart guns and snares were already in her truck, along with a tarp covering and a reinforced net. The zoo hadn't reported any big cats missing, but there were always private owners. It was probably somebody's scared lion. The rich and their pets. She shook her head in disgust.

Didn't they know these types of animals could never be tamed? How many times had she had to put down a cornered half-crazed animal just to keep it from hurting nearby humans? Too damn many. Renewed anger surged through her. These people had no business keeping predators in the middle of a city the size of Los Angeles. Once Katy caught this cat, she'd tell them so. It was her job to clean up other people's messes. Someone was going to get their ass kicked if she had to shoot a cat today.

Katy shoved the truck in reverse and backed out of her driveway. She heard brakes screech and the blast of a horn. She didn't care. She needed to get to La Brea Tar Pits and fast. The ride there was slow going at best, thanks to L.A.'s typical traffic flow of slow, slowest and crawl.

She considered taking to the sidewalks, but decided against it. The cat would probably hunker down somewhere in the brush until nightfall, and then make its escape. Hell, that's what she would do in its place.

Forty minutes later, she pulled into the heavily shaded parking area at La Brea Tar Pits as several police cars exited. The crowd seemed to have dissipated somewhat, leaving only a few hardcore lookie loos around.

Katy shut the door of her truck, then strapped on the holster for her dart gun, slipping the weapon into place. She moved to her tailgate to ensure the cage and tarp were in order before approaching the people.

"Where's animal control?" she asked no one in particular.

A man stepped forward. "They left, since they couldn't find any trace of the animal. One had the nerve to suggest we were making up the whole thing to drum up business."

"Were you?" Katy asked.

"No," he said. "And I resent the accusation."

Grumbles echoed throughout the crowd.

Katy debated whether to get back in her truck and go home. If animal control hadn't been able to locate the cat, then she didn't think she'd have much better luck. Sure, she was a good tracker—great even, but it was next to impossible to track animals in a concrete jungle. She supposed it wouldn't hurt to ask if anyone had seen anything before she left.

"Anyone know where the cat went?" Katy searched the faces around her, but most refused to make eye contact.

"You aren't going to kill it, are you?" someone called out.

The last thing Katy wanted to do was destroy the animal, but sometimes she didn't have a choice. "Not if I can avoid it," she said noncommittally.

A little boy pushed his way through the small crowd, then signaled for her to crouch down so that he could whisper in her ear. "I know where it went."

"Petey, get back here this instant." A frantic mother shoved her way to the front in search of her son.

"Where is he, Petey?" Katy used the child's name in hopes it would reassure him enough to answer.

Petey glanced at his mom, then grabbed Katy's hand and tugged her away from the other people. "I don't want anyone else to hear. The kitty told me to keep it a secret."

Katy frowned. "The kitty told you not to say anything?"

The little mop-topped boy nodded his head, sending brown curls cascading into his face. "Mommy doesn't believe me, but you do, don't you?" he asked, his lower lip starting to tremble.

Katy cupped his cheek and smiled. As a child, she'd been convinced she could talk to the animals. She still remembered the pain and humiliation the kids in school inflicted with their "crazy Katy" taunts. "Of course I believe you. Now show me where he is." She nodded to his mother to let her know everything was okay.

Petey beamed, then dragged her down a path that wound around some of the outbuildings associated with the facility. "He's over there under those bushes." He pointed to an area off the path that dipped slightly into a small ditch.

She couldn't immediately see anything, but that didn't mean the cat wasn't there. "Thank you, Petey. You've been very helpful."

Katy glanced over her shoulder and saw the child's mother waiting, a concerned expression on her face. She motioned for her son to join her, while her gaze scanned the bushes.

"You'd better get going," Katy said. "Your mom's worried about you."

He smiled, showing a missing front tooth. "She worries about everything," he said, rolling his eyes.

"That's her job. Now scoot." Katy rumpled his hair, then sent him on his way. She needed Petey and everyone else to stay clear of the area. Predators were unpredictable, especially when cornered. She didn't want to take the chance of an innocent bystander getting hurt, especially a child, and she damn well didn't want to have to put the animal down in front of an audience.

She inched closer, dart gun in hand, her eyes searching the shadows for movement. A warm breeze filtered through her hair, tearing a few strawberry blonde wisps out of her ponytail. She reached up, tucking the errant strands behind her ear.

Traffic sounds faded, giving way to the rustling of leaves in the trees. Even the birds had suddenly gone quiet. Katy knew something hunted her. She crouched lower and blinked. Intelligent green eyes stared unflinchingly back at her.

No way in hell. Her mind refused to acknowledge what she was looking at. Even as denial fluttered through her head, Katy knew there was no mistake. It *was* a saber-tooth tiger, or cat, as the scientific community more accurately labeled them, since the animals were only distantly related to tigers and close cousins to the lion.

Lying under a branch of the farthest bush, panting in the warm Southern California heat, the cat yawned, displaying his seven-inch serrated teeth. Despite the imminent danger, she took a step closer to get a better look.

The cat didn't move. It seemed to be studying her as closely as she studied it.

Katy knew it was impossible, but she couldn't shake the feeling of intelligent awareness that the animal conveyed. It was almost like it was thinking, trying to puzzle her out. She shook her head at her own foolishness. The cat was smart, but it didn't have awareness beyond the primal. She was a meal to the animal and nothing more. Displacing her emotions and putting them on the cat was something Katy hadn't done since she was a kid.

She stared at the cat, taking care not to look it directly in the eyes. The last thing Katy needed was for it to interpret her intentions as a challenge for dominance.

She took in the cat's appearance as it lounged on its side,

watching her. Tufts of white hair surrounded his massive twelve-inch head and accented his muscular legs and belly much like the tigers of modern day. Yet, the stripes on his body were different, less pronounced. Almost as if they were a genetic afterthought.

Shorter than a lion, but still huge up close, the cat easily weighed in at a thousand pounds of solid muscle, doubling the King of the Jungle's body mass and then some. His fangs, which looked more like tusks, hung down like a walrus over his mouth. The lethal weapons could easily gut the largest land-based mammal on the planet.

He truly was the find of the century. At least she thought it was a he. Katy glanced at the juncture between his sinewy legs and her eyes bulged. Yep, definitely a he. This big cat was going to make some female tiger or lion, depending on his genetics, very happy indeed. Katy radioed for assistance, then raised the dart gun and aimed at the animal's flank.

Don't do it! The command slammed into her mind.

It was so loud that she actually reached for the side of her head to cover her ears and almost dropped her gun. Where did that come from? Katy carefully glanced around, keeping one eye trained on the cat at all times.

Tigers and other big cats had a reputation for jumping their prey from behind. Logic told her that the saber-tooth might react the same way. She didn't want to give it any kind of opening, since all the scientific research done on this animal to date was based on theory, not fact.

She gave one final glance over her shoulder. The path behind her was clear of people. Weird. She could've sworn that whoever shouted was nearby.

Katy raised the gun again.

Please don't. The voice said, but this time it came as a request, not a command.

She frowned, ignoring her quivering fingers. Didn't they say that the first sign of schizophrenia was hearing voices? Petey's innocent words came rushing back to her. He'd said the cat spoke to him. Was that what was happening now?

"Are you talking to me?" she asked aloud, feeling more than a little ridiculous.

The cat simply stared at her in that bored kitty kind of way.

"Of course you're not." She shook her head at her own foolishness. Katy aimed the dart gun and fired.

An outraged bellow echoed in her head before quickly tapering as the cat drifted off to sleep. The sound left Katy shaken.

Her backup arrived in time to help her load the saber-tooth into the cage on her truck. Katy threw the tarp over the cage and shut the tailgate, then slipped behind the wheel. She looked over her shoulder at the cat and trembled under the enormity of her find. Her orders were to head straight to the compound that Bio Tech used to temporarily house the animals that she trapped. The company would notify the owners after their staff vets thoroughly examined the beast and collected whatever reward had been offered.

If the animal went unclaimed by its owners, the company would use the creature for genetic research. Katy went out of her way to make sure all animals she brought in were claimed, even if it took her weeks to hunt down the owners. Unfortunately, the discovery of a saber-tooth fell into a different category altogether. There was no way Bio Tech would hand over the cat to anyone without a fight.

"I need you guys to draw some of the media attention away, while I take the cat to the lab. Throw the tarps over the cages in the back of your trucks, so they don't know which one of us has the animal," she said.

"We were told to stay by your side," the one guard said. "And that's what we intend to do."

Katy knew she shouldn't be surprised that they'd been ordered to escort her, but she was. Since when had she become so untrustworthy? She faced the men. "Do you really want to bring reporters down on top of Roger Sylvan and Bio Tech?"

As expected, their eyes rounded at the mention of her ex's name and they shook their heads. The men were well aware of the value of her find and didn't want to do anything to endanger their positions at the company.

"Didn't think so," Katy said. "Now get going."

The security team threw the tarps over the cages in their trucks, then jumped into their vehicles and sped away, fishtailing out of the parking lot. With any luck, the media would follow them.

She started the engine and reversed out of the parking lot into the main thoroughfare. Katy glanced into the back of the truck, catching glimpses of the sleeping cat under the tarp as the wind lifted the material. He really was the find of the century.

Suddenly, taking him to the compound didn't seem like such a good idea. If she did that, there was a good chance Roger would take all the credit for the discovery. The news choppers circled above, filming her departure, instead of following the decoys. It wasn't like the cat would remain a secret for long.

Katy wanted credit for this discovery. Receiving credit would be the only way she could leave Bio Tech and land another job. Yet even with that knowledge, for some reason she couldn't bring herself to share him right away.

The connection she felt with the big cat burned in her mind. Logically, Katy knew it was crazy to think the cat had been talking to her, but no matter how hard she tried she couldn't seem to get the masculine voice out of her mind. She needed to get her thoughts straight and there was only one place to do it.

She threw the truck in gear and headed for her home. There she'd examine him further to ensure he wasn't a hoax. Katy didn't really have a place for a large cat, but it wasn't like she'd take him out of the cage. That cage was the only thing keeping him from ripping her arm off. Well, the cage and the dart in his muscled flank. The tension in her neck eased a fraction. With the drugs in the animal's system, he was no danger to anyone—at least for a little while.

Katy drove, trying to ignore the choppers following her down the freeway. The last thing she wanted was for people to camp out on her lawn in hopes of catching a glimpse of the cat. Katy took as many side streets as she could.

She'd just about given up trying to shake the pesky reporters, when a broadcast concerning a high-speed police chase on the 405 freeway interrupted the music. The choppers veered off in search of the next hot story. Katy's shoulders slumped and she let out a long breath she hadn't realized she'd been holding.

She glanced into the back of the truck, unable to see the animal. "You and I finally have a little privacy," she murmured, then continued home.

* * * * *

Chapter Two

Forty minutes later, Katy pulled into her driveway and drove straight into her garage. She pressed a button on her visor and watched the door slowly lower, before killing the engine. Katy leaned down, resting her head on the steering wheel for a few moments as she considered the ramifications of this discovery and her departure from protocol.

She knew she could be fired over this incident and in all likelihood would be. It didn't matter that she was the best tracker this side of the Rockies or that she'd dated Roger for a time. The latter would only hurt her chances of keeping her employment. And today, she'd inadvertently given Roger the excuse he needed to terminate her.

So why did she feel so compelled to see this through? It made no sense. Yet, she couldn't ignore the little voice inside her head, driving her on, telling Katy that time was almost up.

She straightened. It was too late now. Katy thought about the animal in the cage. People from all over would come to study this cat and take blood, along with sperm samples. They'd want to know where he came from and if there were any more cats out there like him.

The last question brought Katy up short. Where *had* he come from? It's not like they'd been living in the Hollywood Hills and no one had noticed them until now. Did someone dump him off? That made no sense either. How would you transport a cat that size without being seen? It wasn't possible. And if someone had managed it, why hadn't they come forward with their discovery? It would be worldwide news.

These were all good questions, with no easy or obvious answers. Nothing made sense. The find of the century hadn't just dropped out of the sky.

Everyone knew that saber-toothed cats had disappeared thousands of years ago...at least all scientific data had pointed to that conclusion. Until today that is. This discovery would put zoological study on its ear. The history books would need to be rewritten.

The big cat's discovery also opened the possibility that other creatures the world considered extinct were still around. Katy smiled. This was too good to be true. With that thought, the nerves at the back of her neck prickled with unease. Katy looked around her garage to ensure she was alone.

"You're being ridiculous," she chided.

She then plucked the keys out of the ignition and gathered her tote, before sliding out of the cab of the truck. Walking to the door that led to her kitchen, Katy slipped the lock and dropped her bag inside. She shouldn't need it. She'd given the cat enough tranq to keep him out for at least five more hours. That should be ample time to examine and photograph him in the cage, before turning him over to Roger Sylvan and the Bio Tech facility.

Katy strode toward the back of the truck and opened the tailgate. The hatch groaned in protest, before she dropped it with a loud bang. She cringed. It was a good thing the cat was in a deep sleep. She smiled, then carefully loosened the ropes to remove the tarp. Her gaze swept the steel cage and her mind froze, refusing to believe what her eyes were telling it. Katy pinched the bridge of her nose and looked again.

A naked man lay inside the cage, sleeping soundly, with a tranquilizer dart sticking out of his juicy rump. His deceptively long brown lashes accentuated his chiseled cheekbones and near-perfect mouth. The man had lips that were made for… Katy tore her gaze away from his mouth. She didn't want to think what those sensuous lips could do to a woman's commonsense.

Heart pounding, she drank in the rest of him. A thin line of hair swirled around the flat discs of his nipples before trailing down his chest to his… Her eyes rounded and Katy gulped as awareness spread through her body. Parts that hadn't seen any action in months began to tingle and throb. Her cheeks flamed in embarrassment and she quickly glanced at his face to make sure he hadn't caught her ogling him.

The man took steady breaths in and out, his muscled chest rising and falling evenly. Lucky for her, he remained blissfully unaware of her indiscretion. For a second, he'd made her forget all about the saber-tooth, but thankfully, the moment had passed.

It didn't matter to Katy if she had Adonis himself in that cage and from the looks of him it could very well be the legendary Greek god. Right now, her only concern was finding out what had happened to her prized cat.

She'd watched the Bio Tech team load the cat into her truck. Heck, she'd even helped them and secured the cage afterwards. Katy hadn't imagined the weight beneath her palms or the snuffles the animal made from its drug-induced sleep. It had only taken a minute to get into her truck and pull out of the lot. There was no way anyone had time to remove the cat or switch the cages. Yet, that's exactly what had happened.

It was either that or…

Had she somehow been drugged? Had they all been given a mass hallucinogen? One that made them believe they'd captured an extinct cat, when in fact, it had been a man the whole time. The thought horrified Katy, but how else could she explain the loss?

Even as the questions crossed her mind, she realized Roger would never believe her. Had her boss wanted her gone so badly that he actually planned this whole thing? Katy wouldn't put it past Roger, but she didn't think he had the brains to pull it off. There was only one way to find out for sure. She had to wake up sleeping beauty and find out who'd hired him.

She hoisted herself into the back of her pickup and pulled the key to the cage out of her pocket. Katy slipped the key into the lock, watching the man carefully, even though she knew he'd be out for close to twenty-four hours given the dosage of the tranquilizer dart sticking in his flesh. Whoever was behind this elaborate hoax or theft had thought of everything.

Katy licked her lips as she admired the rounded fullness of the naked man's bare behind. Her fingers quivered as she pulled the latch that opened the cage door. It made a loud creak, shattering her nerves and the silence in the garage.

"You're being silly. It's not possible." She shook her head. "This is someone's idea of a sick joke and this guy's in on it, even if he's out cold."

She scolded herself for hesitating as she threw the door wide, slamming it against the side of the truck. Pistol in hand, Katy dropped to her knees and slowly crawled forward, straining to reach the dart. She needed to do this quick, so she could wake the guy and find out his part in this charade.

Without the saber-tooth, there would be no scientific journals, accolades or job offers. She'd be just another out-of-work tracker on a job hunt.

What job do you think you're going to get without

references? Katy's heart sank. In all likelihood her next job would require her to ask, 'would you like fries with your shake'.

Damn it, she wasn't going down without a fight. This guy was going to help her whether he wanted to or not. He may not know it, but he owed her.

Her fingers closed around the dart and she pulled. The man didn't move. Katy tugged harder and the dart slipped out of his skin. The naked man's hands were on her so fast, removing the pistol from her grip, that Katy didn't have a chance to blink much less pull the trigger.

He came to life like the dart was a mere mosquito bite, not something designed to take down a thousand pound cat. The man pushed her out of the cage and onto her back across the tailgate, keeping his hand firmly locked on her wrists the entire time. His warm muscled body blanketed her before she could even take a breath.

Shocked by the riot of sensations taking place inside her, Katy forgot to struggle. Her sole focus remained locked on the feel of the man above her. It took a moment for her adrenaline kicked in.

"Let go," she said, then fought and scratched him, while her hips bucked against his solid weight in an attempt to dislodge him.

The man didn't seem to notice.

Katy kicked out again and he took the opportunity to settle himself between her thighs, effectively pinning her to the tailgate. Warmth spread through her body and Katy fought harder. "I mean it. Get off me," she snarled.

Be silent!

The command pummeled her mind, knocking the breath from her lungs. Katy gasped. She was losing it. She had to be losing it. People didn't talk to each other using their minds. It just wasn't done outside of the movies and sci-fi-fantasy novels. Didn't he know that? If not, somebody should tell him. She wheezed, drawing in a shuddering breath.

"Who are you and what do you want?" she asked, wiggling her hips until she came into contact with a long, hard ridge of flesh. Katy froze, her eyes rounding as she felt said flesh begin to grow impossibly thicker. She remembered the size of the cat, then unconsciously glanced down, before meeting his gaze once more.

Feral green eyes locked with hers.

Katy felt herself falling into their emerald depths. His breath came in pants, but she doubted it had anything to do with trying to keep her still. The man's jaw clenched and his muscles tightened as his hips moved of their own volition, making a small thrust forward.

She whimpered, as his shaft slid over her cleft, leaving an ache behind. For a moment, Katy couldn't move or breathe as her body responded to his heat, then she panicked. "Get the hell off me!"

She shoved against his hands and he actually had the audacity to grin at her. It was then that she noticed the sharp points of his incisors. They weren't fangs exactly, but they were close.

Will you cease your struggles?

"Fuck you!"

His grin spread wider, flashing more of his unusually white teeth. *If that is an invitation to enter your body, then I accept.*

Katy's eyes bugged. "I-I…" She growled in frustration. "It is not an invitation! Now get off me or I'll scream."

Please don't. I'd hate for you to accidentally harm yourself.

"The only one about to get hurt here, buddy, is you."

His brow shot to his hairline and his sensual lips quirked. She got the distinct impression he was trying not to laugh. He tightened his one-handed grip on her wrists. With his free hand, he brushed the strands of hair away from her face that had come loose in the struggle.

Such an unusual color. He fingered the strawberry blonde tresses for a second, before burying his nose in the side of her head and inhaling. *Your scent is unfamiliar, but I like it.*

"Th-thank you." What in the hell was she saying? Had she really just thanked him for the compliment? Katy was not having a conversation with this…this…man. She refused to think of him as anything more.

He grinned again and her heart fluttered in her chest.

"Are you a mind reader? Is that how you're sending me your thoughts? I'm not psychic, but I've always been a little sensitive." She left off the fact that her sensitivity only extended to animals. Was this really any different? Katy waited for him to respond, but he never did.

He continued to play with her hair, twirling it around his thick fingers. *So soft,* he murmured in her mind.

Any other time, Katy would kill to have this kind of attention from a man who looked like him, but under the circumstances…

"Are you going to let me up?" she asked.

No, he answered softly.

She snarled in frustration. "You can't keep me here."

He glanced down at her body and rotated his hips. Her head dropped back and she bit her lip to keep from whimpering. Damned, if that didn't feel good.

I prefer your current position and it appears you do, too.

* * * * *

Kegar felt her soften beneath him and nearly groaned. Her arms remained tense, but the rest of her accepted his weight as if they'd been joining for centuries. His hips rested between her firm thighs, his shaft cradled by her softly rounded stomach.

He loved the fact that she wasn't small and brittle. Strength was prized by him and his people. A weak mate was useless. He needed someone who'd fight by his side and bear strong babes. Someone who'd stand up to him, despite his great size.

This woman seemed more than up for the task. Sure, it would take some convincing, but he had a little time. Kegar wished he had more, but unfortunately he'd left the ship without permission, which meant he had to work fast. His people were already orbiting this planet. As soon as they located his position, they'd retrieve him, whether he was ready to go or not. Kegar knew he could always contact them, but what fun would that be?

A smile flittered over his mouth as the woman pushed against his hands. She reminded him of the ancient stories he'd heard about a pack of female feral cats that had lived on Zaron long before his people had settled the planet.

When the Phantom Warriors had arrived, several of the women had trapped and captured the males for breeding purposes. Not that the males complained for the feral women were rumored to be beautiful beyond compare. Their offspring were said to be the start of the Claw Clan. Kegar knew it was only a story, but part of him hoped that this woman would want to claim him like those feral women had done to his ancestors so long ago.

"What if I don't like this position?" she retorted, unable to hide the sudden rasp in her voice. He leaned down mashing his chest into hers. Her nipples pebbled on contact.

Kegar's mouth watered at the thought of tasting her. *Your body tells me otherwise.*

"My body is lying whore," she said. "You shouldn't pay any attention to it."

Your lips are lying, not your body. I can smell your feminine heat. It beats at me. Right now your entrance creams in anticipation of my hard shaft. He rocked his hips for emphasis. *I have traveled far to find you. I will not have you deny our connection however swift. Not now. Not ever.*

"What connection? We do not have a connection. I don't even know you." It didn't matter if they were generating enough heat to melt the remaining polar ice caps. Katy was not about to do anything stupid with a complete stranger. This was L.A. after all.

She stared into his green eyes. The desire she saw sizzling in those emerald depths made her ache. The connection she felt was instantaneous. Katy wasn't one of those New Age Californians who believed in destinies and karma, but there was no denying that something weird was happening between them. Something cosmic she couldn't explain. Something she wasn't sure she wanted the answer to at this moment.

I know you feel it. Every time you look at me, the blue of your eyes deepens. Your body heats and begins to ache in a way that only I can assuage.

"Yeah, right. You and any fifty-dollar eight-inch dildo. Rape is still rape, don't try to justify it with some kind of 'woo-woo we belong together' crap." Katy's pulse raced as the words left her mouth. She knew this man would beat any dildo on the market, but the last thing she wanted to do was encourage him. Right now, if she could, she'd pummel him.

His cheeks darkened and his eyes narrowed to green slits. For some reason, his expression reminded Katy of the cat. She snorted. What was she thinking, that this guy somehow turned into a mind-reading saber-tooth? The music from that old-time trippy TV show played in her head. Katy vowed that if she made it out of this alive, she'd go straight to the hospital and check herself in.

I assure you that a toy cannot replace the real thing. His cock throbbed against her stomach, searing her skin right through her shirt. *In the end, you will come to me willingly. No force needed.*

"Tell me what you've done with the cat and I promise I won't prosecute you for theft after you're arrested."

In due time I shall reveal all.

"It has to be the drugs. This cannot be happening. None of this is real—that includes you and your, your mind-reading-speaking thingy."

His nostrils flared and he smiled, then licked his sensuous lips like a cat cleaning its whiskers. His green eyes sparkled in the low light, showing promises of things to come. *Think again, my pet. There is nothing foreign in your system to disrupt your senses. I'm real, very real and I shall prove it.*

She shook her head. "That won't be necessary. I'll take your word for it."

Oh, but I insist. He jumped off the truck, pulling her up suddenly, before tossing her over his insanely broad shoulder like a caveman. Katy found herself hanging upside down, staring at his perfect ass. And oh, what an ass it was. She pressed her lips together to keep from drooling. She should be screaming and beating at him in an attempt to escape.

Her mind stayed indignant, while her body had other ideas. It liked the feel of his muscles shifting beneath her palms, the hot glide of his skin as he walked to the door that led into her kitchen, and the supple cat-like movements he made when he stepped silently on the tile floor. Everything about the man screamed sex and sensuality.

"Where are you taking me?" she asked.

Somewhere more comfortable. Which way to your sleep paddock?

"My what?"

He paused, tilting his head from side to side as he scented the air. Then he moved unerringly to her bedroom.

"How did you?"

I simply followed your ripe scent.

"You can't…I mean…" It wasn't possible, was it? "I don't stink!" she snapped.

No, you don't. You smell delicious.

"Who hired you?" she asked, trying to get her mind back on track.

He didn't answer as they stepped through the doorway into her bedroom. He scanned the room, taking in her meager furnishings, before proceeding forward. He did not put her down until they reached the bed, then he laid her gently onto the covers like she was fragile.

Katy's heart clenched. She didn't want to think about how his caring made her feel. She couldn't allow feelings into the equation. The truth was he'd been part of the deception and the dangerous game they were playing hadn't ended yet.

She scrambled out of his reach, landing on the far side of the bed. Katy made a move for her gun, remembering at the last second that he'd disarmed her. Her gaze shot to his handsome face. His lips twitched as he began to stalk around her oak bedframe, his eyes lazily tracking her jerky movements.

For a second his gaze flashed red, then just as quickly returned to green...or had it? Katy wasn't sure she could trust her eyes anymore. He continued to slowly hunt her.

She got the distinct impression that they were playing a game of cat and mouse. There was no mistaking who was who, all that was missing was for someone to slap a tail on her ass and call her Minnie.

The man circled back, when she scrambled onto the bed to get away, his gaze stroking her body with such intensity that it felt like a physical touch. Katy tried not to respond, but it was difficult given his masculine beauty and the desire pouring off him in waves. No man should look that good naked.

She glanced at his impressive erection and her mouth watered as she imagined what he'd taste like, sliding down her eager throat. Heat infused Katy until her body throbbed with need. This shouldn't be happening. Something was wrong.

Despite his claims otherwise, it had to be the drugs. She shouldn't be responding to this man given the gravity of the situation. Hell, she shouldn't be responding to him at all. Katy had always thought of herself as frigid. That's what Roger had called her right after they'd had sex. She hadn't

been with anyone since, so nothing had changed except...
She stared at her captor.

Why this man? He was a total stranger. What made him
so different, so special?

His movements slowed and his eyes seemed to change
from green to red with greater speed. Some instinct told her
that their game had just come to an end.

* * * * *

CHAPTER THREE

Kegar couldn't believe his luck. He'd only been on the planet known as Earth for a few hours and he'd already found his mate. Her unusual hair color captured him, but it was her strong face that held him. She wasn't a beauty in Atlantean terms, but to a Phantom Warrior such as himself, she couldn't be more perfect. She was a hunter, a skill highly prized amongst the shape-shifters in his society.

His hands itched to touch her, remove her clothing, so he could begin worshipping her body with his tongue. Her scent intoxicated him until he found it difficult to think. The fight she put up in her transport had left him achingly hard.

Unlike most human couplings, which he'd studied intensely before leaving Planet Zaron, mating between pairs amongst his people could be extremely physical. Biting and scratching was common. Kegar had a feeling that this human huntress would be up to the task. She'd have to be, because he intended to claim her. Already his body had begun the mating heat.

Kegar smiled, pacing around the sleep paddock, hoping he could get himself under control before he touched her. He'd told the woman that she'd come to him willingly and he'd meant it. She didn't need to know that his pheromones from the mating heat would aid in her capitulation.

He could smell the changes taking place inside her. The cream between her legs trickled down, moistening her sex. Already blood was beginning to fill the center of her desire. Soon her need would grow too intense for her to control, then she would beg for his cock, beg him to take her.

The thought sent a shard of pain through his groin. Kegar wouldn't be able to wait much longer. Instinct rode him hard. The urge to mate was too strong. His heat had triggered her own. Kegar wanted to roar in frustration. Instead, he continued walking, slowing his steps until they kept time with each exhalation.

What is your name?

"Tell me yours first." She arched a brow in challenge.

He flashed her a smile, curling his hands into fists to keep from reaching for her. *Very well. My name is Kegar.*

"That's an unusual name."

Not where I'm from.

"And just where would that be?" she asked.

Kegar could read her thoughts easily. She hoped to gain enough information to give to the authorities after he left here. She had no idea that they'd be leaving this planet together…the second he finished claiming her. Kegar debated whether to inform her of her fate, but decided against it. She'd learn the truth soon enough. He stopped his pacing and faced her.

I'm from far away. Now what's your name, little one?

She snorted. "No one's called me little since I was twelve years old."

He frowned, not entirely sure what she meant.

"My name is Katy Manfred and you, Kegar, will be in a lot of trouble for keeping me against my will—unless you give me my damn cat back."

I am sure that is what you'd like to believe, but it is not so.

"How do explain my missing saber-tooth?"

I have taken nothing.

"Fine! Whatever! You may not have taken the cat, that remains to be seen, but you've been holding me against my will for the last thirty minutes. On top of that, you've all but admitted that you plan to rape me."

Actually, I believe I said you would come to me willingly. Your body already grows heavy with need. I can see your nipples beneath your shirt. They are hard and aching for my mouth. Already your channel moistens to ease my entrance. He grabbed his shaft, fisting its thick girth, then began to slowly stroke up and down.

Katy's gaze riveted, following his movements. Her breathing deepened and her hands clasped the covers as if to prevent herself from moving toward him. Kegar hid his smile and continued to fondle his length.

After a few moments, his breathing matched hers and his grin faltered as he clenched his teeth. Sweat beaded his skin. Teasing her wasn't working the way he'd hoped. If anything, it had backfired. He released his shaft, refusing to spend himself in his palm.

Katy licked her lips and her fingers slipped between her cloth-covered legs.

You will not pleasure yourself! The command was loud in his own ears. Kegar growled and his big body trembled with desire. *Call to me now!*

"No," Katy said, her hips rocking as she slumped back down onto the bed. "What have you done to me?" Her eyes clouded as lust took over.

I have done nothing...yet. Do you not see that you make us both suffer needlessly? I know you want me as I want you. Your pride is the only thing stilling your tongue.

* * * * *

Katy blinked as the truth hit her. Kegar was right. She did

want him—or at least her body did, while her mind boycotted the decision. No man had ever desired her this way. Roger had wanted sex, but he'd never wanted her. Kegar did.

His every move told her so. If she had any doubt, all Katy had to do was look in his eyes. They burned with hunger and so much emotion that it was almost painful to gaze upon. His intensity left her feeling raw and exposed. He hid nothing and demanded the same in return.

Yet, as much as he desired her, he would not take her without permission. Katy knew that implicitly. The knowledge both frightened and excited her because in the end she knew the decision to sleep with him was ultimately hers to make.

Kegar's muscles shifted beneath his taut skin. Her body throbbed in response. She'd never wanted anybody as much as she wanted this man. She was obviously out of her mind. The old Katy Manfred never wanted a man. Sex was below mowing the lawn on her "to-do" list.

"Who are you really?" she asked.

I told you. My name is Kegar.

"That's your name, not who you are." The need became unbearable. Katy's back bowed off the bed. His scent filled every pore on her body, leaving her delirious. She couldn't stand the feel of her clothes against her skin.

Like a woman possessed, she began ripping her clothes away, her movements frenzied, her normal modesty all but forgotten. Welts rose on her skin where her nails raked.

Enough! Tell me to come to you. I can ease your body. The deep baritone of his voice echoed in her head.

"No!" she screamed, tearing her bra and panties off. "I can't. Sex with you is not worth my life."

On my honor as a warrior, I swear I carry no diseases. I would never put you in harm's way. I'd rather die.

Nakedness didn't seem to help. Katy could smell the musk from her sex as it wept for Kegar. He stood at the end of her bed, his hands gripping the oak frame until she heard something crack. She glanced at his shaft. A fresh glisten of moisture formed at the top. A moan tore from her throat.

"Please," she begged.

I must hear the words.

"Please, Kegar."

Tell me the words and I will end this. Tell me you want me.

She heard the pain that gripped his admission. It tore at her heart. He needed her. And more than that, Kegar needed to know that she wanted him. This was so fast, so insane. She'd always played by the rules. Never one to bend them until now.

The urge to welcome him into her body, into her life was strong and left Katy shaken. Tears filled her eyes and spilled down her cheeks as her body became inflamed with a passion that she never knew existed.

"Damn you," Katy sobbed.

He growled. *That's not enough. Tell me.*

"I hate you," she snarled.

No, you don't, but I have no doubt that you wish you did.

Fire swept through her, an inferno of desire that threatened to consume her. "Make it stop!"

Say it!

"I want you to fuck me. Okay? I admit it. Are you happy now?" She surrendered on a whimper.

No. Kegar shook his head, sending his hair over his shoulders. *Tell me that you want…me.*

Their eyes met, clashed, then seemed to come to an unspoken agreement. "I want. I want." She cleared her throat. "I want you," Katy said softly.

Finally. To his credit, Kegar did not smile. He knelt onto the bed and crawled between her legs, moving like a big cat. He didn't climb on top of her. Instead, Kegar stopped when he reached the junction of her thighs and buried his nose in her moist curls. He shook as he inhaled, then his flat rough tongue spread her folds with one long swipe.

Katy cried out and her body arched to get closer. Kegar did not disappoint. He dropped onto his belly and began to feast upon her, scraping her clit with his teeth, then soothing the exposed nerves with his lips until she was convinced she'd go insane.

Pressure seized her womb as his coarse tongue flittered like a vibrator. Katy gasped, hoping to catch her breath, but he didn't stop, only increased speed. It was too much, the intensity too strong. She couldn't take any more. She reached for Kegar. She needed him inside her. Now!

* * * * *

Kegar lightly nipped her hand in warning, then continued to lick and suckle. He refused to be rushed. He'd waited for his woman, convinced she'd never appear. He had all but given up hope, then he'd seen her and his hearts had nearly burst.

Now that he had her, Kegar wanted to savor her. He wanted to know every inch of Katy Manfred. Hear every sound she made from a gurgle to a scream as he fucked her with his tongue and impaled her on his shaft. They had a lifetime to get to know each other. Right now, he needed this primal connection. He needed to know his mate wanted him, wanted what he could give her. That meant taking his time.

Kegar grasped Katy's hips and spread them wider. Pink and perfect, she bloomed before his eyes like a flower at first dawn, its petals covered in dew. Her scent surrounded him, causing his head to spin and his body to ache. The thought of sliding into her sent fire rushing through his body. Kegar released one thigh and pressed a finger into her entrance.

Katy moaned.

She was tight and oh so wet. The combination left him salivating. He added a second finger, then dove back onto the bundle of nerves. Kegar worried the flesh with his teeth as he slowly stroked in and out of her luscious entrance. Her body gripped him, pulling his fingers deeper inside. It was his turn to groan. Kegar couldn't get close enough.

He devoured her until he felt the first flutters against his fingertips. Kegar rotated his wrist and curled two fingers up until he could stroke the spot he'd read about in Orion's report. The files covered languages, animal life, cultures, currency and human behavior—particularly sex. Kegar's commander had been quite detailed when it came to the anatomy of Earth women and for that he was truly grateful.

Katy screamed as her orgasm slammed her body and collapsed like a rag doll onto the bed. Her skin was drenched in a fine sheen of sweat and her breathing sounded ragged in the relative quiet of her bedroom, matching the uneven pounding of her heart.

Kegar remained between her legs, lapping up her juices and growling deep in his chest. The one hand he held her with had left scratches down her outer thigh. She hadn't even felt it. With one final swipe of his tongue, he rose, his cock looking hard enough to drive nails into the wall.

She gulped as he slowly worked his way up her body. His gaze strayed to her nipples. They beaded in reaction. He lowered his head until he could suck one into his mouth. Katy felt the pull of his lips all the way to her groin.

Kegar continued to tease and flick her with his tongue as he cupped her other breast with his large calloused hand, pinching and twisting her nipple in a dance of pleasure and pain that left her achingly taut.

Katy had never been into pain of any kind, but for some reason Kegar's lovemaking left her breathless. And it was lovemaking, she had no doubt as his red eyes met her gaze. "Your eyes, they're changing color," she said.

It's nothing. A trick of the light, he said, his expression growing stern.

Katy knew that wasn't true. The color held some significance. She stared deep. The emotions swirling in his crimson depths shook her to the core. She didn't want to think about what it all meant. There'd be time enough for that later.

For now, she would focus on the pleasure he brought her. Katy reached up and grabbed his head. The dark hair beneath her fingertips slid like silk over her palms. She burrowed her hands, relishing the feathery sensation.

Something that sounded suspiciously like a purr rumbled from Kegar's chest. He released her nipple with a pop and then looked into her face. *Once we do this there is no going back. Our essences will be joined. Do you understand?*

"I don't think so," she said.

He slipped down to her entrance, his blazing crown searing her skin, turning her molten beneath him. All logical thought left her head.

Katy, do you understand?

"Ah, sure." She didn't, but if saying she understood would get him to slide the rest of the way inside her, Katy would agree to anything.

An expression of triumph softened Kegar's warrior-like features. He smiled as Katy bucked her hips in encouragement.

You are mine.

The words slipped into her mind the second he thrust forward. Katy gasped, as her body attempted to accommodate his sudden invasion. Kegar was huge and it felt as if he was growing larger with each breath she took. He brushed the wet hair away from her face, pushing the strands gently behind her ear.

Relax, huntress. You can take all of me.

"What do you mean all of you?" There couldn't possibly be more.

He laughed and rolled his hips, slipping a couple inches deeper. *There's more.* He couldn't keep the arrogant male pride from entering his voice.

Katy refused to admit that he had every reason to gloat.

* * * * *

Kegar gritted his teeth as he pressed inside her. She was so unbelievably tight that it took the last shreds of his control not to lose himself on entry. He kissed the side of her face, his lips feathering over her brow and down her nose, before finding her mouth.

He nibbled on her lips, until Katy sighed and let him in. Honey and light poured inside him as he gained entrance. Kegar slanted his head and began to explore in earnest. She was so sweet, so intoxicating. She made his head spin. The moment their tongues touched, his hips thrust forward, parting her folds until he'd buried himself in her velvet channel.

Kegar rode her gently at first, waiting for her body to adjust. He continued to kiss and tease her lips, until Katy began to match his movements. The second she did, Kegar swelled some more. She was perfect in every way and she was his. He'd gotten her agreement under duress, but he wouldn't let that little detail deter him.

Put your hands on me. I want to feel your nails score my skin as I take you. He rocked his hips and she gripped his shoulders. *That's better. Do not hold back. I want everything. I will try not to hurt you, but know that it's my people's way to inflict pain, while bringing pleasure.* He threw the last words out in challenge.

Katy's gaze narrowed. "You're not going to hit me, are you?"

Never! Affronted, he shook his head. *My hands will only bring you pleasure.*

She searched his face, then seemed to come to some kind of decision. "Then I can take it."

Kegar smiled. *I knew you could. I'd expect nothing less from my mate.*

She frowned. "Mate?"

He didn't answer. Instead, Kegar bit her lower lip and

drove into her. He caught her gasp, while plundering her mouth. She shifted her hips to better accommodate his size. Kegar took the opportunity to grasp her legs and bring them up over his shoulders. The angle allowed him to penetrate to her soul.

Katy broke their kiss, her head thrashing from side to side as his hips began to piston. Her nails tore at his flesh, leaving streaks of blood behind. The coppery tang scented the air, along with their lovemaking. Kegar's grip tightened, as the fleshy nodes on his cock rose, stroking her internally like a thousand tiny fingers.

"Oh my goodness, what is tha—"

Katy came apart beneath him, before she could finish her question. Her body clamped down on his shaft hard enough to send him over the edge. Kegar bellowed, convulsing as he pumped his seed into her. She milked his life force, drawing it in until he collapsed. Their lungs strained as they reached for air. He forced himself to roll, taking Katy with him. She lay on top his chest, her body soft and sated, dripping over his length like warm honey.

They didn't stir, content to lie in the other's arms. Kegar stroked her back, cupping her bottom to bring her closer to his face. *You are all I'd ever hoped to find. I am pleased and honored that you've chosen to be my mate.*

* * * * *

Chapter Four

Katy's drowsy mind came awake instantly. Kegar had mentioned something about being his mate earlier, but she'd been too distracted to respond. Now she wasn't. Mate was a term used most commonly when referring to animals.

What was he talking about? Even as the question formed in her mind, she had bad feeling that she already knew the answer.

"Kegar, I can ignore the fact that you talk directly in my mind. I can even accept that I was a willing participant during sex. But, I have a problem with this whole 'mate' business. Especially, since I know you're part of some elaborate hoax, concerning the saber-toothed cat. She sat up onto her elbows so she could look into his face. If he lied, she'd know it. "I think it's time to come clean."

He took a deep breath and released it. *You are not going to like what I have to say.*

She glowered. "Tell me anyway."

I am not involved in any deliberate deception. It is against my nature to do such a thing.

Katy wanted so badly to believe him. He looked so sincere. Was it possible that Kegar was a pawn, too? That still didn't explain the whole mate business. "You said I was your mate," she prodded for him to continue. "What do you mean by that?"

My people are different from yours. We do not marry. We mate. Only one time. Our women grow fewer in numbers. Due to this anomaly, our males have been forced to seek mates outside our clans. Earth holds our best chance at defeating extinction.

"Earth?" Katy felt the color drain from her face. Why did she always pick the jerks and the crazies? She sat up and swung her legs over his chest, pulling their joined bodies apart so she could stand by the side of the bed. "The least you could've done was tell me the truth. I'm all for a good gag, but this is pathetic." Hurt, Katy walked toward the door.

Kegar leapt from the bed and landed on her, bringing her gently to her knees. *I have never lied to you. I would never lie to you. That is not how mates behave.*

"Get off me." Katy dropped to all fours and tried to crawl away, but the warmth of his body seeped into her, causing her knees to wobble. The scent of his skin grew stronger and Katy's head spun.

She took another step. Kegar's teeth clamped onto her shoulder at the base of her neck and he growled. The warning was clear. He didn't want her to move. Well too fucking bad. Katy tried to get out from under him, but before she could take one step Kegar entered her in one thrust. The power behind it nearly lifted her to her feet.

Katy gasped as he reached beneath her to pluck at her nipples and thumb her clit. Everywhere he touched, fire erupted. She squirmed, but his teeth sank deeper, piercing the tender skin at her nape.

"Ouch," she gasped. "Okay, I won't move."

He pulled out of her until only the tip of him remained. Katy whimpered and rocked back to capture him, but Kegar held her firm. It was a sheer act of dominance and damn if it wasn't turning her on. No man had ever handled her this way. Maybe that had been the problem all along. She wasn't frigid. Katy simply needed a firm hand.

As if to confirm that fact, Kegar stroked her. Katy flinched, then moaned as her sex flooded, drowning him in her juices. His tongue lapped at her neck, while his teeth kept her in place so he could take her the way he wanted— hard and fast.

Kegar's hips pounded her flesh, driving into her until Katy was convinced she'd choke on his shaft. She lifted her butt higher to meet each frenzied thrust, taking him as deep as her body allowed. He grumbled something she couldn't make out, then raked his nails along her legs until he held her waist. Katy's breasts bounced and her body quivered as he slammed into her over and over, again and again.

She heard whimpers coming from somewhere and realized she was the one making the noises. The suctioning sound intensified as he rode her toward completion. It wasn't just sex, it was possession. Kegar was trying to absorb her body and soul in this feral mating. Something inside Katy shifted, locking into place like a puzzle piece. Instead of fighting the onslaught, she softened and her body readily submitted.

Kegar threw his head back and roared. The hair at the nape of Katy's neck stood on end. The only time she'd ever heard that primal sound was when she'd camped in Kenya. The native guides had told her the lions were mating. Before she could turn to see what was happening, Kegar pinched her clit and sent Katy tumbling into the abyss.

He released his grip on her, but his tongue continued to lave the spot he'd bitten. He was back to making those purring sounds deep in his throat. *I'm sorry if I hurt you, but I couldn't allow you to leave.*

"I wasn't going anywhere." *But you will be*, was left unsaid. As mind-blowing as the sex had been, Katy knew there was no way they could stay together.

We need to talk.

She glanced at him. "What do you think I've been trying to do?"

The phone's shrill ring interrupted their conversation. Kegar slipped from her body, leaving Katy feeling empty and cold. Their combined juices ran down her legs, coating her thighs, making them sticky.

It was amazing how fast sex could turn into something else. Not love, but something. Which was odd since she didn't really know this man. Katy refused to admit that she'd like to get to know him better. It worried her that she was already starting to develop feelings for him. Where could a relationship that started out as lust really lead? Nowhere.

The phone rang two more times. "Kegar, I have to answer that."

Dread filled Katy as she saw the number on her caller ID. Crap! She didn't need this right now. She picked up the phone. "Manfred speaking."

"Where in the hell are you?" Roger's voice boomed. "I've been waiting at the facility for over three hours."

She glanced at the clock on the wall and cringed. "I'm at home, sir."

"I know you're home. What I'd like to know is what you're doing there?"

Katy pictured Kegar's naked body and blushed. "Nothing, sir."

"Where's the cat? You do know if he's authentic. Have you examined him to see if he's been surgically altered? Do we have the find of the century in our hands?"

His rapid-fire questions made it clear that Roger wasn't part of the hoax. Damn, that meant the only person who could locate the cat was Kegar and he hadn't exactly been cooperative in that regard. She glanced back toward her bedroom.

Roger Sylvan let out a groan of frustration. "Why did you break protocol?"

"The site was compromised and I was worried that we'd

lose our find." Which wasn't a total lie, but certainly not the truth.

"I don't want to hear your excuses," he said." I took you in after your parents died, when you had no job and nowhere else to turn. This is how you repay me?"

"Excuse me?" How dare he pretend that she was a charity case. "You hired me because I'm the best tracker west of the Mississippi."

"Save it," he snarled. "You know what this means."

"Yes, I do." It meant she was out of a job. It had been one thing to think about it in the realm of possibilities, but now that it was certain, the reality was disheartening. How was she going to be able to keep her house? Her car? She'd barely gotten by on her Bio Tech salary. Katy couldn't afford a pay cut with the cost of living in Los Angeles being so high.

"I'm on my way over now. I expect you to hand the saber-tooth and your resignation in at the same time. Do we understand each other?" he asked.

Katy closed her eyes and took a deep breath. What was she going to do now? Tracking was her life. She didn't know how to do anything else.

"Are you listening to me?" he asked, shuffling paperwork.

"Yes, I heard you," she said.

"Have the cat ready for transport in thirty minutes or getting fired will be the least of your worries. Bio Tech doesn't take theft lightly."

There was a click and then the dial tone rang in her ears. She needed to find out where the saber-tooth was before Roger arrived. That was the only chance she had of staying out of jail and it was a long shot at best. She refused to believe there was no hope. Katy hadn't had the cat long after she left the Tar Pits. All she had to do was prove it.

She strode back inside her bedroom. Kegar was propped in the middle of her bed with his hands behind his head. His magnificent cock rose like a fist in the air at the sight of her. "Don't you ever get tired?" she asked.

Not where you're concerned.

"Listen, Kegar, we have to talk. My boss is on his way over here to pick up the saber-tooth. I need to know where you put him or I'm sacked."

Sacked?

"Fired…unemployed…finito. Get it?"

I understand, but you won't need the job where we're going.

"Where we're going? We aren't going anywhere. I have a job here—or at least had a job. My life is in L.A. I don't know how to do anything else and in thirty minutes my boss is going to knock on that door and expect to see a saber-tooth," she said. "If I don't give it to him, he's going to have me arrested for theft. So are you going to tell me where you hid him?"

I cannot.

"Cannot or will not?" Katy planted her fists on her hips and glared at him. Didn't he realize he was playing with her future?

Kegar sat up. *It is not that simple.*

She threw her hands up in the air. "Men!" She snorted. "It is that simple. Either you know where your buddies hid him or you don't. It's not like you could've moved him on your own."

You'd be surprised what I can do, but as you said, we don't have much time. So I'll have to show you once we get to Zaron.

"Grr…you are impossible!"

No, I'm a Phantom Warrior.

"A what?"

A Phantom Warrior, he repeated as if that should mean something to her.

"What's a Phantom Warrior and what's a Zaron?" She waved her hands in the air. "Forget it. I don't have time for this game. I have to throw some clothes on and come up with a plausible reason for the cat's disappearance. Emphasis on plausible. If you aren't going to help, then just get your things and get out. The last thing I need Roger to see is a naked man hanging around." As the words left her mouth, Katy realized how ridiculous a notion that was.

Kegar had arrived naked. He had nothing to take. She stared at him a moment, absorbing his magnificence. She couldn't allow him leave like that. The women of Los Angeles would riot. The thought of Kegar with another woman sent an unexpected spike of jealousy through her.

Who is Roger? And why do you wish to avoid his discomfort? His voice was deceptively calm.

"He's my boss." Katy shrugged. "And my ex-boyfriend." She raised her hand to stop him from speaking. "Before you say anything, I know dating my boss was a stupid move on my part. It's not one of my proudest moments."

You've lain with this man. He sat up. *Is he the one who caused you to doubt yourself as a woman?*

"No, yes, no, it's complicated," she said. Kegar was way too perceptive for his own good.

Katy opened her drawers and began to dig through her clothes. She didn't want to discuss Roger or their crappy relationship. She wasn't about to touch their sex life after what she'd just experienced with Kegar. She dug deeper, throwing clothes over her shoulder onto the flow. There had to be something here he could wear. She found a pair of cutoff shorts that she'd bought when she'd been a size sixteen.

"Here." She tossed the clothes at him. "They aren't pretty, but at least they are loose and should provide you with a little cover until you can get to the clothes you stashed."

Kegar caught the shorts. *I'm quite comfortable the way that I am.*

"I bet you are." Katy found clothes for herself and

dressed quickly.

The doorbell rang as she tied her shoes. Roger had given her thirty minutes. He probably lied in hopes of catching her red-handed, except the laugh was on him because she didn't have the cat.

Katy glanced in the mirror at her reflection. Her lips were kiss swollen, her make-up was smudged, and her hair looked as if she'd just rolled out of bed. Pretty accurate all in all. She stepped into the hall.

Kegar stopped her before she went any farther. *Before you go, there is something you need to know.*

She whirled her hand to indicate he should hurry up.

There was no cat. It was an illusion of sorts.

Katy rolled her eyes. "I didn't tranquilize an illusion."

No. He shook his head. *You shot me.*

He was telling her something important, but she wasn't following. "What are you saying?"

The doorbell rang again. Someone pounded on the door before the chime died.

Kegar stroked the side of her cheek with the back of his hand. *So beautiful.*

"Kegar, focus." Katy snapped her fingers and gave him a warning glare that she hoped said she wasn't up for playing any more games.

I have not lied to you. I am a Phantom Warrior from Zaron. Planet Zaron. I am not human, so therefore the rules of this planet do not apply to me. I can run with the beasts by changing my form, walk through your walls and hide myself from prying eyes.

Katy stared unblinking for the longest time, unable to say a word. Her mind replayed the day's events with extreme accuracy. Could what he was saying be true? As much as she wanted to believe him, there was no way.

The pounding grew louder, then she heard Roger order someone to break down the door.

"Wait right here." Katy raced for her front door. She

couldn't afford to fix it if she were unemployed. She slipped the locks and opened the door. "What in the hell is the matter with you, Roger?" She looked past his shoulder and saw two Bio Tech security members waiting in the wings. "Why did you bring them? That's overkill even for you."

Roger wore a belligerent expression on his face. "I needed someone to carry the stolen property. Besides, you've been acting so bizarre that I couldn't take the chance that you might refuse to hand the cat over."

She snorted. "Stolen property? I've never stolen anything in my life." Katy wasn't sure what had gotten into her. She should be trying to keep her job, not baiting the boss.

He pushed his way into the house, leaving the men outside. "Wait out here. This won't take long," he said to them, then shut the door. It locked automatically, but Roger didn't seem to notice or maybe he didn't care.

"I have nothing to hide," Katy said.

"Then you won't mind if I take a quick look around." Roger started his search in the kitchen, then made his way back to the living room. "I see you haven't bothered to make any changes to the place, even after I gave you all those wonderful suggestions."

Katy wanted to tell him just what he could do with his suggestions, but she didn't. "You're not going to find anything." *Except the naked man in her bed.* She prayed that Kegar had found a good place to hide. He'd claimed to be an expert at it. She hoped he was telling the truth.

Roger stormed into the bedroom, then suddenly turned on Katy. His gaze narrowed as he sniffed and took in the rumpled sheets. "You've been having sex," he hissed in disgust.

"I don't know what you're talking about." Katy rubbed her arm and casually looked around to see if she could spot Kegar, but he was nowhere in sight.

Roger took a menacing step toward her. "Drop the act, princess. This room reeks of sex," he snarled. "Who have you been fucking? Is that why you rushed home, instead of bringing the cat to the facility? I can't believe you'd endanger an animal that way, not to mention the public."

Katy's face flushed as she forced her anger down. She'd never, in all her years of tracking, endangered an animal or civilians. To say otherwise was an insult. What she'd experienced with Kegar wasn't mere fucking. The fact that Roger made it sound like a vulgar act truly pissed her off. He had some nerve given their history.

"You know better than to accuse me of animal cruelty and it's none of your business who I see," she said. "We broke up. Remember?"

He snorted and walked back into the living room. "You're right. It's not like he'll be around long now that you've lain like an iceberg beneath him. A guy can only take so much cold before he gets frostbite." He paused. "It was a guy, wasn't it? If not, that would explain a lot."

"You're such a jerk," she muttered

A roar came from the other room. Katy's eyes widened. How had the cat gotten into her house without her noticing? A flash of movement was the only warning Roger got before the giant cat leapt for him. Claws extended and mouth open ready to eviscerate, the saber-tooth brought Roger to the ground, slamming him onto his back. Its ears were pinned and its teeth exposed, daring him to move. Roger shifted a shoulder and the cat growled, slapping one enormous paw onto his chest. It flexed its claws just enough to draw blood.

Roger screamed, then glanced at Katy for help. "Where's your gun?" he asked, his voice coming out in a strained soprano. "You need to kill it."

Katy stared at the creature's face. Green eyes. It had green eyes just like…

I told you I wasn't like your people.

"Kegar?" It couldn't be.

Your heart knew the truth all along.

"But how?" Logically, Katy knew it wasn't possible.

There was no such thing as magic, but she couldn't deny the instant recognition when the cat had looked into her eyes.

"Who are you talking to?" Roger hissed as the cat brought his nose down to his throat and sniffed.

"I'd be quiet if I were you, Roger," Katy said. "You don't want to make any sudden moves. Big cats are unpredictable."

He whimpered.

The security team began to pound on the door, demanding entrance.

Katy glared at Roger. "Tell them everything is okay or that saber-tooth will gut you from neck to groin."

He paled as his gaze slipped back to the seven-inch serrated teeth. "Everything's fine," he choked out. "False alarm."

The pounding subsided.

"I asked you a question, Kegar." Katy stared in awe at the man, the cat she'd made love to.

I answered with the truth. I am not from this planet. I came here seeking a mate and I found her in the guise of a huntress. You will be worshipped and cherished on my planet, Katy. You will never have to want for a thing. You have my vow and my heart…if you want it. We can leave immediately.

"I can't leave L.A." She wrapped her arms around her and felt tears burn her eyes as she glanced at the quiet emptiness of her home. He was offering her love—or at least the chance of it. That was something she hadn't experienced since her parents died. Yet Kegar couldn't be serious. She barely knew him. Katy wanted so badly to believe.

What do you have here? This home? A job? I have a home. It is in need of your touch, but it is comfortable and I know you would like it. You could continue your work there unimpeded.

"You need a tracker?"

No, but my people do. What I need is you.

Could she leave?

I know the home means much to you. We could take all your belongings with us.

Katy looked around. There wasn't much of hers in the house. Only the items in her room. She'd never wanted to change anything. She'd been afraid that if she had, she'd somehow lose the memory of her parents.

Kegar was right about there being nothing left here for her. It would be a miracle if she managed to avoid jail time. If Roger had his say, she wouldn't. Katy watched Kegar for a few moments. He sat quietly, waiting for her decision. She glanced at Roger.

He'd convinced her that there was something wrong with her. He'd told her she could keep her job because he felt sorry for her. She'd swallowed his words like a tonic and allowed them to poison her self-esteem until she was afraid to move, to change her circumstances. He wouldn't be giving her another chance at the job and she didn't want one. Kegar had opened her eyes to new possibilities. It was time for her to shore up her courage and strike out. This time she wouldn't be alone.

"Let him up," she said.

The cat hissed.

Katy took a step forward. "Please, Kegar. If what you say is true, then we don't need him anymore."

The cat eyed her warily, then stepped back, retracting his claws. Blood sprang to the front of Roger's shirt. The saber-tooth walked across the room to stand by Katy's side. She dropped her hand onto its head and began to stroke his soft fur. A strange rumbling purr ensued. Definitely not a sound a lion would make. She smiled, glancing up in time to see Roger stumble to his feet.

He was glaring at her, holding his chest. "I plan to notify the authorities about this incident. Once they prosecute you, that animal will be destroyed."

She tilted her head. "You'd destroy the find of the

century?" she asked, genuinely curious.

He tugged at his watchband. "If it meant that I'd get the first cut on the dissecting table, damn right. Now be sensible for once in your life and step away from that beast."

Katy's blood ran cold. She couldn't allow Roger to harm Kegar. She tried to step in front of the saber-tooth, but he wouldn't cooperate. "I can't let you do that, Roger. What started out as the find of the century has quickly become the love of a lifetime."

He laughed. "Love of a lifetime? That's a bit dramatic, don't you think? What are you going to do? Run away? I'd find you no matter where you tried to hide on this planet." Roger walked over to the door, his intent clear. He slipped the lock and threw the door wide.

"Roger, please wait. You're making a mistake." Katy lunged to stop him.

"Security, come quickly. The animal attacked me. It needs to be put down immediately," he shouted, clutching his crimson-stained shirt for emphasis.

The Bio Tech team burst through the door with their guns drawn. Katy cried out and moved in front of Kegar to block their shots. Suddenly, everything began to move in slow motion. A gun went off, the sound reverberated throughout the room. Katy closed her eyes and braced, expecting to feel searing pain. When none came, she cracked one lid.

Instead of the bullet hitting her, she saw the guard no longer pointed the pistol at her chest. The second man fired a shot. Plaster rained down from the ceiling. Katy screamed and searched for Kegar. He was gone.

No longer in cat form, Kegar appeared briefly behind the two men, only to disappear again. She blinked, unable to believe her eyes. He wrenched their guns out of their hands and threw them across the room. Bones snapped and one man fell with a sickening thud. The other scrambled to his weapon.

The glass frames on the wall that held her pictures

exploded as the security expert fired repeatedly. Katy ducked. The gun dropped to the ground and the man rose in the air, held by invisible hands. His feet flailed beneath him as he clawed at his throat.

"Please don't hurt them anymore," Katy pleaded, rushing forward even though she wasn't quite sure what she was going to do to stop Kegar if he chose to end their lives. He was a force like nothing she'd ever encountered. "They're only doing their jobs."

Kegar materialized. *And I am only doing mine.* He threw the man into the wall as if he weighed nothing at all. Two hundred pounds of flesh hit, punching a hole into the plaster, then he slid to the floor. The other man lay unconscious a few feet away.

"Will they be okay?" She peered at the men in an attempt to ascertain the extent of their injuries.

They will live, but they will not soon forget their encounter with a Phantom Warrior.

"You could've been hurt." Her voice cracked.

My only concern was your safety. They were going to harm you. He indicated to the two men on the floor. *I could not allow that.*

They wouldn't have drawn their weapons if... She looked around the room for her boss. A chair in the corner squeaked. Katy took a step forward and saw Roger cowering behind her recliner.

"You can come out now," she said, unable to hide her disgust. "You've caused a lot of trouble." Katy gathered the photos of her parents, brushing the glass away.

"Who in the hell is he?" Roger asked, gaping at Kegar's naked form.

Katy glanced at her warrior. "That's the man-beast I shot earlier at the La Brea Tar Pits. You know, the one I brought home to fuck. Kegar meet Roger Sylvan."

Kegar turned his red gaze on the man, measuring him without saying a word. His presence filled the space like a black hole, sucking all light and life toward him. When it was clear that Roger did not measure up, he quickly dismissed him and turned his attention to Katy once again.

"That was quite a show you put on," she said, smiling.

You would not have believed me without the...demonstration.

She laughed. "Is that what you call it? A demonstration? You're like a ghost."

His eyes glittered like rubies in the fading sunlight, then he vanished. Katy felt a slight tingling as Kegar passed through her. It was an odd sensation that didn't quite diminish when he reappeared in front of her a second later.

"That felt *really* weird," she said. "In the future, ask before you do that again."

Are you saying we have a future?

Heat radiated from his body, surrounding her in loving warmth. "I'd say there's a pretty good chance." She touched him to ensure that he was real.

What would it take to persuade you?

Katy pulled his head down and whispered the suggestion in his ear.

Kegar grinned. *That can be arranged.*

"Hello, I'm still in the room," Roger said, his fists clenching at his sides.

Kegar tapped a spot on the side of his neck, then turned to face the man. "You may be, but we are not."

Katy gaped. Those were the first words Kegar uttered aloud. They were followed by a loud popping noise and then Roger, the security team, and her living room were gone. Katy blinked several times to get her eyes to focus, then looked around. She was still holding the pictures of her parents.

Lights from instrument panels blinked on and off. She looked out the window at the beautiful blue/green planet below. It was then Katy realized she was standing on the deck of a ship. She dropped the pictures. They clattered to the floor. She stared out the window at Earth. It looked so real, nothing like the sci-fi movies she'd watched over the years.

It is real. That is your home planet. And this is indeed the deck of a ship. Kegar swung the command chair around, his large body looking at home with one leg draped over the arm.

"Why didn't you tell me you could talk?" she asked as if that was the most important thing happening at this moment. It wasn't, but her brain couldn't handle the information overload.

Kegar's lips twitched. *What fun would that have been?* he asked, slipping back into his preferred method of communication.

Katy glared, but it was impossible to stop a smile from spreading over her face. Sure, part of her was freaking out, but the other half was grateful that Kegar had been telling the truth. "Are we really on our way to another planet?"

Yes, we're on course to Zaron. Or we will be soon.

"When will we get there?" she asked, feigning an innocence she did not feel.

It will take seven of your Earth days. Perhaps less. Why? Suspicion and something else flashed in his green eyes.

She shrugged casually as if the question was no big deal. "Just curious," she said, nonchalantly glancing around.

Kegar rose with a cat-like grace, his long black hair fell freely to his shoulders. His gaze never left her as he picked up her photos, then pressed a panel in the wall and placed them inside. He shut the panel and continued to stalk her, a smile playing on his sensual lips.

Katy backed away slowly to what she hoped was the bedroom. She planned to take full advantage of this long flight, starting now. "Here kitty, kitty, kitty," she said, crooking her finger for him to follow.

Kegar's eyes flashed red. He didn't disappoint.

* * * * *

EPILOGUE

Planet Zaron, Eight Months Later...

Life on Zaron wasn't much different than Earth, Katy thought as she crouched over the paw print of a rogue Phantom Warrior. She and Kegar had been tracking him for four days and this sign was the only indication that they were finally getting close.

She glanced over at her mate, staring at his long black hair as a cool breeze lifted it away from his handsome face. Even now, Katy could feel her body readying itself for his invasion.

What's on your mind, mate? Kegar asked, tilting his head to look at her.

Katy widened her eyes and put on her most innocent expression. "Nothing, why do you ask?"

Kegar licked his lips and inhaled deeply. *Because your rich cream wafts on the air, distracting me from our mission.*

She put her hands on her hips. "I am not a distraction. If you recall, I'm the one who found the print."

This is true, he conceded, pride filling his voice. *But you are nonetheless a distraction.*

Katy opened her mouth to protest.

Kegar held up his hand to still her words. *You are the best kind of distraction,* he said, peeling his tracker uniform off his body.

She gulped and took a step back. Katy doubted she'd ever tire of seeing this man naked. Kegar was magnificent inside and out. And he was all hers. "I don't think there's time for that right now." She nodded toward the fresh print.

Kegar grinned. *There's always time for us to join.* He slipped her red uniform off her shoulders, pulling it down, while raining kisses in its wake.

Katy's nipples engorged as his teeth scraped the sensitive flesh. "Kegar," she gasped, clutching his head to her body.

He sucked her deep, worrying and laving until Katy thought she might go mad.

Kegar removed the rest of her clothes, then lifted her into the air. *Wrap your legs around my waist.*

Katy did as he instructed.

Kegar entered her without preamble. *I swear I could drown in your feminine juices and die a happy warrior.*

"I love you, too." Katy kissed him tenderly as he drove them both into the solar system and beyond.

Kegar gave Katy one last kiss, then they dressed quickly and continued their pursuit. The warrior wouldn't escape.

We are close. Kegar shifted into his cat form.

"I am never going to get used to this," Katy said, staring at him in envy.

Yes, you will. Now come on before we lose him.

Katy's body began to tingle, then gradually disappeared until it was replaced by a female saber-tooth with strawberry blonde fur.

Kegar nudged her with his massive head and she swatted him with her paw. He snarled playfully, then they took off toward the horizon, their future in front of them and their elusive prey finally in their sights.

PHANTOM
WARRIORS
Talon
JORDAN
SUMMERS

CHAPTER ONE

A shadow passed overhead momentarily blotting out the warm sun. Lynn Regis shivered as something primal inside of her urged her to run. She ducked instead, then planted her feet on the craggy rocks and tilted her head, squinting against the sunlight. Like debris caught in a whirlpool, two enormous raptors circled above her on a sea of blue, dropping lower and lower until she could see the white 'V' of their feathers clearly beneath their wings. Relief flooded her and tears of joy misted her vision.

Her condors were alive—and safe. After a day and a half of hiking in the Grand Canyon, searching the skies, she'd finally found them.

Even from this distance the birds looked huge. Throwbacks from another age when man lived in caves and feared anything larger than himself. The raise and release program had gone better than expected. Her pair of condors looked to have bonded, which meant her job here was almost done.

Lynn watched them climb, using thermal updrafts. One soared toward what looked to be a small cave in the ridge of the cliff and disappeared. At least she thought it was a cave, but from this distance it could very well be an indented ledge, since condors could roost in relatively small spaces, despite their large size.

The only way Lynn could be sure the spot they'd picked would be safe for any future hatchlings was to climb up there and check it out. She stared at the side of the canyon wall, craning her neck to see the top of the ridge. From this depth and angle, she couldn't immediately spot it.

She glanced at her watch, then checked the angle of the sun. There was no way she'd start the climb in the afternoon. It would take her hours just to reach a spot safe enough to ascend. Hours that would eat the last remaining rays of sunlight. Shadows already clamored along the burnt orange and beige canyon walls and it was barely past two. Soon Lynn wouldn't be able to see her hand in front of her face, much less two black raptors.

The terrain in the canyon's belly was dangerous in the daylight. At night it could be lethal. Several people had disappeared in the Grand Canyon National Park never to be seen again. So many so, that there was actually a book detailing their deaths and disappearances. Fascinating reading, but hardly comforting when she was trekking on her own.

Lynn pulled her backpack off and dropped it onto the rocks. She had enough provisions to last for several days, along with a sturdy tent, small cook stove, solar lanterns and a sleeping bag. She could afford to wait until the morning to find a safe place to climb. The condors weren't going anywhere. Not tonight anyway.

She stared at the bird's nine-foot wingspan and grinned as it followed its mate into their new roost. With the help of conservationists and ornithologists like her, this proud species of raptor just might have a chance at survival. Lynn took out her journal and noted the location of the small cave in the distance, then prepared for the coming darkness.

An hour later, she'd erected the tent and set up camp. A

land of extremes, the desert could be scorching hot in the daytime and freezing at night, depending on the time of year and the location. If a person wasn't prepared, they could easily die of exposure and dehydration.

Sweat dripped from Lynn's forehead and ran along her jaw. She gazed longingly at the Colorado River flowing thirty feet away. She hadn't thought to bring a swimsuit, since she had not anticipated it taking so long to find the condors.

The idea of submerging herself in the greenish-brown waters nearly had her salivating. It might not be ideal, but at least it would be cool. And would certainly do until tomorrow, when she'd reach her favorite campsite in the heart of wild country.

Lynn flicked her gaze up river and didn't immediately spot any rafters floating down. It was late and they should've all set up camp by now, but there could always be stragglers. She bit her lower lip. Could she risk stripping down long enough to wash the sweat off?

She glanced down at her dust-covered clothes. Lynn wasn't ashamed of her body. Far from it. So what if it didn't exactly conform to what was considered ideal beauty these days. How many women could truly say their bodies did? Confidence aside, that didn't mean Lynn wanted strangers stumbling upon her naked size sixteen backside, when she bent over to wet her hair. She did have a modicum of modesty after all.

Despite reservations, she walked forward and trailed her fingers through the current. Ribbons of cool water feathered in their wake. Lynn checked one last time to ensure her privacy, then quickly stripped out of her hiking clothes and plunged into river before she could change her mind.

She yelped as the brisk flow licked over her ample curves, crinkling her nipples and stroking her generous thighs. God, it felt so good. She could stay here for hours, floating in the shallows. Lynn closed her eyes and quietly bobbed on the surface, letting the sun kiss her upturned face.

A breeze whipped through the Canyon, sending a chill through her, making her teeth chatter. Maybe the water was colder than she'd initially thought. Gooseflesh rose on her skin. With it came an unexpected surge of awareness.

Lynn sat up and looked around, suddenly painfully aware of her nudity and isolation. There wasn't another human in sight. So why was her heart racing?

She shook off the feeling of being watched and ducked her head below the surface. Lynn knew she was alone. She'd checked twice. It was only paranoia…or perhaps wishful thinking on her part. *There's nothing wrong with wanting to share your life with someone*, she told herself. Of course, the chances of them wandering into the Canyon to say, 'Here I am' were pretty slim to none. Stuff like that only happened in books and movies, never in real life. And certainly never to her.

Lynn held her breath for as long as she could, watching bubbles float to the surface, then came up sputtering. Her long brown hair clung to her back and lovingly curled around her large breasts, accentuating her pale skin.

The feeling of being watched had dissipated somewhat, but hadn't completely gone away. As much as she wanted to stay in the water, Lynn couldn't ignore her instincts any longer. She rose, paying no heed to the sensual caress of rivulets trickling over her bare flesh.

Lynn resisted the urge to brush the droplets away. She was afraid if she touched herself at that moment it would only make the ache inside her worse, since it had been months since she'd had a lover.

How many times had she promised to work less and make more of an effort to date? Too many to count.

"This time I really mean it," she muttered, knowing that in all likelihood the promise would fall by the wayside much like her New Year's resolutions to lose weight. It wasn't like she had time to worry about such things now anyhow. Lynn had come here to do a job. The sooner she focused on finishing it, the better.

She waited a few more seconds, allowing the air to dry her, since she didn't have a towel. The gentle juniper-scented breeze brushed through her wet hair, causing her skin to prickle. Lynn spread her arms and slowly turned in a circle, soaking in the sunshine.

The feeling of being watched returned.

Lynn's body tensed. She opened her eyes, half expecting to see someone standing in front of her. The sensation of being observed was stronger this time, sweeping over her skin, leaving scorch marks behind.

Definitely male...

Her gaze darted up and down the river, but she still couldn't spot anyone. In the Grand Canyon, that didn't really mean anything. Someone could be watching her with binoculars from up on the ridge. Talk about an unfair advantage. Lynn rushed forward and dove into her tent to get dressed.

* * * * *

Talon stared out the bridge viewport at the blue-green planet below. The ship would continue to orbit Earth, while teams of Phantom Warriors were dispatched to the surface to find mates. Nerves tightened his stomach, twisting his gut into a Zaronian stew. Soon it would be his turn to venture onto the planet.

Already several Phantom Warriors had returned empty-handed. Talon forced his mind away from the possibility that he, too would return mateless and focused instead on having a successful hunt like Bacchus and Kegar.

Those two warriors had already returned to Zaron with their new mates in tow. The men had received a hero's welcome for bringing hope to the Phantom people. Although hesitant, the women had done their best to settle into

Phantom society. Their acclimation and acceptance had been helped by the fact that both warriors had successfully passed their genetics onto the women.

Even the most cynical of the Phantoms had been unable to deny the truth of Bacchus' and Kegar's claims, when their mates had shifted form into their respective clans.

Seeing the women change had given the other Phantom Warriors hope for their future. Talon took that newfound hope and turned it into determination the likes of which he'd never experienced before. He wasn't about to blow his allotted three days on Earth and come back alone. If his commanding officers could find mates in a matter of days, then so could he.

He glanced at the map of the world and his two hearts sank. Though smaller than Zaron, Earth was still substantial in size. Talon had no idea where to begin his hunt for a mate.

Being part of the Wing Clan meant he'd need a lot of space to roam. He needed to test the thermals in the alien atmosphere before narrowing down his hunting grounds. Talon didn't want people in the cities spotting him, when in his other form. At least not at first. That meant he had to go somewhere remote. But where?

He pressed a button on the bridge and the map of the planet grew larger and more detailed. It may take several trips to cover it all. Perhaps he was being a little overoptimistic about finding his mate the first time around. It might take several trips to the planet to succeed.

No! He shook his head. He couldn't think that way. He would find a mate. And not just any mate. Talon was determined to find his *true* mate. He might be desperate, but he wasn't so desperate that he'd attach himself to just any female. He was looking for something different, *someone* different.

He scanned the map, staring at the illuminated sections that indicated dense populations. There were so many places that had been conquered on this planet, leaving very few wild spaces untouched.

Talon pressed another button and the heavily populated areas disappeared. That elimination should help narrow his search some, but not enough. He glared at the map. He needed a place where he wouldn't readily stand out. Talon walked to a console and hit a separate screen. With a few deft strokes, he brought up the list he'd been searching for.

There were several species of raptor on Earth. None near his size in his other form, but a few like the Wandering Albatross and the Andean Condor were close enough…if viewed from far away. Despite their low numbers, Talon chose to go with the condor, since they were closer in coloring to his other form. He hit a few more buttons and the locations of these giant birds appeared. There weren't nearly as many as there should be, but several held the remoteness he needed.

Now all he had to do was choose.

Such a simple task for something that posed such great personal risk. Not that Talon feared for his safety. He was a Phantom Warrior after all, but he couldn't exactly convince a woman to mate with him if she was terrified of him. He sent out probes to take images of the areas. It would only take a few seconds to receive the information he needed.

When the first images appeared, Talon quickly ruled out the California locations. The state was far too heavily populated for his needs. He moved onto the pictures of Baja, which seemed promising, before finally settling on the Vermilion Cliffs in Arizona. The vast expanse called to something deep inside of him. The cliffs were located near a place known as the Grand Canyon.

Intrigued, Talon pressed a point on the map and the probe zoomed in, sending back even more images. His breath caught in his lungs as the craggy geography came into view.

The area was beautiful. Perfect for soaring on thermals and testing the atmosphere. He touched the map again and it took him into the depths of the canyon down to the swirling water below. He scanned the canyon for condors and found two, making lazy circles above a pale object on the ground.

Perhaps they'd spotted their next meal? Seemed likely since condors were expert scavengers. He wondered what had the birds so fascinated.

Talon hit another button and the probe zoomed in on the image. That's when he saw *her*. Naked. Wet. And mouthwateringly lush. Rising like a goddess from the abyss. Every muscle in his body shot to attention. Talon's breathing deepened as he gazed at her long brown hair and full figure. He couldn't seem to swallow as his flight suit suddenly constricted, choking off his air supply.

The skin on Talon's neck and shoulders tightened as the *change* threatened to overpower him. It was a good thing he couldn't smell her or he'd probably end up embarrassing himself in front of the other warriors, wandering the nearby corridors.

They'd never let him live a slip up like that down. Only a child couldn't control the change and he was far from being a child. Talon glanced around to make sure he was alone. It had been years since a woman had forced a change upon his body. So long in fact, that he couldn't recall the last time—if ever it had occurred.

Interesting…

He reached out and touched the viewer screen, stroking a finger down the woman's tempting image. Talon watched her pale nipples pucker and firm, as if she'd truly felt his touch. Was it a sign from the Goddess?

His gaze traveled longingly over her luscious curves. The hair between her thighs matched the color on her head. He wondered if they'd be of equal softness. His mouth watered at the thought of tasting her, running his tongue along her moist seam.

Talon couldn't stop himself from touching her image again. The woman glanced around and shivered, then rushed forward into some kind of dwelling. He jerked as hundreds of years of instincts urged him to take chase.

"Mine," he growled.

The flap of the dwelling closed behind her, concealing her gorgeous form. Disappointment flooded him, along with a stronger, more dominant emotion. The woman might be able to hide for now, but she wouldn't be able to hide from him for long. Talon marked the spot on the map, then shut down the image, his purpose clear.

He now knew exactly where he needed to go and what he was looking for. He'd find her with or without the map. Once Talon did, there would be no place she could run where he wouldn't follow. His cock hardened at the thought. It was only a matter of time before he claimed what was rightfully his.

Someone cleared their throat behind him. "Commander?"

Talon stiffened at the sound of the deep voice and slowly turned. He hid his embarrassment behind a mask of open hostility. Given his raging emotions, it was easy enough to do. He'd been so wrapped up in the woman that Talon hadn't heard the young warrior approach.

"How long have you been standing there, Arctos?" he asked, his voice deadly still. Talon didn't care that the question gave away the fact that he'd let his guard down. He was operating on pure instinct now.

The junior officer flushed, then lowered his head, sending silvery white hair into his face. His flight suit barely contained his broad shoulders and massive bulk. "Not long," he murmured.

The lie hung between them, adding mass to the silence. The urge to gouge out the young warrior's eyes with his talons was strong. If he didn't know for a fact that Arctos was from the Tooth Clan, Talon would've acted upon those urges. But Arctos was, which meant that the man could shift into a creature that bore both the characteristics of a bear and a wolf, becoming much more than the nightmarish creation human legend spoke of. Of course, he'd probably stick with his bear form, when he hunted for a mate.

Talon glanced at Arctos' hands. Deadly claws had already sprung from his fingertips. It wasn't so much a direct challenge as an indication that Arctos had difficulty controlling his emotions. Talon was pretty sure he could take the young recruit in combat, but it wouldn't be an easy victory or a painless one.

The last thing he wanted was to appear bloodied and tattered when he presented himself to his potential mate. It was for that reason, and that reason only, that Talon dismissed Arctos' imprudence.

"I suggest you retract your claws…unless you plan to use them. Now what is it?" Talon barked. "You know I'm scheduled to depart shortly. I don't have time to settle another dispute."

If that were why he was here, then Arctos would make the third warrior today to present a case of misconduct. Mating always brought out the aggressive side of Phantom Warriors. Talon had broken up more fights since they'd arrived on Earth than he had in the entire previous year on Zaron.

As time passed, the aggression only got worse. If it continued at this rate, there'd be no choice, but to send some of the men back. Talon didn't want to be the one who gave that order or chose who got to stay and who had to go.

Sensing the danger, Arctos dropped into a quick bow. "Forgive me for the intrusion. I come with news that I am to accompany you on your journey to the planet. My name was chosen."

Talon stilled. He wasn't prepared to take a traveling companion. If anything, that would make his hunt for a mate more difficult. Phantom Warriors were territorial by nature. If they remained in the same area around an available female, blood would spill. Deaths, though rare, were known to happen.

"I think there's been a mistake," Talon said quietly.

Arctos' red gaze met his. "No mistake, sir. Orders have come down from Commander Bacchus."

"I cannot allow you near the female that I have chosen to...*investigate*." Talon's muscles tensed as his body prepared for battle.

Arctos' lips twitched. "I believe you misunderstand me. I am to travel with you down to the Earth's surface. From there, I will head north to a place called Alaska. I believe one of the women said it was a state. Whatever that means. I have located the land mass on the map." He pressed a button on the console and a snowy image popped onto the screen.

"I see," Talon said.

"It is too warm for me to exist comfortably in anything above fifty degrees," Arctos added quickly.

Talon kept his expression blank. He knew the young officer had told him the latter to reassure him. What Arctos didn't know was that Talon didn't *need* reassurance. He would fight any man to the death, be they Phantom Warrior, Atlantean, or human, until he could discern whether this woman would turn out to be his match in every way. Deep down in his gut, Talon knew she was already. He'd seen how her body reacted and he hadn't even touched her yet.

He let a fraction of his power rise to the surface until he felt his eyes glow, too. The skin along Talon's shoulders, neck and back began to burn as his wings pushed to be released.

Arctos took a step back, his claws lengthening as he did so. "I meant no disrespect, Commander."

Talon took a deep soothing breath and forced his muscles to relax. If he attacked an underling, then he was no better than the rest of his squabbling men. His jaw clenched and his body shook as he fought for control. "I will see you in the departure bay," he gritted out between clenched teeth. "Dismissed."

Arctos nodded, but didn't turn around to leave. Instead, he backed out of the room.

Smart warrior, Talon thought. He shook off the last of his power, forcing it once more inside his body. The appearance of the female was already messing with his rigid self-control. What would it be like when he finally stood before her? A shiver of anticipation trickled along his spine and Talon grinned in anticipation. He couldn't wait to find out.

* * * * *

CHAPTER TWO

Lynn woke to the sound of splashing coming from the nearby river. She poked her head out of her tent and spotted three rafts going by filled to the brim with sunburned tourists. The people waved and raised their beers in salute. She glanced at her watch. It was barely past six thirty in the morning. Talk about a 'Breakfast of Champions'. Lynn gave them a half smile, then slipped back inside her tent. She needed coffee…bad.

It didn't take her long to dress. Lynn hurried into her shorts and slipped on her windbreaker. The sun hadn't touched the bottom of the canyon yet, so the air still held a faint chill. Okay, more than faint. It was downright nippy. She primed her small cook stove, then poured some water from her canteen into a pan to boil. The smell of fresh brewed coffee filled the air a few minutes later.

While she sipped at her first cup, Lynn scanned the sky for her condor pair, but didn't immediately spot them. They were probably out hunting for breakfast. Her stomach growled, reminding her that she needed something to eat, too. She dug into her backpack and pulled out a couple of energy bars. They would do until lunch.

Lynn devoured them while she savored the hot smoky taste of coffee. She watched the sun's long red fingers slowly creep along the rock. If she were going to make it to the condor-nesting site, she'd have to start now. She sighed, not looking forward to packing up camp and the hike ahead.

Talon watched the woman from the canyon's rim. She looked tiny from this distance, but he could tell that she was preparing to leave. Fear spiked through him. It was quickly followed by determination. She would not get away so easily. At least not until he'd gotten the answer to the question he'd come all this way for.

The warm air caressed his face, sending his dark hair into his eyes. Talon reached inside a pouch for a tie to secure it, then glanced around to ensure he was alone. Reptilian creatures scurried nearby. A few hawks circled lazily overhead. He caught the soft footfalls and musky scent of a large predator cat, but no sign of any other humans.

Satisfied, Talon took off running and leapt into the air, shifting as he did so. It was time to hunt his prey.

* * * * *

Lynn had been hiking for over three hours and didn't seem to be any closer to the bonded pair. They had looked so much closer yesterday when she'd first spotted them. She'd set up camp at her favorite spot. Her tent looked like a small red speck next to the glistening aqua blue water from this distance.

She stared up at the canyon wall calculating how much farther she had to go before her hike turned into a full on climb. Lynn had brought the right harnesses and enough rope, but despite her love of all things winged, she wasn't much for heights.

In fact, being up high without more than a safety harness scared her silly. But Lynn had learned to conquer her fears. Okay, maybe not conquer, but she'd certainly gotten to the point where she no longer froze and that was saying a lot given where she'd started. Soon it wouldn't matter. Fieldwork would be a thing of the past.

The next generation of researchers preferred to track the birds by computer program. It allowed them to follow their progress without disturbing the birds' nesting sites. At the ripe old age of thirty-two, Lynn, with her boots on the ground approach, was as close as she cared to get to being deemed obsolete.

A dark shadow passed overhead, pulling her out of her maudlin thoughts. Lynn shaded her eyes and saw one of the condors soar by not even twenty feet away. The bird circled back, riding the thermals to check to see if she was a predator. She'd needed proof before, but this confirmed her suspicions. The birds were definitely roosting together. Now all she needed to know was had they mated and managed to lay any eggs yet?

Lynn looked at the cliff face. There was only one way to find out. She pulled out her climbing shoes and helmet, then stepped into her safety harness. She slipped the strap holding her spring-loaded cams, nuts, and quickdraws over her head before grabbing her dynamic and static ropes, then started the long climb.

It took four hours to reach the nesting site. Drenched in sweat and exhausted, Lynn took off her sunglasses and peered into the large nest and spotted one lone egg. It wasn't much, but at least it was a start. Would've been better if it were two, but success was success, especially when it came to bringing a creature back from the verge of extinction.

Lynn made sure not to touch anything on or around the nest as she took out her smartphone to document the find. She had just taken her last picture when a dark shadow blotted out the sun.

She twisted around in her harness in time to see a large bird streak across the sky. Scratch large. Make that humongous bird. She'd assumed by the cast of its shadow it had flown right over her head, but it had been at least thirty feet above her. Lynn squinted, trying to get a better look at the massive raptor, but it was gone as quickly as it had appeared. She'd never seen a *bird* fly so fast.

Lynn glanced back at the small—by comparison—egg. Her stomach twisted. She didn't like the idea of another predator so close to her mated pair. Especially since she hadn't been able to identify the species yet. She scanned the sky, searching for the large bird, but it was as if it had disappeared in mid-air. Which of course was impossible.

She knew better than anyone that there weren't raptors *bigger* than the ones she'd released in the Canyon—at least not in the area. And she was darn sure that a Wandering Albatross hadn't gotten lost this far inland. She pinched the bridge of her nose, then put her sunglasses back on. Maybe she'd been in the sun too long. It had probably just been the mama condor checking to make sure that her nest was undisturbed.

Yeah, that had to be it.

Lynn made a few more notes before beginning her descent. It would be almost dark by the time she hiked back to camp. She knew she'd have to be extra careful if she didn't want to end up as another statistic.

* * * * *

Talon's hearts swelled as he soared out of sight and faded into the clear sky. The woman was even more beautiful in person than she'd appeared in the viewer. He knew it wasn't smart to get so close, but he'd been unable to resist the temptation of her clinging to the cliff face.

Though he still didn't understand why she'd been perched so high up, dangling by a thread. As far as he could tell, humans didn't have wings. One sharp tug and she could have plunged to her death. The thought chilled him. He wouldn't have allowed that. Couldn't have. Even if it meant exposing what he was before it was time.

He recalled her upturned face and warmth blossomed inside him. Her dark lashes had accentuated her wide green eyes and fully kissable lips. She'd tied her long hair back, but Talon had been able to detect its shine despite her attempts to conceal it beneath a helmet. He wondered if her hair would be as soft as Zaronian silk when it flowed over his chest. He shivered in anticipation of fisting the long locks in his hands as he rode her lush body.

The woman wasn't small like Queen Rachel of Zaron, but then again, Talon never cared for tiny women. He wanted a woman he could hold onto, one who cradled him against her rounded body. One who was sturdy enough to care for their young, yet soft to the touch. He wanted a woman whose breasts spilled out of his hands, whose nipples were the size of flower blossoms.

Talon's mouth watered at the thought and he licked his lips in anticipation. He could almost taste her sweetness and he hadn't even touched her yet. He sighed. It had been next to impossible to find one such as she on Zaron, where the women tended to be overly tall and built like warriors.

He had nothing against warrior women. He respected their strength and had lain with his fair share, but that didn't change the fact that he just wanted to come back to his dwelling and be embraced by a soft plushness that only came from someone with ample curves. He glanced down at the ridges of muscle packing his frame. His body would be hard enough for them both.

Talon was smart enough to never confuse softness with weakness. Any mate of his would never be weak. Could never be weak. His demands were too great. He was not a selfish lover. Far from it. But he was aggressive. Aggressive enough to know that he wanted a partnership, not a simpering female who could not care for herself.

That said, Talon knew he wouldn't mind having someone to care for. He wanted someone to call his own. Someone to want him as much as he yearned for them.

From what he'd seen of the woman, she was more than capable of taking care of herself. After all, she'd come into this wilderness without an escort and had managed to climb halfway up the cliff face on her own.

As far as he could tell, the only thing missing were her wings. If things went as he planned, she wouldn't be missing those for long. Talon grinned and began to formulate how to meet his destiny.

*   *   *   *   *

Lynn was shivering by the time her tent came into view. She couldn't believe how low the temperature had dropped since the sun disappeared. Most people made the mistake of thinking that only the heat could kill you, but exposure to the cold would do just as good a job.

She glanced up ahead at the lone tent pitched by the placid pool of water. All she wanted to do was climb inside and burrow into her sleeping bag, but Lynn knew she needed to hydrate and get something to eat or she'd end up cramping during the night.

Despite strict camping rules forbidding fires below the rim, Lynn dug a hole and built a small blaze using driftwood. Warmth exploded in her limbs relaxing her tired muscles for the first time that day. She heated some water, then tucked into a package of instant chicken and rice. Reconstituted food had never tasted so good.

It took thirty minutes for her fingers to stop aching from the climb. She flexed them, then picked up her notepad. She wanted to make sure she had everything down while it was still fresh in her mind. She switched into scientific mode and began to write.

Lynn prided herself on her meticulousness and observations skills, when it came to charting the condors' progress. She'd spent thirty minutes replaying the moment the unidentified raptor soared over her head, but no matter how many times she envisioned it, Lynn couldn't recall the white spot that should've been there had it been one of her tagged birds.

So if the raptor wasn't a condor, then what was it?

She ran through her mental Rolodex of all the large birds on the planet, but none seemed to fit. "Maybe if I draw it," she murmured.

Lynn made a quick sketch of the bird on the paper, then examined her work. If she had to guess, she would say the wingspan had been at least fifteen feet across and the body over six feet long, but how was that possible?

She shook her head. It wasn't.

Her mind circled back to her original thought. Maybe she *had* been suffering from heat exhaustion. She'd kept hydrated during the climb, but she'd still been dripping by the time she'd reached the nest. Being overheated was known to cause hallucinations.

Lynn was pretty sure she hadn't imagined the bird. As a scientist, she'd never had that good of an imagination. But she conceded that she might have *imagined* its size. After all, the only creature known to have that kind of wingspan was extinct.

Hey everyone, I saw a dinosaur today. It flew over my head. There was no way she was putting that into any report. As one of the few female ornithologists, it was hard enough to get respect from her peers. She wasn't about to give them a reason to discount her further.

Lynn polished off her dinner and made a couple more notes, before calling it a night. Tomorrow she'd take another look to see if she could spot the bird and photograph it. She didn't have a lot of time to look, since she'd only prepped for staying a week and it would take at least two days to hike back out of the canyon. If she hoped to succeed, then she'd need to get an early start.

Talon stared down at the soft glow of the woman's fire.

He dared not get closer for fear his mating instincts would take over. The last thing he wanted to do was shift accidentally and scare her senseless.

He inhaled and looked up at the stars. Somewhere up there, the Phantom Warrior ship circled, cloaked against the primitive radar systems Earth employed. Talon thought about his fellow warriors, waiting for their chance to find their mates.

Many would succeed and many more would fail. He would not be among the failures. His future lay on the canyon floor tucked inside the primitive dwelling. Like those waiting warriors, his days were limited.

He slowly dragged his gaze away. She would be his. There was no other option. Tomorrow Talon would make his move.

* * * * *

CHAPTER THREE

Talon woke to the screech of a hawk as it swooped down to catch a field mouse. He watched life play out before his eyes, reveling in the raptor's speed and agility. He stood, stretching his muscles from a night spent on the hard earth. It was a very good thing he could regulate his body temperature or he'd have froze to death last night.

He rolled his stiff shoulders and glanced up at the sky once more. He so wanted to take to the thermals and glide over the canyon, but Talon resisted the temptation. Today was the day he'd finally get to meet the woman. Unfortunately, that meant approaching her in his *human* form.

Talon reached into his small sack that contained his meager supplies. He hadn't intended to stay in the canyon for long. Just long enough to meet the woman and mate. He took out the rations.

Despite their small size, they carried enough nutrients to satisfy his hunger. He popped them in his mouth and grimaced. Too bad they tasted like dirt. He brought out a flask of water to wash the vile food down, then slid it back into his pouch.

It would take at least thirty minutes to reach the woman walking. Less if he flew. But Talon wouldn't. He couldn't risk the chance of her spotting him again in bird form. Not yet anyway. He'd scouted the area. Knew the route he needed to take. With any luck he'd reach her campsite before she rose.

Talon tossed the pouch over his shoulder and began his hike. Anticipation rode him hard, making him pick up the pace, despite his determination to approach cautiously. He inhaled as he neared the tempting pool of water, catching the scent of *his* woman for the first time.

His eyes flashed red as need savaged him. He stepped carefully around the water's edge. He didn't want to send rocks into the liquid and give his position away. It was important that she didn't know he was here until just the right moment.

Talon wasn't altogether sure what that moment would be, but he had no doubt he'd recognize it when it arrived.

The skin on his back began to itch as the beast fought to get out. Talon forced it back in and crouched near the ground, waiting. It wouldn't be long now. The sun was racing toward the canyon floor. The animals had already started to make their presence known.

The woman's scent grew stronger as he made his way to a small outcropping of brush. It wasn't thick enough to conceal him, but then again, he didn't need such things to hide in plain sight. He was a Phantom Warrior after all, a being capable of bending light to disappear and shifting his molecules until he could pass through solid objects.

He heard shuffling inside the structure and knew it wouldn't be long now. Talon quickly stripped out of his flight suit and slipped into the lipid pool. The cool water rippled around him as he sank low, leaving only his eyes and nose peeking out.

The woman stepped out of her tent and slowly stretched. She stared longingly at the water, unable to see his faded form. She bit her lip and looked around, then slowly began to strip her clothing off.

Talon couldn't seem to catch his breath as second after second revealed more pale skin. He had no idea how she'd react once she realized he was in her territory. If she were a warrior, it would be easy to determine. But she wasn't. She was a luscious gift that the Goddess herself had delivered into his hands and he wasn't about to refuse her.

It seemed to take an eternity for the woman to finish stripping. By the time she had, Talon's body bore more resemblance to the canyon wall than it did a man. He closed his eyes and prayed to the Goddess for strength.

The woman dipped her toe into the water, then whipped it back out and sucked in an audible breath. For a moment, Talon feared she'd change her mind, but then suddenly she grinned and raced into pool.

He waited until she broke the surface and pushed her hair out of her face, then he slowly rose like a leviathan from the watery depths.

* * * * *

Lynn nearly swallowed her tongue, as she watched the man surface from the aqua blue water like the god Neptune surveying his kingdom. Droplets clung lovingly to his bare muscled chest, glistening in the sunlight as the water settled around his trim waist. She'd never seen perfection like this up close.

Heat blossomed inside her and her body came alive in an instant, swelling and moistening in equal parts. He moved closer, causing those magnificent muscles to ripple and flex. Lynn's heart stuttered in her chest. Was she imagining him, too? She closed her eyes and quickly opened them again. Nope, he was still there.

The man swept his dark hair back with a casual brush of his hand, exposing a face that could only have been summoned from some woman's darkest fantasy. Lynn made a mental note to find her and thank her, whoever she was.

Speechless and more than a little in awe, it took Lynn a moment to stop gaping and remember why his being here was a bad thing. She looked down and yelped, then plunged into the water to cover her nudity. The cool waves lapped at her swollen breasts, causing her to gasp.

"What are you doing here?" she snapped, ignoring the need threatening to overwhelm her.

One dark brow rose. "I could ask you the same thing," he said in a voice made for late nights, cool sheets, and sinful secrets.

"This is…" She broke off. What could she say? *This is my favorite spot and you're not allowed.* Just because not many people came here didn't make it a private area. It was a public park after all. Lynn frowned. "How long have you been here?" she asked instead. Was it too much to hope that he'd just arrived and she hadn't put on a striptease in front of him?

Despite her ingrained modesty, the idea of stripping in front of him didn't seem totally *unappealing.* In fact, something about him brought out a daring side that had somehow stayed dormant until now. Just her luck.

Lips that were made for kissing canted at her question. "Long enough to enjoy the stunning view," he said, eyeing her as if she were standing before him naked, not concealed by the water.

Lynn ducked down even further. "You need to leave," she said.

He grinned then, flashing stark white teeth. "I was here first," he said, then looked around at the large pool. "Besides, I think the spot is big enough for the both of us. Don't you?"

She couldn't fault his reasoning, but this was her spot, darn it. She didn't want to share, even if that meant sharing the spot with a man who was too gorgeous to truly exist on this planet. Heck, in this universe. Maybe he really was a god. "Are you an actor or model or something?"

It would be just her luck that she'd get stuck naked with a male model, when she had more than a passing acquaintance with cellulite. Well if that's what he turned out to be, Lynn felt obligated to downgrade his 'god' status.

He laughed. The rich infectious sound rolled over her, and then burrowed deep. "Is that your way of telling me that you find my appearance pleasing?" he asked, practically preening under her regard.

She winced when she realized that she'd unwittingly fed his already healthy ego. Despite his false modesty, Lynn had no doubt he was used to being ogled or at least stared at all the time. She, on the other hand, wasn't. "Do you mind turning around?" She twirled her finger in a circle for emphasis.

His gaze sharpened. "Why?" he asked.

"Because I'm not exactly dressed for company," she said in exasperation.

Something feral flashed in his unusual colored eyes. The blue appeared to be ringed with red, which was odd...and quite possibly a trick of the light. Lynn scrubbed the water out of her face and looked again. The color didn't change, if anything it seemed brighter.

"I don't mind." He took a step closer and all thoughts about eye color fled from her brain.

Lynn frowned. "You may not, but I do," she said, crossing her arms over her large breasts.

The man shrugged casually, then said, "From what I saw, you have nothing to be ashamed of." He all but purred his response.

Lynn's body flushed with warmth and she blinked. Was he flirting with her? Men that looked like him *never* flirted with her. Her first thought was to dismiss him outright, but what if he *was* really flirting with her? Would that be so bad?

She'd never been the type of woman who went for casual connections. Up until this moment, that hadn't been much of a concern, since men weren't exactly beating down her door. Sure, she'd taken care of her 'needs' when they'd cropped up, but she didn't jump into anything lightly. It just wasn't in her nature. She preferred to analyze, deduct, then once all the data was in—act.

Look where that's gotten you? The pesky voice in her head whispered.

Maybe it was time to shake things up. Lynn stared at the man. He'd moved closer while she'd been contemplating what to do. Could she act without thoroughly examining the situation? More importantly *should* she?

"Don't come any closer." She held out her hand. The man stopped instantly.

"I will not harm you, I swear it." Gone was all the flirty humor that had been there before. He seemed genuinely hurt that the thought of harm had even crossed her mind.

Something inside Lynn melted. Maybe he wasn't quite as secure and egotistical as she'd first imagined.

"You never answered my question," she said.

He visibly relaxed, causing the muscles in his abdomen to ripple enticingly. "What question was that?"

"What are you doing here?" she asked.

He tilted his head. "I wanted to spend time at my favorite spot in the canyon." He spread his arms wide, giving her an eyeful of his extraordinary biceps. "This is it."

Lynn swallowed hard. She watched a lone drop of water snake between his pecs and slowly make a beeline down the slight indent that bisected his perfect stomach. It disappeared into his nearly invisible navel. Lynn had the sudden urge to dip her tongue inside and taste that drop. Would it be salty like his skin or would it taste like the man?

"Okay." Not the brightest response, but it was all she could manage as lust soaked her brain.

The man took a step closer and held out his hand. "My

name is Talon," he said.

She'd have to rise a little to take it. Did she dare? She hesitated.

A musky aroma washed over her. Lynn wrinkled her nose as the wild scent teased her nostrils, daring her to inhale. She did. A second later, heat swept through her like a flaming tsunami. Lynn closed her eyes on a moan and inhaled again, deeper this time, taking the enticing smell as far into her lungs as she could get it, then swayed.

"Are you all right?" Talon asked, watching her closely.

Lynn's gaze flicked to him and she gave him another quick once over. The need that had been simmering below the surface shot to the forefront, nearly buckling her knees. This would probably be her last time in the field. She had no idea when or if she'd ever get back to this spot. Why not make her last time here memorable?

The scientific part of her brain was screaming at her to stop, figure out what was happening. The woman in her quickly gagged that logical voice and shoved it into a dark recess of her mind. She wanted this man. And he miraculously appeared to want her, too. They were both consenting adults. As long as they kept things simple, they could both walk away satisfied.

Lynn kept one hand pressed against her chest in a poor attempt to cover herself. She reached out with the other and took Talon's outstretched hand. A slight tremor ran through his body on contact and his nostrils flared.

An unexpected thrill shot through her. She'd never really turned men's heads or made them lose control. What would it feel like to have that kind of power over a man like Talon? Lynn shivered as his large hand enveloped hers. His grip was firm, but not crushing, like he considered her something precious.

Wow, what a concept!

For someone standing in cool water, his skin was unbelievably hot, like he was generating a fire from the inside out. Lynn knew exactly how that felt, since she was pretty sure without the water that she'd spontaneously combust if they got any closer.

"Nice to meet you." She paused. "Talon? Is that a family name?" Before he could respond, she added, "Saddled with something like that, it must've been a challenge growing up."

He shook his head and a few strands of dark hair fell into his face. He brushed them back casually. She watched the muscles in his arm flex. "Not so much," he said, with a sly smile. "I've always been very good at taking care of myself…and anyone else under my care."

Lynn blew out a breath. She just bet he was. Her body swayed toward him subconsciously, seeking that delicious fragrance that seemed to cling to his skin. "My name is Lynn. Lynn Regis." *And I want to jump your bones.*

Talon grinned as if he'd read her thoughts. "The pleasure is all mine, Lynn Regis." Her name rolled off his tongue in a savoring of syllables.

She blushed. "Um, I really need to get dressed. Do you mind?" Lynn turned to leave, but his next words stopped her.

"Sure you want to go back?" The musky fragrance came again. This time stronger, body slamming the last of her resistance. "I was hoping we could go for a quick swim together," he said, a little too innocently.

Lynn glanced over her shoulder. There was nothing innocent about the look Talon gave her. His gaze scorched every inch of her exposed skin, drinking her in, devouring her without laying a finger on her. Lynn's heart thudded hard against her ribs. Now she knew what Eve felt like when that wily snake offered her that apple.

"Unless you're…*chicken*," he added, all but daring her to act.

* * * * *

CHAPTER FOUR

Talon knew he was cheating a little. At the last second, he'd decided to test her reaction to his pheromones. The faint scent would only affect her if there were a possibility that she could be his mate. Talon knew he should've given her more time to get used to his presence, but time was something he couldn't afford to squander. If Lynn turned out to be incompatible, then he needed to know before this went any further, so he could search elsewhere.

His body rebelled at the thought of walking away from her. He'd waited a lifetime to find her. She was everything he'd been looking for in a woman, yet the last thing Talon expected to find. Lynn was an odd mixture of shy, courageous, modest and sexy. The perfect woman. The perfect mate.

How had he grown so attached so quickly? Maybe he wasn't the only one cheating with pheromones?

Indecision danced in furrowed lines across her forehead, before eventually smoothing. Her expression went from reluctant to euphoric in a blink. Lynn inhaled again and giggled. She slapped a hand over her mouth to stifle the sound.

"Sorry," she slurred, flushing crimson. "Just thought of something funny." Lynn was definitely affected more than she was letting on.

Hope made his two hearts swell. Talon knew he was getting ahead of himself. More tests needed to be done, but it didn't stop him from anticipating what was to come. He'd served his people well, along with the Atlanteans. Talon had never asked for anything in exchange. Now he did. He wanted this woman. Longed to pull her into his arms, lay her beneath his body and claim her for all time.

From the videos that had been created upon Queen Rachel's arrival, he'd learned a lot about Earth. Talon had been keen to understand the customs. Being from the Winged Clan, he'd learned all he could about the flying creatures that populated the planet. He'd also learned the subtleties of the English language. He knew calling Lynn a 'chicken' would goad her into acting. Chickens were one of the few birds on this planet that really couldn't fly—at least not far.

Talon tried to imagine what that would be like and his mind blanked. The thought was inconceivable. He'd never want to be a chicken. And to think, people on this planet actually *ate* them. He shuddered.

Lynn gave him a shy smile. "Race you to the other side," she said, then dove under the water.

Talon watched her swim. It was easy enough to track her movements. Lynn surfaced a minute later to try to locate him. She frowned when she noticed he hadn't followed.

"What are you doing?" she asked, treading water.

Talon grinned. "Giving you a head start," he said, hoping the distance would diminish the effect his pheromones were having on her. He wanted Lynn sober when he took her.

She snorted. "I don't need one," she said, then swam hard for the other side.

He threw his head back and laughed, then slipped beneath the water. His strokes were clean and strong. It helped that he didn't need to breathe as frequently as she did. Talon caught Lynn easily. Thanks to the water's aqua blue color and overall clarity, he'd been able to spot her legs as she kicked her way to the shore. Oh, and what legs they were...

Talon reached out and slid his hands over her firm calves, following them up until he brushed the inside of her soft thighs.

Lynn squealed loud enough for him to hear her beneath the water.

He surfaced with a smile on his face. "Caught you," he said, then pulled her into his arms.

For a second, Lynn struggled. The moment her back made contact with his hard chest, she gasped in shock, then her body sagged. He could feel her heart racing, but she didn't try to pull away.

"What happens now?" she asked in a voice so quiet that Talon barely heard her.

He slowly turned her in his arms. "Now I do what I've been longing to do, since I laid eyes on you."

"And what's that?" she asked.

His gaze locked on her lips and Talon lowered his head. The first brush across her petal soft skin made every muscle in his body tighten. His hands flexed and he pulled her closer.

On the second swipe across her mouth, Lynn's sweet taste hit him like an Atlantean energy blast to the groin. Talon groaned and sank into the embrace, deepening the kiss with a swipe of his tongue. His hands roamed over her lush curves, exploring every inch of her bare skin. He couldn't wait to taste everywhere he touched.

She slanted her head, giving him better access. Talon didn't think. He simply took, conquering her mouth, laying siege to her senses, while he sought to capture her heart. Their connection was greater than he'd imagined. Lynn was beyond perfect.

He growled, a habit he'd picked up from the Claw Clan

on Zaron. Lynn quivered and her nipples stabbed his chest. Talon longed to take the hard kernels into his mouth and feast upon them. He knew he could bring her to orgasm by his mouth alone and he planned to...again and again and again.

Before he finished, she'd be begging him to take her.

* * * * *

Lynn's head spun. She'd never been kissed like that in her life. Talon's mouth didn't just move, it teased, tasted, coaxed, and devoured. She'd tried to retreat, but he wouldn't allow it.

Instead, Talon chased her tongue, pursuing it as he explored the deepest recesses of her mouth. His hard shaft dug into her soft belly as he rocked his hips forward. If the *feel* was anything to go by, then the rest of Talon was as impressive as his magnificent chest. *Oh my...*

The kiss became maddening. Talon's wild flavor filled Lynn's mouth, overpowering her senses until she craved it, craved him. The man was addictive. One hit and she was hooked. A little voice inside her head warned her not to take too much. If she did, she'd never get him out of her system. Lynn knew it was already too late.

His hands seemed to be everywhere at once, setting her body aflame with a gentle stroke here and a rough pinch there. He played her like a man familiar with a woman's body, like a man who appreciated and adored pleasing women. A surge of jealousy struck out of the blue. At least that's what she thought it was.

She'd never been jealous before and frankly, she didn't like it one bit. Lynn pushed the unwarranted emotion away. As a woman of science, she wasn't naïve enough to believe that a man like Talon hadn't been with a stable of women. Her minor in anthropology served her well in that regard.

She knew the score going into this...this...whatever was

happening between them. She wasn't about to turn shrew and demand he give up his potential harem for her. Lynn might want to, but she'd never do it.

Talon's grip on her tightened and he groaned deep like a man tortured.

"I need you," he whispered, between gentle swipes of his tongue. "Goddess knows I want you." His hot breath brushed her cheek as he blazed a trail to her shoulder and began to nibble in earnest. "Tell me that you want me, too." It was a plea and a confession.

Lynn's breathing hitched. Had anyone ever needed her? She truly couldn't recall. Did she dare admit that she wanted him, too? Would that scare him if she did? She didn't know. This was all foreign territory for her. Lynn wasn't used to dealing with feelings, unless they were directed toward birds.

"Kiss me," she said, instead of admitting something that she might later regret. She knew it was the coward's way out, but Lynn wasn't feeling all that brave. An unfamiliar vulnerability had crept in when she wasn't looking and was currently doing its darnedest to derail her normally robust confidence.

Fortunately, Talon didn't need to be asked twice. His lips latched onto hers and pulled her into a maelstrom of sensations, wiping away her concerns and insecurities with a swipe of his tongue.

Lynn's skin felt too hot and far too tight for her body. Her fingers dug into his shoulders. It was like trying to cling to granite using thumbtacks. She wrapped a leg around his thigh and whimpered when his hard cock brushed her sex.

The last thing she wanted was to put a stop to this, but they needed to get back to her tent before this went any further. Lynn didn't want someone to wander by and catch them mid-performance. It was one thing to act upon her racy thoughts in private, quite another to put on a show for strangers. Talon was turning her into an exhibitionist. Lynn nearly giggled as the thought crossed her mind.

Who would've ever thought that she, Lynn Regis, a shy, science bird geek, would be jumping a stranger in the Grand Canyon? Certainly not her friends, who liked to tease her with the name 'Rigid Rules Regis', back home.

She forced her lips away from Talon. It was hard, but one of them had to keep a level head. At least until they got back to her camp. "We should go. Someone might see us," she said, gasping for breath.

* * * * *

Talon was panting, his chest rising and falling rapidly as he blinked to clear his head. He hadn't heard a word Lynn said, his mind and vision remained too fogged with lust to concentrate. "What?" he asked, praying she hadn't asked him to stop.

"My tent. Let's go back to my tent where it's a little more private." She licked her bottom lip.

Talon followed the movement with his eyes, longing to capture the pink tip with his teeth before sucking it back inside his mouth. He shook his head again and looked around. They were exposed to the elements. Exposed to anyone who happened to stumble by.

The idea of Lynn being seen naked by another male sent a surge of possessiveness through him. It was followed by a wave of aggression that left him trembling. Talon knew in that instant that he'd kill any male who came near her. He grasped Lynn's hand gently and led her into the deeper water.

"Care to race back?" he asked, his voice gruff to his own ears. "Winner takes all," he added before she responded.

Lynn hesitated only for a moment, then smiled. "See you on the other side," she said, then slipped into the water, swimming hard for the shore.

Talon watched her go. Her lush bottom broke the surface

with every other stroke. His mouth began to water at the thought of tasting the rest of her. Already, she'd left her gentle scent upon his skin and her sweet flavor in his mouth. Talon planned to do the same and more once they reached her dwelling. He smiled, then slipped in behind her, his gaze tracking her progress like the predator he was.

* * * * *

Lynn reached the shore first. She knew Talon had let her win, but she didn't care. She pulled herself out of the water and grabbed her clothes, drying off as quickly as she could before slipping inside her tent.

There wasn't a lot of room to maneuver, but at least she'd remembered to bring a small blowup mattress to tuck beneath her sleeping bag. Not perfect, but a whole lot better than messing around on the rocks.

She picked up her backpack and rummaged inside. There had to be a condom in there somewhere. She usually used them to keep her memory cards dry. As soon as she found one, Lynn set the prophylactic aside and tossed the backpack through the narrow opening.

She expected to hear a thud as it landed on the rocky shore, but the sound never came. Lynn poked her head out of the tent and saw Talon holding her gear. Her journal had fallen out of the bag and was in his hands. He had a strange expression upon his face as he stared at the sketch that she'd made yesterday of the giant bird.

"That's part of my work," she said absently as she stepped out of the tent and took the items from his loose grip.

"What is this?" he asked pointing to the drawing.

Lynn shrugged, but wasn't sure how to answer. On the one hand, there was a very good chance the bird had been one of her condors. If that were the case, then the sketch would be no big deal. But if it turned out to be a new species, one that hadn't been documented yet or one that science thought was extinct, then the news would make her career. Like any good scientist, Lynn wouldn't make an announcement until she had all the facts. She decided to play it safe.

"It's just a bird. Nothing special," she said with a casualness she didn't feel. All birds were special to her. Each unique in their own way.

Talon's expression hardened, but he didn't reply.

Had he changed his mind about getting together? Her body protested at the thought. She knew she should say something to break the tension, but what?

Talon looked at her for a moment longer, his gaze searching her face, then he slowly smiled. "You won," he said. "What would you like for your prize?"

* * * * *

Chapter Five

Talon could smell her lie on the air. He couldn't decide what made him angrier, the fact that she'd lied or her casual dismissal of his other form. She'd called him nothing special. *Nothing special?*

He had half a mind to tell her to kiss his tail feathers. If he weren't so achingly hard, he'd do just that. Talon knew he was being ridiculous given Lynn's limited knowledge of the universe, but her careless words still stung.

He wanted her to be impressed by his other form. Show him the same interest that she had her condors. Was that too much to ask?

Lynn stepped out of the tent and held the flap open wide for him to enter. Talon hesitated, then glided into the cramped space and sat. He was far too tall to stand. Lynn followed, zipping the entry up behind her. She turned to face him and dropped to her knees.

"Did you really mean it?" she asked.

His brow furrowed. "What?"

"That I could have any prize I wanted?" Her gaze dropped to his lap.

Talon didn't bother to hide his body's response to her

nearness. Despite his anger, he still wanted her. He'd told her as much. So why hide it? "Yes," he said, his voice growing husky. "Anything you want."

She shook her head. "I can't believe I'm about to do this. I don't normally…I'm not normally…"

"This is different," he said.

"Yes, it is." Lynn crawled forward on her hands and knees. She paused, then her lips descended upon his collarbone.

Talon forced himself to remain still despite the urge to pull her down, roll her beneath him, and mount her like a wild beast in rut. It was important for Lynn to know that she was the one in charge—at least for now. It would ease her adjustment later, when he staked his claim…at least he hoped that it did.

Mating was something he'd never done before. Talon had expected it to be like any other joining, but he'd been wrong. He'd known that the second he'd laid hands on Lynn's lush curves.

Her lips were feather soft as she traced his collarbone up to his shoulder. She nipped him gently at the juncture of his neck, marking him. Talon's body tensed. Had Lynn done that on purpose? Did she have any idea what it meant to bite him there? He didn't know, wasn't sure, wasn't about to ask. Some things weren't that important.

He took a deep breath and curled his fingers into tight fists. The last thing he needed was for his talons to come out and scare her half to death. Lynn licked his neck and then dipped her tongue into his ear. Talon growled.

"A man only has so much control," he said, praying she *didn't* heed his warning. Talon had never given himself permission to let go completely. There'd always been a part of himself that he'd tucked away from the others. A part he'd specifically saved for his future mate.

"Let's see how long yours lasts," she said, then reached down and grasped his hard cock. She slowly stroked to the tip, circling the thick crown, before sliding back down.

Talon sucked in air with an audible gasp. "Do that again and you'll find out."

Lynn repeated the move. She knew she was playing with fire, but she couldn't seem to stop herself. She'd been so scared that Talon had changed his mind that she'd come frighteningly close to begging him to stay. When had she become so desperate? She'd never begged for anything in her life, except grant money.

Luckily, Talon hadn't let it come to that—thank goodness. Lynn wasn't sure she'd have ever lived that down.

She tightened her grip and stroked his hard satiny flesh, using her palm and fingers. Talon's shaft seemed to grow even larger. How was that possible? If he got any bigger, the Magnum-sized condom wouldn't fit. Lynn licked her lips and continued to tease him. She pressed a kiss to the corner of his mouth.

Talon snarled, then whipped his head around to capture her lips. He hadn't touched her beyond that, but he held her just the same. Lynn's pulse kicked as she sucked his tongue into her mouth. God, he tasted like heaven. It was wrong that a man should taste so good.

He deepened the kiss and she let him. Her hand moved faster now, gripping and releasing, pumping him hard. A cry broke from his lips and Talon shoved Lynn back onto the sleeping bag.

"Enough," he snapped. For a second, his eyes appeared to glow bright red, but the color was gone so fast that Lynn knew she'd imagined it.

"I'm not finished," she said, ignoring the little voice that told her that she was in over her head.

"My turn." Talon snarled and lowered his mouth to her aching breasts.

The first swipe of his tongue had Lynn's back bowing off the mat. Rocks shifted beneath their weight as he pressed his body down upon her and latched onto her nipple. He sucked hard enough to curl Lynn's toes. Instead of pushing him away, she grabbed his hair and pulled him closer.

Talon grinned around her flesh, then proceeded to tease her into submission. His hands seemed to be everywhere at once, plucking her nipples, then pinching them to the point of pain before soothing them with his mouth. Lynn's thighs clenched as her sex moistened. Her body tightened, ready, wanting, but he never let up.

She cried out in frustration. She wanted him inside her now, but no amount of urging got him to move. Lynn rocked her hips, brushing his shaft. Talon's breath hissed out, but he kept on lavishing her breasts with all his attention.

Her orgasm came out of nowhere. One second she'd been balancing on the precipice, the next, she'd tumbled over the edge. Lynn gasped and her body shuddered as the release continued to ripple through her in wave after glorious wave.

How in the world had Talon managed to do that?

Her expression must've have betrayed her unvoiced question because he said, "We're only getting started."

Talon couldn't get enough of her taste, her scent. The musky aroma of hot, moist woman filled the small space, making his head spin. Her nipples were now flushed deep red and swollen. He longed to devour them again, but there were other places he wanted to explore, places that called to something primal inside of him.

He kissed Lynn soundly on the lips, then slid down her body, wedging his wide shoulders between her thighs so she couldn't close her legs. Her rich spicy aroma was thicker here, more enticing. Talon leaned forward and inhaled. His eyes closed in ecstasy and he gave thanks once more.

"Do you have any idea how beautiful you are?" he asked, his voice a harsh whisper.

Lynn looked suddenly uncomfortable and she started to shift away from him.

"Don't!" His hand came down upon her abdomen to hold her in place.

"Why ruin the moment by saying stuff like that?" she asked, then quickly averted her gaze, but not before he'd spotted the pain lingering in the green depths.

Talon wondered what was wrong with the men on this planet. Didn't they have eyes? Couldn't they see the gifts before them?

"I told you that I wanted you," he said. "That hasn't changed." And it wouldn't. Sure, it was always *possible* that Lynn would turn out not to be his mate, but Talon didn't think so. Every instinct inside of him recognized her for what she was—*his*. "Look at me," he demanded. There was no way he'd allow her to hide from him. Not now. Not here. Not ever.

* * * * *

Lynn didn't move. Couldn't move. She was afraid to. What if when she met his gaze it was filled with lies? No, Talon hadn't given her any indication that he wasn't telling the truth, but Lynn knew men. More importantly, she knew herself. She didn't command this kind of attention from anyone, much less a man like him.

"I said look at me!"

The command made her jump. Lynn met Talon's gaze. It was hard and uncompromising. The intensity she saw there both thrilled and frightened her. "What do you want from me, Talon?"

"Everything," he said unflinchingly, then lowered his head and began to feast.

Talon's tongue seemed to dance on her skin like hummingbird wings as he fed voraciously upon her sex. He teased and licked, nipping at the hidden bundle of nerves, worrying it with his teeth, before sucking hard. Lynn's thighs clenched around his head and shoulders.

The sensations were too much, too intense. She squirmed in his grasp. Lynn wanted to get nearer, while at the same time her body struggled to get away. Talon never let up. Like a starving man denied access to a banquet, he plunged his tongue into her entrance, fluttering it faster than she thought humanly possible.

A keening cry was ripped from her throat. One thick finger replaced his tongue. Lynn bucked beneath him, clenching the sleeping bag. "Talon!" She gasped his name, then bit her lip as he sucked her clit between his teeth, while he continued to stroke in and out. "I can't," she murmured.

"You can. And you will," he said, biting down hard.

Lynn screamed as her body convulsed. Blood roared in her ears and the world dimmed around her.

Talon moved fast. He knew he didn't have much time. Lynn's eyes were closed, but they wouldn't be for long. He focused on his form, manipulating his molecules into nothingness, then slid through her body as easily as he walked through walls.

He appeared beneath her for a half second, then reversed direction, so he was staring down at her once more. Her lashes fluttered and a frown furrowed her delicate brow, but she didn't open her eyes.

Information from Lynn's memories flooded his mind, nearly blinding him with the sensory overload. In his heart, he'd known. He'd *always* known, from the moment he'd laid eyes on her. And now it was confirmed. Lynn was indeed his mate. His true-mate. His *only* mate.

Talon pulled her close and kissed her soundly. "Are you still with me?" he asked.

She cracked open an eyelid. "I've never felt an orgasm like that," she said. "It was like it went right through me. Wonderful, but weird."

He grinned. "There's more," he said, as joy filled his hearts. Talon winked, then positioned the head of his shaft against her dripping channel. He couldn't wait to get inside her, fill her empty womb with his seed. He nudged forward, his thick crown breaching her entrance. She was tight, oh so tight, and beyond perfect.

Lynn's eyes shot open and a look of panic crossed her face. "Wait!" she said and rolled to the side to grab something small.

"What's that?" he asked in confusion.

"Protection," she said as if that explained everything.

Talon's brows shot to his hairline. "Protection from what?" He jumped up and ripped the tent flap open. Crouching low, he quickly scanned the area with his predatory senses to make sure they weren't in any danger. Other than a few creatures nearby, Talon couldn't detect a threat.

"What are you doing?" It was Lynn's turn to look confused.

"Searching for the threat you spoke of?" he said, glancing over his shoulder at her.

Lynn laughed. "You're joking, right?"

His face heated. "I take your safety *very* seriously. I would never jest about such a thing."

She snorted, then beckoned him back inside the tent. "What planet have you been living on?" she asked, slipping something out of the small package and gently grasping his shaft.

Talon decided it was best not to answer that question. He didn't think Lynn was ready for the truth yet. Soon, all would be revealed. Her soft hands continued to pump his rigid flesh. The tension left his shoulders, only to return when she placed the stretchy substance onto the tip of his phallus. "What are you doing?" he asked.

"What do you think?"

He had no idea, but as long as she kept stroking his cock he wouldn't stop her.

* * * * *

CHAPTER SIX

Talon watched Lynn roll the strange material over his hard length. He didn't understand why she'd insisted on putting it on him, but he wasn't going to complain. She stroked him again, this time harder. He waited until she'd finished, then gently pushed her back onto the soft padding.

Her breath hitched as he positioned himself at the entrance of her moist opening. "Ready?" he asked.

She nodded.

His jaw clenched as he inched inside. The sensations were muted, but still strong. He slid in deeper, then waited for her body to adjust to his size, before pushing further.

Lynn gasped.

Talon stilled. "I haven't harmed you, have I?" he asked, fighting the need to thrust.

She shook her head and her lashes fluttered open. "You're just big... And it's been a while."

He trembled at her admission. Happy beyond words that she hadn't lain with another male in a long while and that she found his size more than acceptable. Talon had never had any complaints from females before, but this time was different. This time was the first time he was joining with his mate. He wanted their first time together to be perfect. He wanted to bring her nothing, but pleasure.

Lynn canted her hips and he slipped in deeper. Talon groaned as her vise-like channel held him tight.

"You feel incredible," he bit out, as sweat covered his brow.

"I swear I won't break," she said, then reached around him and sunk her fingernails into his ass.

Talon's body jerked, sending him surging inside her.

Lynn's lungs heaved as her body clamped down on him. "Don't move," she said.

He froze, his muscles trembling as he fought for control.

A few interminable moments later, her body relaxed. "That's better," she said.

"I will try to be gentle," he grit out from between clenched teeth.

"The time for 'gentle' ended thirty seconds ago," she said, then blushed.

Talon's nostrils flared. Incited by her provocative words, he pulled back, then thrust deep, watching with pure male satisfaction as her eyes glazed with passion.

"You're mine," he growled, then began to ride her in earnest, branding her with his body, while he savaged her with his mouth.

Lynn couldn't seem to catch her breath. Talon caged her with his broad shoulders, his gaze intense and heated. She forced her body to relax as she took him deep. He was so massive that for one crazy moment she'd thought he wouldn't fit. Luckily he had. Now she was getting the full brunt of his deliciously large cock. The man had talent. She'd give him that.

Somewhere inside of her a little voice admitted that once with Talon would never been enough. He knew just where to touch her and exactly how to please her. It was as if he'd been given a skeleton key to unlock the secrets to satisfying her body and her body alone. One bout of lovemaking, and he'd as good as ruined her for other men.

He surged forward, driving straight to her soul, taking her to heights she'd never imagined reaching. Had never reached before. Silk encased in steel, his cock battered her senses, demanding entrance to her heart.

This was a fling. Only a fling. She told herself in hopes that it would help when he walked away. Lynn wasn't foolish enough to believe there was more than sex happening here…even if it *felt* like it.

She searched his passion taut face for clues to his thoughts. His lashes lay at half-mast, keeping secrets, hiding truths. Did he mean it when he said that she was his? In the heat of the moment, lies easily slipped from tongues.

Lynn didn't care. If this were all they'd ever have together, she'd take it. Savor it. Store it away in her memories for the rest of her life. She wanted this man. She wanted Talon. As if reading her thoughts, he thrust hard, taking her breath.

"Who do you belong to?" He grunted, as sweat dripped from his brow.

"No one," she lied, while her traitorous body sought a deeper connection.

Talon's eyes narrowed until she could barely make out the glints of color beneath his lids. "Wrong answer," he said, rolling his hips and taking her mouth in a searing kiss that demanded her submission, her surrender.

Lynn's breath shuddered as her body threatened to shatter into a million pieces. "I don't need promises," she said, ripping her mouth away.

"I do!" he growled. Talon reached between their bodies and found her hard, swollen, and receptive. He stroked the tiny nub once, twice. On the third swipe, Lynn flew apart, taking him with her.

She barely felt his teeth lock onto her shoulder and bite down. The quick sting from the bite was followed by a wave of pleasure, as his tongue licked the spot, soothing the tender skin.

"Tell me that you are mine," he murmured, planting soft kisses on her neck.

Lynn couldn't seem to focus. Despite finding the kind of release that women dream about—hell, write sonnets about, her body moved restlessly beneath him, wanting more, needing more. What was happening?

She pushed up and he slipped out of her. The emptiness created an ache that wasn't about to be wished away. Lynn had never been a nymphomaniac. Sure, she'd enjoyed sex, even managed to orgasm with her partners, but it had never been like this. This was all encompassing, all consuming. This was the kind of thing that could change a woman for life…or scar her. Probably both.

For some reason, she couldn't get enough of him. "More," she said, and barely recognized her own voice when the husky request spilled out.

The musky sweet scent on Talon's skin poured over her, leaving her euphoric, but far from satisfied. Lynn's nipples beaded, hungry for his mouth, his touch. She arched her back to brush against his chest in hopes it would ease a fraction of the desire storming through her. It didn't. If anything, the move made her even more ravenous. It should've been impossible, but she actually felt her clit swell and her sex flood again.

Her body was acting like he hadn't just fucked her to within an inch of her life. She whimpered, then leaned forward and latched onto Talon's lower lip, sucking hard. He groaned and followed her back down onto the sleeping bag.

"What did you do to me?" she asked, pulling at his hair, trying to get closer, while her body took on a life of its own.

"I made you mine," he said without remorse.

She writhed beneath him, teasing his flaccid flesh back to life. Talon's cock rose hard and thick from the light nest of curls covering his sex, swelling even bigger than it had the first time.

"I need to feel you," she said, rocking to sooth the emptiness inside her. "All of you." Lynn knew what she was about to do was utter insanity, but for some reason, she couldn't stop herself. She reached down between their bodies and pulled the used condom off Talon's shaft. "I'm clean. Are you?"

He gasped, then grabbed her hand before she could pull it away and curled it around his growing girth. Lynn teased him, slowly at first, then faster. His pupils dilated and his gaze seemed to sharpen.

"You carry my scent." Pleasure filled his voice. "You are now part of me. No harm will ever come to you from me— or anyone else."

Lynn inhaled, but all she could smell was the aroma of hot, sizzling man. "I want you again."

"Tell me that you're mine," he said. It was a demand.

She shook her head and Talon pulled back. "No!" Lynn shouted. "Please, I need you." Her body was making demands she had no idea how to meet. All she knew for sure was that Talon held the key.

He teased her breasts, making delicate circles around her nipples without touching them. It was like heaven and hell combined. She needed more. Lynn needed his hard shaft back inside her. Skin to skin. Breath to breath.

"I will give you all that you want, but not until you admit the truth," he said.

Lynn's head thrashed in frustration. She rose up and tried to force him inside her. Talon's breath hissed, but he held firm though she could tell it cost him to do so.

He pinned her down, dominating her with his hard body. His firm touch sent licks of flames dancing over her skin. "Tell me!"

"I'm yours," she whispered. It was the truth, but Lynn knew she'd pay later for admitting as much. Now he held all the power. Talon could destroy her heart with the drop of one careless word and she had no way of recovering.

Instead of gloating, Talon smiled. "Was that so difficult?" he asked.

"You have no idea." Lynn scooted down trying to get closer to him. Before she could move into place, Talon grabbed her and kissed her hard. When she opened her eyes, he was lying beneath her and she was straddling his thick thighs. "What just happened?"

He shrugged. "I rolled us over."

It hadn't felt like he'd rolled her over, but Lynn wasn't going to complain since this put him exactly where she wanted him.

Before she could move, he stopped her. "I swear on my Clan's honor that your heart and body are safe with me," he said, gently running the back of his hand over her nipple.

Tears welled in her eyes. Embarrassed by the sudden swell of emotion, Lynn scrubbed them away and prayed he'd been too preoccupied by her large breasts to notice. The last thing she wanted was for Talon to know how much those words had meant to her…even if they weren't the truth.

Lynn grasped Talon's hard shaft, then lifted herself over him and slowly slid down. His jaw clenched and his cheeks flushed, but he did nothing to stop her—or help.

Talon had crossed the line between agony and pleasure an hour ago. Every muscle in his body clenched as Lynn melted over him, swallowing his hard length until they fused together as one.

As he'd suspected, the strange substance she'd rolled onto his shaft earlier had muted the sensations. Now there was nothing between them. Nothing to hold back the pleasure. Nothing to keep them apart. Nothing to prevent the bond.

Every instinct he had screamed at him to pump hard and get his seed into her, but he locked them down before he could act. Already, he'd lost form and passed through her. The first time, he'd done it on purpose, but this time it had been because she'd made him lose control. Talon had *never* lost control before. The realization shook him to the core.

Still, he had no regrets. Talon knew the more times he passed through her, the more his essence would imprint on her and strengthen the bond that had started to build between them.

Already her body recognized his, demanded his touch. Soon the mating frenzy would take over and she'd become insatiable. It was only fair, since he was already. The need to join with him would continue until her first shift, which wouldn't be long now.

Her green eyes already held a hint of a red ring around them. It would eventually darken, then her wings would sprout and the urge to fly would be undeniable. And then Talon would finally be able to admit the truth about who he was and why he was here.

There was no doubt that Lynn suspected something was up, but her need had been too great to question him. Talon knew that wouldn't last. His mate had a sharp mind. He'd thought so before, but now he knew for sure. She deserved answers, but they'd have to come later—after her first shift.

* * * * *

Lynn saw the flash of desire in Talon's eyes as she took him into her body, cradling him tight. His rapid breathing matched her own. She waited only a moment, then began to move. The skin on skin contact sent shivers up her spine, crinkling her nipples into hard round nubs.

She reached up and pinched them. The pleasure-pain made her gasp. Talon's eyes widened, then a slow smile spread across his handsome face as he watched.

"Do that again," he said, his voice a dark rumble.

Lynn did, enjoying the power that came with having a man's complete and undivided attention. His hands clamped down on her hips as she rocked back and forth, pinching and pulling at her beasts with nimble fingers.

"Offer me a taste." He swelled inside her.

She held out one nipple and waited, breathlessly for him to take it.

Talon sat up and swiped his tongue over the rigid flesh, then blew warm air over her. Lynn sucked in a breath, but didn't pull away. He leaned forward and latched onto her, sucking gently at first, then harder. His hips rose with each pull of his mouth, going deeper and deeper.

Lynn's breathing hitched, then she lifted, slamming down on Talon as he thrust up. They both gasped, then repeated the move. "You are an amazing man," she said, snaking her hand down his rugged chest, sliding her fingers between their bodies. "A girl could get used to this, you know?"

He let go of her nipple and looked up at her. His odd colored eyes warmed on contact, shimmering with an emotion that Lynn didn't think possible given the short period of time that they'd known each other. "I certainly hope so because I intend to give you this every day for the rest of our lives."

Her heart leapt in her chest. Lynn knew it was the lust talking, but for just one moment she allowed herself to believe. "Shut up and kiss me, Talon," she murmured.

He did with a slow slide of tongue along the seam of her lips. Lynn sank into the embrace, savoring it like a greedy child with a full bag of Halloween candy. He tasted so good and smelled even better. If it wouldn't make her insanely jealous to know other women were wearing his scent, she'd bottle it.

She continued to ride him until her body quivered and her channel fluttered in a final rapturous release. Talon watched the ecstasy color her features. His hearts pounded. Whether it was one or a hundred lifetimes, he'd never get over the joy of seeing Lynn draped in his arms like this.

He waited for the last ripples to end, then rolled her beneath him. He was too exhausted to pass through her, so he did it the human way. Her arms were relaxed, but remained loosely wrapped around his shoulders. Talon closed his eyes and inhaled. The scent of sweet satisfied woman teased his nostrils as he began to move. It wouldn't take long now.

Lynn raised her legs and locked her ankles around his thighs. Talon felt the tension build deep within him. She placed her lips on the side of his jaw, then licked and kissed her way to where his neck and shoulder met. Lynn swirled her tongue over that spot, teasing him, driving him to the point of madness.

Talon's balls rose, pulling tight against his body. "Bite me," he hissed.

She kissed him again, sucking a little.

"Do it!" he ground out. "Hard!"

Lynn smiled against his skin, then bit down. Her flat, blunt teeth broke the skin.

Talon's body shook and he bellowed as his release rushed out in a surge so powerful it nearly blinded him. "You are mine," he gasped. "Now and forever."

* * * * *

CHAPTER SEVEN

Lynn's body ached in all the right places as she and Talon dressed, then made their way out of the tent. She didn't know about him, but she was ravenous. She was pretty sure she could eat a water buffalo by herself.

Unfortunately, the buffalo would have to wait until she got back to civilization. Instead, dried chicken and rice would have to do. She still couldn't believe that she'd brought a stranger back to her camp for sex. She'd never done anything that crazy. Ever. Not even in her wild college days.

To make matters worse, she'd actually bit him until he'd bled. Completely unsanitary, not to mention dangerous. If Talon knew how many germs were lurking in the human mouth, he would've never asked her to do it. Of course, she did and that hadn't stopped her.

Maybe he had a vampire fetish. She looked at him. He really didn't seem the type, but you never really knew what people did in the privacy of their own homes. Lynn didn't like vampires. The whole undead thing was a real turnoff, so why had she enjoyed biting Talon so much?

She glanced his way again. He truly was gorgeous. The

fact that he was sitting on the shore staring at her like she was the most beautiful woman he'd ever laid eyes on, only made him more so in her mind. Lynn wanted nothing more than to rush over and fall into his arms. But she couldn't, wouldn't—at least not yet.

Despite having *intimate* knowledge of his body, Talon *was* still a stranger in so many ways. Lynn knew nothing about the man. Where did he come from? Did he have any family? What did he do for a living? What was he doing here in the Canyon? Did they have anything in common other than great sex?

So what if it *felt* like she knew him. That was just her hormones talking. Everyone knew they couldn't be trusted, when it came to making rational decisions. The last few hours were proof of that. Hormones were a bunch of slutty little Benedict Arnolds if you asked her.

Lynn finished heating the chicken up, then dished it into two bowls. "Lunch is ready," she said. Even though this was lunch and breakfast for her. She poured herself a cup of coffee, then held one out for him.

Talon took the cup and the bowl, then sat down next to her. He sniffed the food, then asked, "What is this?"

"Chicken," Lynn said. "Sorry, I didn't bring much of a variety."

Talon blanched, then took a small bite. His face slowly turned green as he swallowed.

Lynn laughed. She couldn't help it. The look on his face was priceless. She half expected him to spit the food out, but his good manners prevented it. "You don't have to eat it if you don't like it. I'm sure I have a protein bar in my pack somewhere."

Talon looked relieved, then handed the bowl back to her. "Sorry, I'm afraid I don't have much of a taste for fowl."

"That's okay," she said, then handed him the bar.

He took it gingerly, then dug in, sipping the coffee as he ate. "This is really good," he said, holding up the cup.

"What's it called?"

Lynn blinked. Was he serious? She searched his face, but couldn't find any humor hiding in his expression. She shrugged. "It's just regular coffee."

"May I have more?" Talon asked.

"Sure." She refilled his cup.

They ate in silence, each lost in their thoughts. Finally Talon spoke. "What are you doing in the Canyon?"

"I came here to check on my birds," she said, placing the bowls off to the side.

"Your birds?" he asked.

Lynn smiled, happy to discuss something besides what was going to happen next. "I'm an ornithologist."

Talon frowned.

"I'm a scientist who studies birds," she said to clarify.

His expression brightened. "That's wonderful."

Lynn got the impression he'd been about to say something else, but she didn't press. If Talon thought what she did for a living was boring, she could live without knowing the truth. "I'm part of a condor reintroduction program. We released two condors into the Grand Canyon last year and I'm here to see how they're doing."

That explained why she'd been perched on the cliff face, when he'd first spotted her in person. "And is your program a success?"

"Yes!" She beamed. "They've successfully mated."

"How do you know?" he asked.

She brushed her hands off on her pants. "I found their nesting site."

"Is that why you were up the side of the cliff?" he asked.

She took a sip of coffee. "How did you know that I climbed one of the cliffs?"

Talon kicked himself for saying too much. There was no way he should've known about the nest and her climb. After all *he* hadn't been there. "Where else would birds nest in this rugged terrain?"

She nodded, but he could practically see the questions forming behind those wide green eyes. "The nest looks sound and will be a secure place to hatch a baby condor."

"Ah, yes, the egg," he said absently.

Lynn put her cup down. "I didn't say there was an egg in the nest."

"Are you sure? I could've sworn that you'd mentioned it," he said, placing his empty cup beside him.

She shook her head. "No, all I said was that they'd successfully mated and that I'd found the nest. Not that they had an egg."

"Perhaps, I just assumed…" Talon was having a difficult time keeping track of their conversation. He kept getting distracted by her delicious scent and the rise and fall of her luscious breasts.

Lynn's eyes narrowed. "What did you say you were doing in the Canyon again?"

"I came here to get the lay of the land," he said, not wanting to lie to his mate. It was the truth. Just not the whole truth.

"What's that supposed to mean?" she asked. Despite her growing attraction and the connection she felt between them, warning bells were going off in Lynn's head. She'd heard them before, but having Talon naked in her sleeping bag had made it so easy to dismiss them.

Clothed, he was still distracting, but at least she could think clearly one again. Something about Talon's arrival didn't add up. Why was he being so evasive? Was he embarrassed about what he was doing here? Had he come to the Canyon with someone? A female someone? The thought sent pain spiking through her heart. Surely, if he'd come here with someone he would've said something.

Yeah, right, Lynn. Being honest is the first thing men think about when they stumble upon a naked and willing woman.

"Where are you camped?" she asked, praying she was

wrong about Talon. If he had someone waiting, he'd probably make an excuse to leave soon.

"Not far from here," he said, giving her another non-answer.

Lynn stood, gathering what was left of her pride. "Sorry to call an end to the afternoon, but I need to get some work done. I still have a ton of documenting to finish."

"Yeah, I should probably go check on my campsite," he said, glancing around as if he couldn't get out of there soon enough.

She nodded and her stomach soured. She was such a fool. "Sure, I understand." Lynn picked up the bowls and swirled some water around them to give her trembling hands something to do. "Guess I'll see you around." An ache started in her chest and spread through her body as the words slipped from her lips. The thought of never seeing Talon again hurt more than she imagined it would.

Cut your losses now before you can't walk away, the insidious little voice inside her head whispered. *You knew going in it was just a quick fling.*

Logically, Lynn knew that was the truth, but that knowledge didn't change the feelings he'd managed to stir up in the few hours they'd shared together. No wonder she'd avoided one night stands all these years. She wasn't wired to sleep with someone, and then walk away.

Lynn sensed more than saw Talon approach. She looked up when he was nearly upon her. Before she could speak, he pulled her into his arms and kissed her, taking her breath from her lungs and giving her some of his own. His tongue barely brushed hers, but it was enough to send tingles trotting along her spine. Her traitorous nipples hardened and her channel clenched, betraying her need.

"I must go," he said. "But I shall return. Soon."

She didn't trust her voice enough to respond, so Lynn nodded and forced a smile. As much as she wanted him and couldn't imagine life without him, she knew this was for the best. Today had been a mistake. One she'd never forget.

Talon gripped her chin and tilted it up until their eyes met. "Be safe, mate." He gave her another quick kiss, then turned and left.

Mate? What did he mean by that?

Lynn held her tongue. Her heart hammered in her chest as she watched him go. She had the overwhelming urge to run after Talon and beg him to stay, which was reason enough not to.

She shook her head and forced herself to get her climbing gear together. She wasn't a weak woman. So what if she'd had the best sex in her life? So what if it felt like her heart was breaking?

She'd get over it like she'd gotten over all the others. It just might take a while longer with Talon. Okay, make that a lot longer. Determined to overrule her emotions and bypass her raging hormones, Lynn forced her brain to focus on her work. She finished packing in record time and hit the trail.

* * * * *

Talon made sure that he was out of sight before he shifted and took to the sky. It had taken every fiber of his being to walk away from Lynn Regis, but he'd had no choice. He had to contact the ship and let them know that his hunt for a mate had been a success.

He'd planned to tell Lynn the truth before he left, but he hadn't been able to. At first she'd seemed so vulnerable, then that vulnerability shifted to anger. He still didn't understand what had made her mad or why she'd grown suspicious, but he'd find out eventually. Lynn was changing quickly. Quicker than he'd anticipated. The red ring that had begun to form when they were making love was now complete.

Talon had watched it darken while they ate. Soon the rest of her body would follow. He needed to be there when that happened. No one should experience a shift on their own, especially a human not used to seeing such things.

He hurried to the rim, then opened a pouch on his flight suit. A small communication device glowed inside. Talon took it out and set it on the ground, then pressed a button. A Phantom pilot from the Claw Clan appeared in three-dimensional form before him.

"Commander, are you ready to return to the ship?" He leaned forward with feline grace.

Talon shook his head. "Not yet, but soon. I have found my mate. She's in the process of transformation now. Once that's complete, we'll be ready for extraction."

The pilot smiled. "Congratulations, Commander."

"Thank you! May you have the same luck upon your arrival, Linx."

The Phantom Warrior blinked, then gave him a lazy smile. "From what I hear, I'll have many to choose from. Perhaps I'll have to give a few a try before settling down."

Talon laughed. "Be careful, warrior. The women here might not like your alley-cat ways."

Linx grinned. "I've never had any complaints."

"That may be true, but cross the wrong woman and you might end up neutered," Talon said and laughed at the young warrior's confused expression. He'd learn the score soon enough.

* * * * *

CHAPTER EIGHT

It only took an hour for Lynn to realize that she wasn't going to make it in time to the cliff-side to get in a climb. She'd spent too many hours fooling around with Talon. Just the thought of his muscle-strewn body sent a rush of desire through her. Between the brush of her T-shirt and the slide of her khakis, Lynn was convinced she'd go out of her mind.

Her body seemed hypersensitive and far too revved for someone who'd just spent the afternoon having mind-blowing sex. Shouldn't she be sated by now? She hitched her backpack higher and began the slow journey back to camp. As much as she'd enjoyed her day with Talon—okay more than enjoyed—she couldn't allow him to distract her tomorrow. Lynn had a job to do.

She picked her way along the trail wondering not for the first time if he'd be waiting when she returned. He'd told her that he had to check on his campsite. Was that the truth? Or was it just a polite way to blow her off? Lynn didn't know. She shouldn't really care…but she did.

She'd never let a man get under her skin. Had never met a man capable of doing so until she'd met Talon. Something inside of him called to her. As sappy as that sounded. There was a familiarity, a comfort that she felt around him that had never existed in her life before now—at least with people.

Lynn didn't connect with many people. In fact, she connected with very few. Most people didn't get her. And to be honest, she didn't get most people. She was far more at ease in the company of her birds.

She'd certainly never fallen into bed at the drop of hat. No, she was the watch first, calculate, analyze, then leap kind of girl. So why had she thrown caution to the wind and jumped at the chance to be with Talon?

She was still asking herself that question when she returned to camp. Lynn had just rounded the final boulder when her tent came into sight. It was immediately apparent that Talon had not returned. Or if he had, he'd left again. Her heart sank at the thought that she might have missed him.

You're pathetic. Snap out of it, the voice inside her head shouted. *What did you expect?*

So maybe she *had* hoped he'd return. Maybe she'd hoped that this morning and afternoon meant more to him that a quick roll in her sleeping bag. Lynn wasn't disappointed, darn it. She wasn't...and she would just keep telling herself that until she believed it.

Lynn went to work cleaning up her campsite. If she were busy, then she'd have no time to think about Talon. She cleared brush and re-washed her clean dishes, then took a quick swim. The water was warmer now—thanks to hours of direct sunshine. She stroked back and forth across the expanse until exhaustion threatened and her muscles quivered. If nothing else, being tired would allow her to sleep better.

She made a quick meal of mushrooms and rice, then got ready for bed. The sun had already sunk behind the rim, leaving the lower Canyon draped in shadows. When she ran out of things to do, Lynn slipped into her tent and zipped it closed behind her.

Inhaling, she instantly realized her mistake. The whole

tent smelled like Talon. Her sleeping bag, the mat beneath it, even her floor held a hint of the spicy scent that he carried on his skin.

She groaned and threw the sleeping bag open. As much as Lynn wanted to unzip the tent door, she couldn't afford to since there were predators who hunted in the Canyon...not to mention snakes and scorpions. Nope, she'd just have to suck it up for the night or maybe plug her nose with tissues. She punched her pillow and closed her eyes.

The second sleep yanked her under the dreams began. They were foggy at first, smudged images on a dirty lens that refused to come into sharp focus. Stunning battles played out between giant winged creatures and lizard-like beings that were barely humanoid in shape.

The foes changed, but the large raptors remained as the battles raged on. Outstretched talons gripped bits of flesh. Blood covered dark feathers. Fierce cries pierced the green sky.

Scene after scene, fight after fight, Lynn watched in fascinated horror as the creatures took on enemies twice their size. The fact that they had wings didn't seem to matter. They fought just as hard, if not harder because of it.

Eventually, the blood faded and the birds' proud faces morphed into men. One of those faces she recognized instantly. It was Talon. He stood before her, his head held high. Eyes, once so familiar, now glowed bright red.

"Now you know," he said quietly.

"Know what?" she muttered in her sleep. Where had the beautiful bird gone?

Talon knew Lynn was asleep, when he returned. He'd sensed her restlessness, heard her incoherent mumbles. He thought about waking her, but decided against it. She needed her rest and so did he. Tomorrow was going to be a very trying day. The Phantom ship would reach them and Talon had to somehow convince his mate to come with him.

He didn't relish having to do the latter. Lynn was a

logical woman. Telling her that he was an alien wouldn't sit well with her. Humans believed they were alone in the universe. Talon knew better. Still, there had to be a way.

Already he could sense the changing taking place within her. Her skin no longer held the honeyed aroma it once had. Now Lynn smelled like a combo of them both. A rich earthy fragrance that he more than approved of. No Phantom Warrior would be stupid enough to go near her now.

Talon wondered if she'd missed him as much as he'd missed her today. They'd only been apart a few hours, yet he felt as if it had been eons. Is this what having a mate felt like? Or was this unique between them? He hoped it was the latter. Talon liked the idea of his mate needing him, wanting him—and only him, while they were apart.

He listened to her steady breathing for a few minutes more, then slipped away, taking to the sky. Talon perched himself on the rim so he had a good view of her camp and could see danger coming from any direction.

"Sleep well, mate," he whispered on the wind. "For tomorrow you'll need all your strength."

* * * * *

Lynn awoke alone. Being alone wasn't a surprise, but the disappointment that followed sure was. Regret snapped doggedly on its heels, leaving her in a grumpy mood. It didn't help that her neck had crick in it. She threw the sleeping bag back and climbed out of the tent to stretch.

A dark shadow glided over her. Lynn glanced up and saw the strange bird soaring above the Canyon rim. It was back. She shielded her eyes to get a better look, but once again it was gone as quickly as it had arrived.

"Not today you don't," she said, throwing her clothes on. She'd left her gear packed from the previous night, so within minutes she was dressed and ready to go.

Lynn caught sight of the massive bird thirty minutes into

her hike to the condors' nesting site. It seemed to be making large loops in the sky, circling back around to look at her. She took out her camera and shot a few photos. The first image looked like a black smudge on the screen, but the second one was clearer. Lynn enlarged it hoping to identify the bird. But no markings gave it away.

"What are you?"

She reached the condor-nesting site thirty minutes later. She'd lost sight of the big raptor again, but if it stayed true to form it should be circling around in a few more minutes. Lynn wanted to get up the cliff before it did. She wanted a better look—a closer look at the bird. She also wanted to make sure it hadn't disturbed the condors' egg.

She gathered her gear and began the slow climb up the cliff face. Like before, the climb took her way longer than she would've liked. Lynn was sweating and her face was flushed by the time the outcropping came into sight. She cleared the remaining feet that separated her from the condor nest, then clamped down on her rope.

Lynn could tell by the dark head popping out of the nest that one of her condors was sitting on the nest. She dare not get any closer. She didn't want to startle the bird and have it crack the egg. She pulled out her camera and took a few photos, then put it away to retrieve her notepad.

"Beautiful, isn't she?" A masculine voice said from behind her, sending her heart rate rocketing.

Lynn yelped and fumbled with her notebook, nearly dropping it down the cliff. Despite her immediate disbelief, she'd recognize that voice anywhere. She twisted in her ropes until she could see Talon. He looked even more beautiful perched on the side of the cliff than he had rising out of the water. How was that possible?

"Wh-what are you doing up here?" she sputtered. He hadn't been there before. She was sure of it. She would've seen him as she ascended. Had he repelled down? She scanned the cliff face.

He shrugged. "Climbing."

Her eyes narrowed as she took in his strange attire and the fact that he had no ropes to speak of. Okay, so he hadn't repelled. Well he darn sure hadn't flown. "How did you get up here?" she asked, checking for climbing spikes.

"I'm quite nimble when I want to be," he said, a secretive smile forming on his lips.

Surely he wasn't crazy enough to free climb this rock face. Didn't he know how dangerous that was? What if he fell? "You're insane," she said, trying not to let the fear creep into her voice.

Talon frowned. "I thought you'd be glad to see me."

"I was." She paused to align her thoughts. "I mean I am. You just startled me. I thought I was up here alone. What are you doing here?" Lynn needed to know. Nothing made sense when it came to him. She'd overlooked a lot thanks to the mind-shattering sex, but not now. Not halfway up the Canyon side. Lynn wanted answers.

Instead of giving them, Talon went into a summery of condor history and breeding habits that would shame any ornithologist. Well, any ornithologist, but her. By the time he'd finished his little educational speech, Lynn had moved from surprised to downright suspicious.

The only people who knew that much about condors were either ornithologists or egg thieves and Talon had already hinted that he wasn't in her field of study, which made him…a thief.

Was that the reason they'd met? Had he planned the whole thing just so he could get close to her and find the nest? Talon was a gorgeous man. He could have anyone he wanted. Yet, he'd picked her. Why? The truth stung, hurting way more than Lynn wanted to admit.

"What's wrong?" he asked, watching her closely.

"I don't like being lied to," she replied. Lynn's back started to burn like a fire ant colony had suddenly taken up residence under her skin. She swung around, trying to scratch it against the rock, but it didn't seem to help.

"You need to get down." Talon inched closer.

Lynn held out her hands. "Just stay right there before you fall. I'll be fine," she said, but she didn't feel like she was going to be fine. Something was wrong. Very wrong. Lynn glanced up and saw that the rim was only six feet away. It would be easier to climb the short distance, than to rappel down.

"You need to get on level ground." He followed her line of sight. "Yes, up will do nicely."

She didn't know what Talon meant by that last remark and Lynn didn't care. Whatever was happening to her was getting worse. She did need to get onto solid ground fast or she was going to fall. "What about you?" she grit out between clenched teeth.

"Don't worry, I'm used to heights. I'll be right behind you," he said.

* * * * *

CHAPTER NINE

Talon was waiting for Lynn when she pulled herself up and over the Canyon's rim. She flopped onto her back, panting from the exertion. The crunch of loose rock caught her attention and she whipped her head around.

"What are you…how did you?" She sat up and glanced over the side. No way had he beat her up here. She'd had ropes. He was free-climbing and he darn sure hadn't passed her. The warning bells that had gone off earlier now chimed like Big Ben in her head.

"It's time," Talon said, not answering her question.

Lynn slowly climbed to her feet. "Time for what?"

"Have you ever dreamed of flying?" he asked, instead.

"Sure, hasn't everyone?" she said, not liking the direction this conversation was taking.

"What if I told you that you could fly without the use of a plane?" he said.

Lynn paused. "I'd say you were crazy."

Talon didn't respond.

The pain in her back increased, doubling her over at the waist. "What's happening?" she gasped, twisting and turning to try to get a better look at her shoulder blades. Fat tears welled in Lynn's eyes, then spilled down her cheeks. "Did you drug my water or something?" The thought terrified her, but she didn't know what else could be causing so much pain.

Talon flinched at the accusation. He'd never drug his mate. If she weren't in agony, he'd explain as much, but he didn't think Lynn was up to listening to reasoning at present.

Every cry that ripped from her throat shredded his soul. If he could take it away, he'd gladly do so, but there was no avoiding this part of the transformation. It mattered not that Lynn was a human. Even Phantom Warriors experienced this growing up.

"I'm sorry," he said, meaning every word. "The first time is painful, but it does get easier."

Lynn glared at him. "The first time for what? You'd better start explaining what you've done to me."

"I can't. You wouldn't believe," he said, hoping that the process hurried up. Talon couldn't stand to see her like this, especially knowing that he was the cause.

She took a step toward him and swayed on her feet. "Why would you do this to me?"

"It was the only way to know for sure." Talon had been dreading this since he'd found Lynn. How could he explain that he was from another world without convincing her that he was mad? He couldn't. Already she believed the worst. "Words are inadequate. I think it's time to show you the truth." He walked toward her.

Lynn tried to stop him. "Don't touch me." She was afraid if he did, she'd crumble. Or do something really stupid like let him hold her. God, somehow Talon had turned her into one of those simpering heroines that were too stupid to live.

He stopped a few feet away, watching her like she was a dancing amoeba under a microscope lens. "I can help you, but I must get closer to do so," he said patiently.

Lynn vowed to kick his perfect butt, when she was feeling better. Until then, could she trust him to come closer?

Fire sliced down her back, taking the choice out of her hands. She screamed. "I don't care what you have to do. Fix it! Fix it now!"

Talon took a deep breath and approached. He gently slipped his arm around her shoulders and held her tight. "I'm sorry, but this *really* is the only way," he murmured, placing a kiss on her temple a second before he flung them both over the side of the Canyon rim.

Rocks raced past her head, blurring into a swirl of orange and beige, as they plunged toward the Canyon floor. Lynn went through shock, heartbreak, and terror all within a span of a second as she realized they were about to die. How could she have been so stupid?

The pain searing her back exploded, ripping her shirt in the process. One second she was falling, the next Lynn found herself gliding over the Colorado River, her body supported by a set of massive wings. It wasn't possible. She blinked and looked again. Yet, the wings remained, protruding from her back.

It took her another minute to realize she was no longer looking at *her* back, unless she'd somehow sprouted black feathers. Was it possible she'd hit the Canyon wall and died? Or maybe she was still dying? That would explain the odd hallucination.

Lynn hadn't lied when she'd told Talon that she'd dreamed of flying, but none of those dreams involved growing wings and gaining feathers.

She looked around for Talon, but didn't immediately spot him. Lynn searched the Canyon floor, expecting to see his body lying amongst the rocks. The thought made her chest clench. Even though he'd pushed her off the cliff, she didn't want to see him like that. Not Talon. He was too vibrant, too alive.

A cry sounded to her right. Lynn swung around and saw a large raptor coming straight for her. *Talon!* The name whispered in her mind, even though logic told her it wasn't possible.

Yet, even in this other form, Lynn would recognize him anywhere. And she did. He was her missing bird. The bird she'd spotted in the Canyon two days ago. Had it really only been two days? It seemed like a lifetime ago. She also recognized him from the *dream*.

Lynn watched him soar over the Canyon rim and circle above her before dipping close. She opened her mouth to speak, but the only thing that came out was a piercing screech.

Just relax and think about flying, Talon's sexy voice floated into her head.

You have a lot of explaining to do, buddy, she sent the thought back, hoping he received it. *You owe me that much after the stunt you just pulled.* Lynn had so many questions. How had this happened? Where had he come from? How long could they remain airborne? She needed answers, but knew the questions could wait until they got back onto firm ground.

For now, she'd do as Talon suggested. She flapped her wings hard, then caught the first of many thermals, allowing her to glide over the Grand Canyon for miles. Despite her fear and anger over being deceived, this was the first time in Lynn's life that she felt light as a feather and totally free. The woman in her rejoiced, while the scientist took copious amounts of mental notes.

She watched mice scurry along the rough terrain, seeking refuge as they passed by overhead. The wind was warm against her feathers, even though she knew it should feel cool given the temp.

Talon circled her, enticing her to play. Lynn managed to hold onto her 'mad' for another three loops, then gave up and enjoyed herself. They soared together, dipping close, then pulling out, wings barely brushing in the process.

In human form, that touch would've sent heat searing through her. But in her current avian state—okay, maybe it was the same, but Lynn wasn't about to admit as much. Despite the thrill of flying, she *was* still mad at him or maybe she was in shock. That would explain her odd acceptance of the situation.

Sure, explaining that he was some kind of birdman might've been difficult. And if she were being honest with herself, Lynn realized she might not have immediately believed him. Okay, so she wouldn't have believed Talon at all. She'd have actually thought he was insane, if he'd come right out and said something when they'd first met. But none of that justified lying to her. He could've eased her into the truth had he wanted, but instead, he'd given her non-answers caged in cryptic phrases.

Lynn's heart began to pound when she thought about the unprotected sex. Was that why she'd turned into a bird? Oh my god! She tumbled from the sky, beak over wing. Before she hit the ground, Talon grabbed her with his sharp claws and pulled up.

No, not claws...*talons*.

Maniacal laughter bubbled up inside her, but the only sound that came out was another loud squawk. This couldn't be happening.

Land! The command boomed inside her head a second before Talon released her.

Lynn flapped her wings and aimed for the rim of the Canyon. She landed hard, sending up a spray of rock. Not bad for her first time, she thought in her *unbiased* opinion. Before she could move, Talon was on top of her, pinning her to the ground.

You are mine, he growled in her head, then held her with his beak and entered her.

It was an odd sensation, not nearly as pleasurable, but strangely enticing given the primitive nature of their sudden joining. Still, sense memory kicked in and her body responded to his savage touch. The mating in this form didn't take long. A few wing flaps and a swish of her tail and it was over.

Talon hopped off her back. As Lynn watched, his shape shimmered and morphed. Feathers were absorbed inside his skin, along with the massive wings that had sprouted from his body. His beak compressed, leaving a sharp nose behind. The process left him panting, covered in sweat—and naked. Lynn glanced down and squawked. Talon was still sporting a massive hard on.

Heat enveloped her. This time there was no pain, only an odd stretching and pulling sensation. When it was done, Lynn found herself lying on her back, her body trembling. She wiggled her hands and felt her fingers move.

Talon's gaze heated as it swept over her body. Despite her resolve to get answers, Lynn felt her sex growing moist as he stepped closer. His hand glided from her foot to her knee and Talon licked his lips. He hesitated, waiting, watching. Lynn wasn't sure what he was looking for, but he must've fount it because he parted her rounded thighs with one finger and moved between them.

He didn't speak. Instead, Talon lowered his head and swiped his tongue along her aching seam. He groaned on contact. "You have every right to be mad at me, but please, I need this. I *need* you."

The admission came with such raw hunger that Lynn couldn't say no. She also couldn't say yes, so she just nodded.

* * * * *

Her taste exploded on his tongue. With one swipe, Talon savored her heat, her anger, and her passion. There was no denying that she was mad at him. She wouldn't be his mate if she weren't. But there was also no denying her need for him...her want. Talon felt it in every touch, every taste. Lynn may not realize it yet, but they were *made* for each other.

Though they'd only known each other for a couple of

days, she was as familiar to him as his other form. He knew her fears, her hopes, her wishes—along with her darkest desires. And she knew his, if she only chose to look. Talon was determined to spend a lifetime fulfilling Lynn's fantasies. But for now, he simply had to have her.

He placed his lips over her engorged flesh and slowly circled it with his tongue, before gently sucking it between his teeth. Lynn's back arched off the ground and her body shuddered. She sank her fingers into his hair and pulled him closer, burying his nose in her satiny curls.

Her thighs trembled against his shoulders as Talon licked his way down, then plunged his tongue inside of her. She mewed, her hard nipples stabbing skyward as he plundered her depths.

He cupped her breasts, rolling her nipples between his fingers and thumbs. She gasped, then moaned, begging incoherently as she sped toward completion.

The sounds she made sent an arrow of need through Talon, driving straight for his heart. Lynn was everything he'd ever imagined, but hadn't dared to wish for. He'd cherish her above all others, including himself and his Wing Clan brothers.

He continued to drink from her bounty, allowing his fingers to take over, teasing her. He circled the sensitive bundle of nerves, until her hips began to rock and her muscles tightened. She was close. So close.

Juices spilled from her channel, running down his chin. Talon licked them away as his body grew tighter with need. His actions took on a newfound urgency. He pinched her nubbin, then began to worry it once more with his teeth. Lynn gasped. Before she could relax, Talon shoved two fingers deep inside her, then slowly pulled them back out, only to return once more.

Between the steady glide in and out and the suction he applied, it didn't take long for Lynn to spiral over the edge. She came with a wild cry and a shuddering breath. Talon continued to ride out those ripples until the last one faded. As soon as it did, he grasped his cock and entered her in one long, hard stroke.

Their eyes met and held. An unspoken understanding passed between them, then he began to move. His hips rolled, shafting her deep, then deeper still as his cock kissed her cervix. She was so tight. So hot. And so incredibly wet. If this were his last moment in life, Talon knew he'd die a very happy warrior thanks to this amazing woman.

Lynn couldn't seem to catch her breath. She wanted to look away, but Talon held her trapped within his gaze. And what she saw floating in his eyes scared her more than being tossed off the cliff. The emotions were raw, new, and beyond intense. Lynn had spent her whole life searching for a man who'd look at her that way and now that she'd found him, she wasn't at all sure what to do with him.

It didn't help that Talon wasn't exactly a normal 'man'. His hard muscles glided over her chest, scraping her nipples. Lynn bit her bottom lip to keep from crying out in sheer ecstasy. Oh sure, he felt like a man. As if to prove it, he thrust hard, driving his massive cock straight to her soul.

But real men didn't change into large raptors and fly.

Lynn reached up and grabbed the back of his head, her fingers brushing through the dark satiny strands of hair. She pulled him down, using his ears as leverage, until their lips fused in a searing kiss. Tongues met, retreated, then met again in a tangle of desire. He tasted so good. Felt so good inside her. Like he was made for her body. And her body alone.

Talon's steady thrusts lost their rhythm as she clasped her thighs against his hips. Lynn released his head and trailed her hands over his smooth back, then sank her nails into his sides. Every muscle in his body tightened. A second later, he grunted and she felt the warmth of his release inside of her.

No panic this time. Even the anger had subsided, leaving only peace behind and an odd contentment Lynn had never felt before. They laid there for a few more heartbeats, each trying to catch their breath. Talon recovered first. He rolled off her and stood, then held out his hand to help her up. His eyes closed and a second later a strange skin-tight material appeared on his body.

"I think I deserve to know the truth now," she said, as awe warred with fear. Technology like that shouldn't exist. Didn't exist.

His lips thinned, then he nodded. "Indeed, you do, but we don't have much time. I am being summoned back."

* * * * *

<h1 style="text-align:center">CHAPTER TEN</h1>

Lynn didn't like the sound of that. It sounded suspiciously like Talon was being forced to leave, which was impossible since she hadn't heard a phone ring and they were out in the middle of nowhere.

"Maybe you should start from the beginning," she said, trying to calm the panic threatening to overwhelm her.

"As you know, I am not like you," he said, glancing at the sky. "Or at least I wasn't when we first met."

Lynn followed his gaze, but other than a few random white fluffy clouds, didn't immediately spot anything. "Yeah, I kind of got that when you threw me over the cliff and shape-shifted into a bird." She was proud of herself for sounding so calm while recalling the most terrifying moment in her life.

"I knew that if I told you the truth, you would not believe me. It was best to show you," he said, flushing at the reminder.

She crossed her arms over her chest. "Can we have this conversation after I've dressed? It's getting drafty," she said.

Talon glanced down at his body and frowned.

"Normally, I wouldn't mind, but I'm feeling a little over-

130

exposed here. Your clothes seem to be *specially* made for…for whatever. Mine on the other hand, came from Wal-Mart. They're not designed to disappear and reappear at will."

His jaw clenched and he glanced up at the sky once more, then said, "I'll be right back."

Good to his word, Talon came back within minutes, carrying her backpack. It was stuffed full of her clothes and her journal. Lynn dressed quickly, then looked at him. "Okay, now spill," she said.

Talon stared at the sky.

"What are you looking for?" she asked. Were there more bird people like him nearby? Female bird people? Maybe that's what he meant when he'd said he had been summoned back. Lynn chided herself. Why in the world was she worried about that when she had way bigger problems?

Something Talon had done to her had changed her. She was no longer the person she'd been when she hiked into the Canyon. Was the change temporary? Or permanent? What if it was permanent and Talon left her? Lynn didn't think she could deal with this alone.

"Who are you?" she asked, staring at him. No more lies. *Tell me the truth.*

Talon took a deep breath. "I am a Phantom Warrior."

Lynn blinked. There was a military group of some kind that went by the same name. Was he part of some secret government experiment that had gone awry? Was the *X-Files* real? She'd never been a conspiracy theorist, but that made as much sense as anything else.

He shook his head. "I am not part of that brave group of soldiers."

How did he?

"Read your thoughts," he finished.

Lynn took a step back. "Okay, that's just freaky. How are you doing that?"

"I'm able to speak to you in various forms because we

are now linked," he said, scrubbing a hand over the back of his neck.

Lynn watched the nervous action. Talon was telling her the truth, but not all the truth. "What do you mean by linked? Is that why I was able to shift into a bird?"

He exhaled. "It's hard to explain, but yes, that is one of the reasons."

One of the reasons? Meaning there were more? "Who do you keep looking for?" she asked. There was no doubt in Lynn's mind that Talon was searching for someone in the sky. *It had better not be his wife,* she thought, running through all the ways she'd pluck his feathers off if that were the case.

He grinned. "You are jealous," he said, sounding more than pleased by the realization.

"I am not!" she lied. "I just don't want anymore surprises." That was the truth.

A soft humming noise reached her ears. "What is that sound?" she asked, looking around.

Talon stepped forward and grasped her hands. "I know this is going to be a lot to accept in such short notice, but I am a Phantom Warrior. That is the truth. I am not part of any government experiment. I am not part of any government on *this* planet."

"Meaning you are part of a government somewhere else?"

"Yes, I'm a soldier of sorts," he acknowledged. "I come from a place called Zaron. The noise you're hearing is my ship's approach."

Lynn's mouth fell open. She knew Talon was speaking English, but the words coming out just didn't make any sense. This had to be some kind of cosmic joke. Things like this didn't happen to people like her. "Are you telling me that you're an…an…alien?" The theme to the old *X-Files* show grew louder in her head.

He nodded. "Not a term I prefer, but yes."

This was too much. What could she say to that? How did he expect her to respond? "How did you turn me into a bird? Did you use some kind of mind control? You didn't probe me, did you?"

Talon's brow rose. "I did not use mind control to mate with you," he said with more than a smidgen of agitation. "As for probing, as I recall, you welcomed *my version* of a probe—and you will again once we get aboard the ship."

Lynn's hands moved to her hips. "Do I have a choice in the matter? Because frankly that sounded more like a command than a request."

Talon bit back the word 'no'. It took every fiber of his being, all the skill he'd acquired as a warrior over the years to do so, but he managed with only a slight tremor, giving away his true emotions.

He didn't want to force Lynn to come with him. He wanted her to choose him. Just like he'd chosen her. Yes, he'd had to do it in an unorthodox way, but he'd had no other options. Three days on Earth wasn't exactly a lot of time to find a woman, test her, and if all went well, mate with her. His journey might have started out clinical, but the rules had gone out the escape hatch the second he met Lynn.

All Talon had wanted to do from that moment on was hold her and tell her the truth. He'd hated lying. It mattered not that they were lies by omission. He wished he could say that given the chance he'd change the course he'd taken, but Talon knew that wasn't the case. He'd do it all again and more, if it meant there was a chance he could have Lynn Regis as his mate.

The sensors in his flight suit indicated the ship's steady approach. It was still cloaked, but would be over them in a matter of minutes. He brought her hands to his lips and pressed a soft kiss onto the back of her knuckles.

"I know I am not who you would've picked to be in your life given the choice. I understand that I'm asking more of you than you may be able to give. But know that if you choose to come with me to Zaron, I will do everything in my power to become the man you want. The man you desire," he said, then slowly dropped her hands and stepped back. "I will make you happy. Promise..."

Lynn's heart was beating so loud, she'd almost missed his last words. Joy blossomed in her chest, along with hope. Talon might have lied to her in the beginning, but he wasn't lying now. "What about my condors?" she asked.

Disappointment flashed across his handsome face, but was quickly replaced by a warrior's stoic continence. "They will be cared for in your absence or if you'd prefer we could take them with us."

She glanced up at the sky and caught a black smudge riding the thermals. Her life's work had been spent bringing these noble creatures back to the Canyon. She knew there were others, younger researchers waiting to take her place.

The sky shifted and suddenly a massive ship appeared above them. "I must go," Talon said. "It's your choice, Lynn. Come with me or stay. If you choose to stay, I *will* wait for you. Forever if need be."

She stared at the ship. "You'd find someone else," she said, even though it hurt to do so.

Talon gave her a sad smile, then shook his head. "Now that we've mated, there is no one else for me. Only you."

"I can't just drop everything and leave," Lynn said. *Could she?*

A beam of light appeared out of the bottom of the ship. Talon took a step toward it.

"Wait!" she cried out. "Will I stay this way, even if you go?"

He nodded. "Yes, consider it a gift. Something to remember me by. I'm sure it'll be of help while you study your birds."

Lynn watched Talon step into the light. He touched his heart, then raised his hand to wave goodbye. Something inside of her shattered. She'd spent her whole life reading about connections like this in romance novels. At first she'd dismissed them as pure fantasy, but a part of Lynn had always held out hope that she'd experience one for herself. Now that she'd been offered that chance, was she really willing to throw it all away just because she was scared?

Definitely not.

Lynn didn't even realize she was running until she tripped and fell. It didn't take a rocket scientist to know that she'd made a huge mistake by letting Talon go. She pushed to her feet and kept going. Just a little further. Almost there. The light blinked off as she reached it. Lynn looked around, but Talon and the ship were gone.

"No!" she shouted at the sky. "Come back. You can't leave me." Her voice broke as she realized she'd just lost the best thing that had ever happened to her. Once again, she'd allowed her logical mind to get in the way of her happiness.

A warm hand touched her shoulder. Lynn ignored it at first, afraid that she was imagining it. The touch firmed and she spun around to find Talon behind her. "I thought I'd lost you." She sniffled, then fell into his arms, holding on for dear life.

"Never," he said. "I disobeyed a direct order just so I could see you one more time."

A huge sexy beast of a warrior appeared out of thin air, prowling behind him. His gait was lethal as he silently stalked forward, his golden eyes sparking off the fading sunlight.

Lynn yelped and held onto Talon tighter.

Talon turned and nodded to the man.

"Does he fly, too?" Lynn whispered, trying to imagine the size of *his* wingspan. He would make one fierce raptor from the looks of him. She pitied any woman who happened to land in his sights. There'd be no escape.

"Fly?" Talon snorted. "Hardly. Cats might be able to land on their feet, but they can't fly."

"Lynx," Talon said, casually, but Lynn felt his muscles

tense.

"Talon," the warrior said in response. "There seems to be a problem with the transporter."

Talon's lips twitched. "Yes, you'd better run a diagnostic when you get back."

Lynx's amber eyes glittered dangerously. "Already have. It's good to go now." He pointed to a flash of light a hundred yards away. "I suggest we get a move on before Area 51 scrambles jets to check us out." He strolled toward the beam. Without looking back, the cat shifter added, "Try not to forget your mate this time."

Talon pulled her close and Lynn snuggled against his warmth. "Don't worry, I won't."

# # #

CUT SCENES FROM TALON

Robbing the Flagstaff, Arizona bank had been easy enough. Getting away afterwards had turned into a pain in the ass--thanks to their twitchy getaway driver who'd panicked before the job finished and drove off.

Earl had, had to carjack a college student. He hadn't wanted to, but he and Henry couldn't exactly walk out of Flagstaff carrying a duffle bag full of money. Especially since Henry had managed to go and get himself shot by the bank guard.

At least the wound didn't appear to have hit anything vital, but he was still bleeding like a stuck pig, which was more than he could say for the dead college student in the trunk. Earl kept to the speed limit as he carefully made his way to Grand Canyon State Park.

If the student were still alive, Earl would've thanked him for the backcountry camping permit he'd found in his glove compartment. What better place to lay low than in nineteen hundred square miles of wilderness? The cops wouldn't think about looking for them there. All he and Henry had to do was get there without being noticed.

Henry moaned. "It hurts Earl," he said.

Earl glanced in the review mirror. "Are you putting pressure on it like I told you to do?"

"Yes, but it won't stop bleeding." Sweat poured from Henry's brow, leaving his mud brown hair pasted to his head. He dabbed at it using the contents of the college student's gym bag.

"We'll pick up some bandages later tonight. We have to get to the canyon and get out of sight first." Earl shook his head in disgust. Henry should've shot the guard while he'd had the chance, but he'd hesitated and now they were both paying for his mistake.

"Okay, Earl. I'll hang on," Henry said.

Earl glanced back at the road. Worst came to worst, he'd just have to shoot Henry and dump into the Colorado River.

* * * * *

"Slow down, Earl. I can't see a thing." Henry slid on the loose rocks.

Earl scowled. "We have to keep moving, unless you want to turn yourself in."

Henry yelped.

"Keep your voice down, you idiot. Sound travels for miles in the canyon," Earl said.

"Can't we stop for a minute? I think my leg has started to bleed again." Henry bent at the waist, resting his hands on his knees, and took big gulping breaths of air.

Earl sighed. "All your yapping is going to get us caught, if we're not careful." He glanced down at his watch. It was only eight o'clock, but already the night was black as pitch and colder than hell.

He scanned the trail they'd taken. He'd nearly walked off the edge twice and they still had a long way to go. Why had he thought it was a good idea to enter the Grand Canyon? He looked back at Henry, who was wheezing from the exertion. Stupid bastard shouldn't have gone and got himself shot.

Earl cocked his head and listened. He hadn't heard any helicopters—at least not for the last hour. Maybe they couldn't fly at night? He shook his head. That was doubtful. He'd seen plenty of cop shows with them circling the suspects at night. They used spotlights and heat sensors. Maybe the police figured no one would be stupid enough to go into the Grand Canyon to hide? That's what Earl had been counting on. What he hadn't anticipated was how hard it was to get into the canyon. They'd been hiking for hours and still had a long way to go.

It didn't help that he had to keep slowing down for Henry. It was either that or risk his leg bleeding again. A pool of blood would certainly alert their fellow 'hikers'. It was bad enough that they weren't dressed for hiking. Fortunately, there'd been plenty of poorly dressed tourists for them to blend in with.

Still, they'd passed a few who'd grown suspicious and had been a little too observant. They'd been dealt with swiftly…and quietly. The last thing they needed was to leave a trail of bodies behind. People fell into the canyon every day. Hopefully they wouldn't be found for a few weeks. Long enough for he and Henry to get to California.

Earl glanced around to get his bearings and saw a flicker of light in the distance. He turned to his partner. "Do you see that Henry?" He pointed to the spot.

Henry straightened and looked past Earl. "I don't see anything," he said. "I never knew it could get this dark."

"Follow my finger, moron," Earl said in frustration. If they weren't kin, he'd have killed Henry long ago.

"Is that a wildfire?" Henry squinted into the darkness.

"Don't think so. It's too small, too uniform to be a wildfire. I think it's a campsite," Earl said. He damn well hoped it was. They needed supplies and a place to rest for a while.

"Think they have food?" Henry's stomach growled before the last of the words had left his mouth. "This kid packed nothing but granola bars. I can't be expected to live on those."

"Only one way to find out." Earl grinned, anticipating hot food and warming up next to the fire. "Think you can make it?"

Henry nodded and scrubbed a hand over his stubbled jaw. "Lead the way."

Earl hoisted the duffle bag full of money higher onto his shoulder. Maybe their luck had finally changed.

* * * * *

Lynn was fast asleep when they entered her tent. She didn't even get a chance to scream as a grubby hand came over her mouth muffling her cries. In her sleep addled state, it took her a minute to figure out what was going on. There were two of them. Men. They stank of sweat and desperation. The shorter of the two was bent over, grasping his leg. Her brain kicked in when the one holding her spoke.

"We don't want to hurt you, but we need a place to stay. If you promise not to scream, I'll remove my hand," he said.

Even though every instinct inside her was screaming, Lynn nodded. If she screamed, there was a very good chance that no one was near enough to help her. As it was, her voice would bounce off the canyon walls, making it nearly impossible to determine where the cries were coming from.

"Good girl," the man said.

Lynn shuddered as he pulled his hand away. She drew her legs up close to her body, wrapping her arms around them protectively.

"Does she have any food?" The one gripping his leg asked.

Lynn squinted to see the man near her. The fire cast shadows inside the tent, obscuring his features.

"You heard the man. Do you have any grub?" he asked.

She nodded once and pointed to her backpack. There

wasn't much there--only enough food for one person for a few days. Well she'd been hungry before, she could be hungry again. Just like dieting. The important thing was to stay alive until she got a chance to escape. Despite what the man had told her and the reassurances he'd given, Lynn knew he was lying.

They used some of her climbing rope to tie her hands and feet before securing her to one of the boulders that had fallen from the canyon walls, then shoved a dirty sock in her mouth to keep her from calling for help.

Lynn supposed she should be grateful that they'd used her sock and not one of their own. The boulder was tucked near the canyon wall, keeping her just out of view of anyone coming down the river.

Thanks to the firelight she could clearly see the men's features. The one in charge—and there was no doubt he was in charge since he continuously barked orders at the other man—was dark haired with cool slate-colored eyes and dark brown hair. He had a wiry build that hinted of strength without really showing any muscle. He was the kind of man that people could easily underestimate…once.

The other man was overweight and balding. He'd combed what little hair he had left on the sides, up and over the top of his head. Fooling no one, but himself into thinking he had hair. His blue shirt was untucked and he had a dark stain covering one of his pant's legs. Dried blood caked his hands, making him look like he'd been digging in clay dirt. The injury looked bad, but not the kind that tended to occur in the canyon. The canyon loved to break bones and twist ankles.

How had this man been hurt? Better yet, where had he been hurt? From the stench, they'd been traveling for a while.

Instead of finding comfort in the fact that she'd finally seen her captors' faces, the realization sent a spike of fear deep into Lynn's bones. If she could see them, then she could identify them, which meant these men had no intention of letting her go. Her intuition had been right. It was escape or die. She yanked at the ropes. They didn't budge. She continued to struggle until she wore herself out.

* * * * *

Lynn woke to a swift kick to the bottom of her foot. She stretched her neck, trying to loosen the kink that had settled in overnight.

"Time to get up," the man who'd been bleeding said. In the daylight, the dried blood covering his leg looked like rust. He hobbled around the boulder.

A second later the ropes loosened and Lynn groaned. He wasn't the only one stiff this morning. She rubbed her arms and flexed her fingers trying to get feeling back into her limbs.

"Get your stuff packed," he said. "We're leaving in ten minutes."

Lynn pulled the sock out of her mouth. Her tongue was so dry it stuck to the roof of her mouth. It took three tries to speak. "I thought the other man said you were going to let me go." She struggled to her feet. Her thighs cramped and she reached out for the rock to steady herself.

"Change of plans," the leader said as he stepped out of the tent. "We need someone who's familiar with the canyon to get us to the other side. From the looks of your setup, you'll do."

Lynn opened to her mouth to contradict him, but thought better of it. At least as a guide she was useful to these men. If they thought otherwise, she'd be dead. "I need to go to the bathroom."

The man's dark eyes narrowed. "Make it quick." He went to work pulling the tent down.

She relieved herself and then walked to the river to rinse her hands. Lynn splashed water on her face, shivering against the cold, then swept her hair back in a ponytail. She didn't hear the man approach, but she felt pain when he grabbed her arm and jerked her away from the water.

"You really don't want to test me," he said, through gritted teeth. "Now help us pack up the camp. We have a long way to go."

Lynn eyed the swirling greenish brown water. It was swift enough to carry her downstream, but then what? The only supplies she had were inside the tent. She wasn't even sure if she could make it to shore before the hypothermia set in. No, it was best to go along for now.

She helped pack up the tent, rolling everything into her backpack. It was clear within minutes that neither man had ever been camping—or if they had, it had been inside a cabin. They looked to her for guidance, which should've been a relief, but wasn't since it made the man in charge twitchy.

"I'm ready." She rolled the final blanket up.

The leader pointed deeper into the canyon. "After you." He flashed the butt of his firearm.

Lynn swallowed hard, then began the slow, treacherous hike.

* * * * *

Lynn saw the shadow before she spotted the bird. It was the same raptor that she'd seen on the cliff face, except this time it was cruising on the thermals above them. If she didn't know better, Lynn would swear the bird was following them, but that was impossible. It probably just equated people with food droppings. It was going to be really disappointed if that were the case. The two men were making quick time with her remaining supplies.

She'd thought about asking them for some food, but had thought better of it. Anything that kept them occupied was good in her mind. Lynn stumbled as the bird dove for their heads and swept by them.

"What the hell!" The man in charge cried out.

"What is that Earl?" the wounded man asked.

The leader shoved the balding man against the rock face. "I told you not to use my name, you fool," he said.

The hurt man winced. "Sorry, Earl. I forgot."

"Don't worry about it, Henry," he said.

Lynn pretended not to hear them. It only drove home the fact that they planned to kill her, when she outlived her usefulness. The bird dove near them, its wings nearly scrapping the side of the canyon wall.

"Look out!" Earl shouted.

Henry ducked and so did Lynn. She'd never seen a bird act this way. Maybe they were getting near its nest. She looked around, but didn't immediately spot a nesting area. The man named Earl took out his pistol.

"The next time that bird swoops by it'll wish it hadn't," he said.

Lynn stopped. "You can't shoot it. They're protected."

Earl's brow dropped over his eyes. "Do you think I give a shit about a bird, lady?"

"My name is Lynn. Lynn Regis," she said.

"I'm Henry and this here is Earl," the chubbier man said.

Earl shoved him aside.

Henry scowled and rubbed his arm.

"Stop talking to the prisoner, Henry." Then his gaze landed on her hard. "As for you," he pointed the gun barrel in her direction, "I suggest you keep walking and worry about your own health, not the health of some damn bird."

Lynn glanced at the sky to the magnificent winged creature soaring high overhead, willing the bird to go away before it got hurt.

* * * * *

Talon's fury continued to build at he got a look at his

woman. Even from this distance he could sense her fear, smell it, feel it like a palpable entity reaching out to snatch the air from his lungs. Whoever these men were, they would pay. He'd make sure of it.

# # #

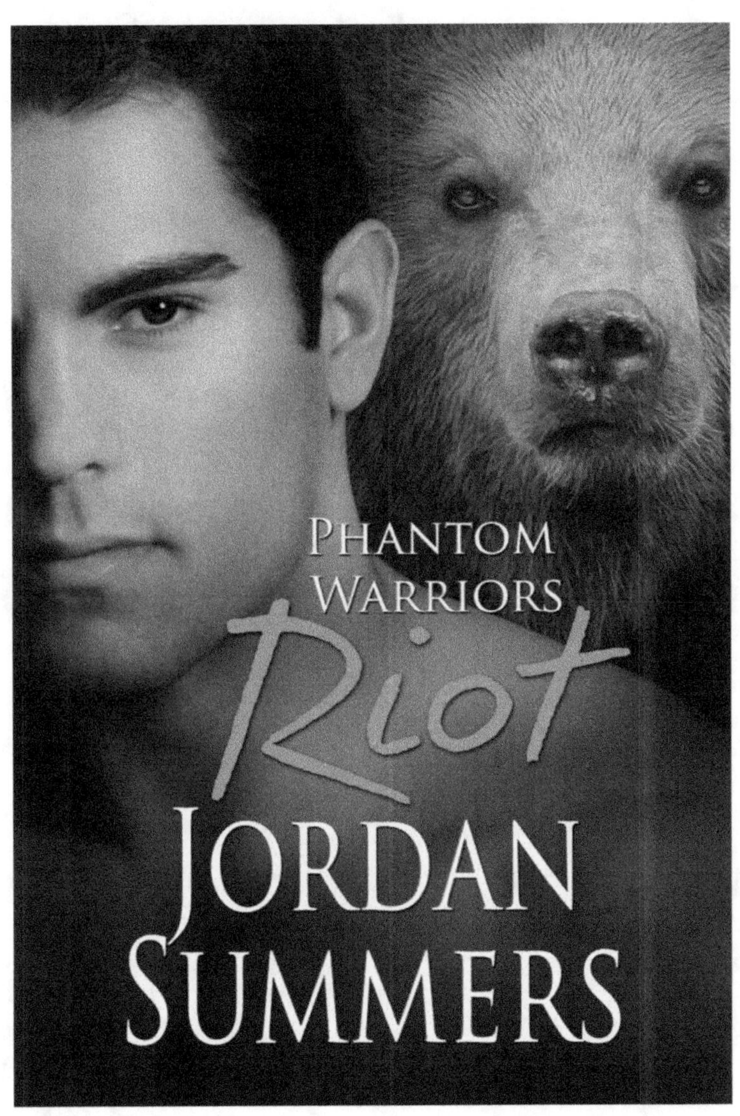

Phantom Warriors
Riot
Jordan Summers

CHAPTER ONE

Riot clenched the summons in his hand and glared at it. In all his years as a Phantom Warrior, he'd never been summoned before the Atlantean King until this week. Nor had he been summoned before any other king for that matter. He scowled at the missive. This made the third one in a matter of days, since he'd returned from Earth. His mind flashed to his brethren, Phantom Warrior Linx. It was that damn cat's fault that he was in this mess.

He should've never allowed Linx to talk him into smuggling Taylor Shelley onto the ship. Riot had only done so because the woman would've been killed had she stayed on Earth. In his mind, the threat of death superseded the actual 'rules' put in place by the Atlantean people for gathering fertile females. Not that he expected the King to see it that way.

The fact that Taylor's sister was Linx's mate…well, that simply complicated matters.

Riot stared at the giant rock slab doors that guarded the Throne Room and took a deep breath. Deceiving the King was wrong. He knew it. But for him, honor and friendship trumped fealty. Riot had no doubt that the King would disagree. He made a mental note to beat some sense into Linx the next time he saw him, then growled under his breath and threw open the doors. He stepped into the Great Hall and scanned the long aisle that led to the crystal throne. This might be his third visit, but he didn't like it any better than the first two.

Long tables fanned out on both sides of the aisle, separated by only a few feet in order to accommodate large crowds. Today, they were empty. Perhaps this would be a private meeting. The thought had barely had time to settle in Riot's mind, when he spotted a small group of people orbiting the throne. So much for a private meeting.

Riot's massive shoulders tensed a notch. He didn't want an audience, but if there were others here, maybe he'd been summoned for a routine reason—not because of the mistakes and bloodshed that had occurred on his last mission to Earth. He glommed onto that remote chance, minor though it may be.

Linx, that lazy good for nothing cat, still hadn't bothered to petition the Atlantean King for permanent residence for their stowaway. Instead, he'd dumped the helpless woman on Hades, the Dark King, knowing she wouldn't be discovered.

Hades only ruled a small part of Planet Zaron, but the Dark King was formidable. No one crossed him and lived. Fortunately, Riot hadn't had to deal with the Dark King…yet. King Eros was bad enough.

As Riot approached, the people hovering around the throne parted, revealing a large, blond-haired man dressed in a loincloth. His chest was bare and softened hide enclosed his feet. Perched upon the glowing green and blue crystal throne, the man leaned forward, as if in anticipation of his arrival. One look at the Atlantean King and Riot's tension skyrocketed, twisting his muscles into tight knots.

King Eros' gaze appeared lazy, which belied his intense scrutiny.

Riot dropped to one knee and bowed his head. "You summoned me, Your Highness?" The question was a formality. They both knew that he wouldn't be here if he hadn't been summoned. Riot glanced up and met the King's eyes. His thoughts immediately turned to food, though he was not hungry.

The King might look soft with his long hair and pretty features, but he was a powerful Atlantean. And like *all* Atlanteans, he could read thoughts.

Eros' blue eyes brightened with amusement. "Are you hungry, Phantom Warrior Riot?"

"Yes," Riot said, automatically thinking of platters filled with roasted meats.

Eros' eyes glittered and his mouth pressed together as if to seal off laughter. "It's strange that you're always in need of nourishment when I call for you."

"Yes, Your Highness. Truly odd coincidence." Riot purposely kept his expression blank as to give nothing away.

The amusement vanished from Eros' handsome face. "Do you know why you're here?"

Riot slowly shook his head and pictured an apple pie. "No, Your Highness."

Eros shifted, his thick muscles flexing and tightening as he moved forward on the throne. "I read your incident report about the violence that occurred during your last mission."

Riot remained silent and thought about the hamburgers he'd had on Earth. He'd especially loved the ones covered in ketchup and extra pickles.

Eros' brow furrowed. "You really should eat before you come here." His gaze flicked to Riot's stomach, then back to his face. "As I was saying, I wanted to speak with you about the deaths that occurred. You said in your report that they were unavoidable."

They'd gone over this multiple times. So many in fact, that Riot wondered if the King expected him to change his story. That wasn't going to happen. Riot rose from his kneeling position. "My Phantom brother, Linx was fighting for his life and the life of his mate when I arrived. He was outnumbered. The humans were armed with weapons made of steel. They fired metal rounds that were meant to lodge within the body."

Eros' mouth tightened. "I am familiar with guns," he said. "What I can't figure out is why a gun would have been a problem for a Phantom Warrior."

"It wouldn't have been, if not for the safety of the women—woman," Riot corrected.

Eros rose from the throne. "Women? Your report stated that there was only one woman."

Riot thought about fries smothered in gravy and his stomach growled. Several of the Atlanteans present took a step back as if they expected him to shift into his bear form and eat them. Riot nearly snorted. None here were to his liking. Besides, they'd be far too tough.

The King's lips twitched and Riot stiffened. His last thought must've gotten through. He immediately went back to thinking about ice cream shakes and toasted buns with thick burgers wedged in the middle.

"I misspoke, Your Highness. There was only one woman that I can recall," he said. "Phantom Warrior Linx later claimed her in order to save her life. Had I not arrived to help, we might have lost her."

Eros' muscles tensed and his nostrils flared. Anger radiated from his pores. Like Riot, the King wanted to kill the men all over again for what they'd done to Linx's mate, Tabitha. "I trust there will be no further incidents," Eros said.

"Definitely not, Your Highness."

Eros nodded. "Good," he said. "You're dismissed. I expect you to be on the next transport back to Earth."

"But, Your Majesty, I just returned. Shouldn't a few of the other warriors have a chance before I'm sent back out?" This was punishment for omitting information. Riot knew it, but he couldn't exactly call the King on it without implicating himself.

"Are you questioning a direct order?" Eros asked.

Riot felt his face pale. "No, Sire." He turned to leave. Eros' next words stopped him short.

"I trust if any new details of the event jar your memory that you will let me know immediately," he said. There it was, the suspicion that had been lurking under the surface the whole time.

Riot looked back over his shoulder. "Of course."

"Oh, and Riot," Eros said.

He swiveled to face the King once more. "Yes, Your Highness."

"Do get something to eat. Your hunger is mentally…*distracting*." The King's lips twitched.

He knew. There was no doubt in Riot's mind, but somehow he managed to keep his composure. "Yes, Your Highness. Right away."

Before Riot made it three steps, the stone doors flew open and a small brown-haired woman swept into the room. "There you are." Her gaze bypassed Riot to settle on the King. A golden-haired boy, the future king of Zaron, and a beautiful chestnut-haired girl, whose curls hung halfway down her back were hot on her heels.

The little girl saw King Eros sitting on his throne and squealed, "Daddy!" As she raced forward, arms outstretched.

Her brother watched Riot closely as he passed, his green eyes as off-putting as his father's aqua blue ones.

Riot bowed. "My Queen," he said.

Rachel smiled at him. "I swear I will never get used to people calling me that." She shook her head and glanced at her husband. "We've been looking all over the palace for you."

The second the King's gaze landed on his wife, his blue eyes began to glow. People may have questioned his return after so many years away, but there was no denying the love he felt for the human woman standing before him.

Something in the vicinity of Riot's hearts throbbed. He hadn't experienced any kind of connection with the women on Earth. Certainly nothing like the kind he saw between the royal couple. Oh, he'd tried. His body had been more than willing to 'test the waters', but his size seemed to intimidate the females of the species.

Riot couldn't really blame them. Even among the Phantom people, he was considered large and rather intimidating—not that anyone would be able to tell that from the King's reaction to him. But Riot had heard his Phantom brothers joking about him on the ship. The harsh words would've hurt, if there hadn't been a thread of worry laced with the humor. They hid their concern with laughter, while Riot hid his pain with silence.

He stopped at the stone doors and glanced one final time at the King and Queen. They appeared to be so happy. Riot was under no illusion that he'd find the same happiness.

* * * * *

Nina Whitetail walked down the sterile hall toward her grandfather's hospital room. The smell of urine, blood, and antiseptic cleaners battered her nose and soured her stomach. Why did all hospitals smell the same? No matter how much they cleaned they could not cover up the odor of death. It clung to the walls, the light fixtures, and the very skin of the workers with its sticky cold fingers. She shuddered and took a deep breath through her mouth. It did little to help. She pressed on, trying not to gag. When she reached the nurse's station, she stopped.

"How's Harold Twofeathers doing today?" she asked.

The nurse recognized her and gave her a wan smile. "He's hanging in there, but there's been no improvement."

No improvement was better than him getting worse. Right? The lie slipped easily into Nina's mind because she wanted so desperately to believe it. "Thanks for taking such good care of him."

Compassionate eyes met hers. "He's a wonderful man."

"Yes, he is," she said. Nina reached her grandfather's room and paused long enough to paste a smile on her face. The act was as much for her benefit as it was for his. It helped ease the dull pain of impending loss. She'd been dealing with the grief for over six months.

Nina knew when she walked in the room that she'd find him propped up in bed, his once strong muscles wasting away. It was like an invisible monster took chunks out of him while she was at work. She couldn't stand to see him like this and would change places with him in a heartbeat if she could. Not that he'd let her. Her grandfather, Harold Twofeathers, was a proud man, who believed in the old ways. Life circled and that was how it should be.

"Stop hovering outside my door like the coyote, Little Deer," his warm voice called out, even though there was no way he could've known she was there. The cancer might be eating his body, but it hadn't touched his mind or his Shamanic abilities.

Nina stepped forward, forcing her legs to move her into the room. "*Shi-yo*, Grandpa. You're looking better today," she said.

"Hello." His warm chocolate-colored eyes sparkled as he patted the lumpy chair beside his bed. "Did you know that your nose twitches when you lie?"

Her hand rose to her face to cover her nose. "Does not."

He laughed. "Come here, Little Deer. My eyes are not what they used to be."

Warmth spread through her at the continued use of the endearment. "Your eyes might not be, but your hearing is just fine." Nina grinned at him and did as he asked.

The second she sat, his large hand reached out to cover hers. His copper skin stretched like crinkled paper over his boney knuckles. Life may have beaten the padding out of them, but you wouldn't know it from his warm gentle touch. Nina carefully squeezed his hand, then didn't let go. Maybe if she just held onto him, death would be unable to take him away. It was a child's hope. She knew that, but in her heart she couldn't stop praying that somehow a miracle would occur and her grandfather would recover. She needed him.

His soft brown eyes crinkled at the corners. "Don't be sad, Little Deer. There's no need to fear the Great Spirit. I have spoken with him many times. He waits on *Kuwah' hi* for me to join him."

"Well, he can wait on the Sacred Mountain a little longer. You're not going anywhere." Nina sniffled and quickly wiped all hint of wetness away.

He patted her hand. "Not yet. I must remain until you're settled."

Nina rolled her eyes. "Then you're going to be here for a while."

Harold chuckled. "So what have you been doing today?"

Nina sighed. "Stocking up on bandages and antibiotics. The bear hunts are about to begin."

He looked at her, his warm expression quickly turned serious. "Stay out of the woods. I don't want the sheriff to arrest you again."

"You know I can't do that. Too many animals need me." He'd never told her to stay out of the woods in the past. Oh, he'd warned her not to get near the crazy white hunters because they might mistake her for an animal, but he'd never told her to stay out of the Smoky Mountains and the surrounding areas. It was tantamount to saying 'stop breathing'. "I'll be fine, Grandpa. You know I'm always careful."

"It's not you that I'm worried about," he said. "The spirits have been whispering to me. They tell me that powerful magic is coming."

"You know magic isn't real, Grandpa." Perhaps the cancer had spread to his brain after all. Her heart dropped as she battled the pain to keep it from showing on her face.

"Oh, it's real." He touched her heart. "You just need to open your eyes to see it."

Nina knew she could keep her eyes open forever and the most that she could hope to see was a rerun of *Harry Potter*.

"The ancestors are singing The Bear Song. I hear it most everyday," he said. "I think this time it's going to draw the Great Bear out of hiding."

Her grandfather had always loved The Bear Song. In his youth, he'd gladly joined in to sing along. Talk of it usually made her happy, but now it just frightened her.

As a veterinarian, Nina could logically understand the ritual of performing the song, but she hated its end result. Every bear season brought an increase of dogs and horses being shot, along with too many bears for her peace of mind. She was always inundated with injured animals this time of year—most of which she couldn't save.

Hunting wasn't allowed in the Smoky Mountain National Park and was highly regulated on the Qualla Boundary, but that didn't stop a few hunters from wandering into places they shouldn't be. Bear season also brought out the poachers. Not satisfied with killing just one bear, they had to trap and kill as many as possible. Of course, it was illegal, but that didn't stop them. The mountains and the woods were vast. Hunters could easily evade law enforcement.

"You are frowning again, Little Deer." Harold Twofeathers smiled. "Let me tell you a story."

Nina had heard the story about the Great Bear hunted by the four brothers. They'd chased the monstrous creature into the sky where they remained to this day. But she listened to her grandfather as if it were for the first time. Some of the Eastern Band of Cherokee Indians, or *Tsalagi* as they called themselves, believed that bears were violent, and that there were monsters the size of woolly mammoths that resembled bears, roaming the woods. These creatures regularly attacked people and could only be slain by heroes.

Others, like her grandfather, believed that bears possessed strong medicine magic, which aided in healing. Nina didn't believe either story, but she implicitly trusted her grandfather and his power. She just couldn't, in good conscious, stay out of the woods.

He finished his story and looked at her. "Do you understand now?"

Nina's brow furrowed. She'd listened to the story, but she wasn't sure what lesson she was supposed to take away from it, other than don't chase bears. "Um…"

Harold shook his head. "You must remember the stories. They will help you through life."

She squeezed his hand. "I know, Grandpa. I will remember, and just to be safe, I promise not to chase any bears."

"Not *any* bears." Harold shook his head. "The lesson I was trying to impart was that if you chase the Great Bear, he will take you with him into the sky." His pained gaze met hers. "There's no coming back from the sky, Little Deer. Once the Great Bear lures you there, you are his for eternity. The four brothers found that out the hard way."

A shiver tracked down Nina's spine. The chances of her running into any bear, much less the Great Bear while she was out sabotaging bear traps, were slim to none. "I'll remember, Grandpa." Nina glanced at her watch. "I have to get back to work now. Do you need anything?"

He smiled. "Only your visits, Little Deer."

"I'll come by again after I get off work." She slowly rose from the chair.

His hand snaked out with surprising speed and grasped her wrist. "Remember what I said. The Great Bear has powerful magic. He can mesmerize you and convince you that he's not dangerous, but in the end, he is still a bear."

This whole conversation was making Nina uncomfortable. She knew going into the woods and messing up traps was dangerous. The sheriff had only let her go after her grandfather promised him that she'd pay for all the damages. And she had, but not until after bear season ended. This year would be no different, except she had no intention of getting caught. "You've always told me that bears aren't naturally violent," she said. "If I leave them alone, that they'll leave me alone."

"This is true." His gaze sharpened. "But the magic that I see coming is no ordinary magic. And since bears hold the most magic, it has to be the Great Bear that the ancestors are warning me about. The Great Bear is like nothing you've ever seen before."

Nina didn't believe it, but she nodded all the same. "If he's as big as you say that he is, then it sounds like the hunters are the ones that should be worried."

"This magic is not coming for the hunters, Little Deer," Harold said. "It's coming for *you*."

She chuckled and kissed his forehead. "The magic is going to have a hard time finding me, unless it comes to the office and knocks on the door." Nina glanced at her watch again. "I really have to go. I have a Rottweiler coming in at 1:00. I'll see you later, okay?"

"I'll be here." Harold laughed, then started to cough violently as he waved her out of the room.

Nina rushed out before he could see the fresh tears forming in her eyes. Harold Twofeathers, healer, shaman, and all around best grandpa ever, had raised her when her mother decided that she cared more for alcohol than she did her only daughter. She'd died ten years ago in a drunk driving accident. The state troopers had said that she'd driven off the side of the mountain on her way back from Gatlinburg, Tennessee.

Her mother had never made it to Cherokee, North Carolina. Nina hadn't cried when she'd learned the news. It was hard to cry over someone that you didn't really know, but her grandfather had wept. Her mother was his daughter. His only daughter. That meant something to him. And now

Nina finally understood as she faced her grandfather's impending death. If only the stories about the Great Bear's magical powers were true… She'd follow it anywhere, if it meant saving the only man that she'd ever loved.

* * * * *

CHAPTER TWO

Phantom Warrior Riot spent the night in La Push, Washington, staying only long enough to admire the pounding waves and the Quileute Tribe's totems. The community was welcoming, but too small for what he needed to accomplish. For that, he needed a much larger population, one full of females of various shapes, sizes, and colors. He made his way through Forks, a small town that seemed to be obsessed with something called 'Twilight', before continuing on to Olympic National Park.

Riot ran across a few black bears in the park, but nothing near the size that he was in his Other form. The bears had sensed danger and quickly scampered off. As a Phantom Warrior—an alien shape-shifter species—and a member of the Tooth Clan, he was expected to find a mate. Women were few in number on his home planet of Zaron. Without the aid of women from Earth, his people would quickly become extinct.

Fortunately, the Phantom people had found a solution to their problem, when a lost group of Atlanteans returned to Zaron after having been stranded on Earth for hundreds and hundreds of years. The news of a planet full of compatible women had spread quickly. Soon warriors from the Tooth Clan, Wing Clan, Claw Clan, and Blood Clan were lining up to travel to Earth.

They'd banned together with the Zaronian Atlanteans, who also battled extinction due to intergalactic wars, to go on expeditions in search of viable mates. Like his Phantom brothers who'd gone before him, Riot had to do his part, which was why he found himself strolling into a bar in downtown Seattle near the wharf.

The moist sea air gave way to the warm press of too many bodies within the narrow room. The crowd parted, giving Riot plenty of space. Too much space. He smiled in the direction of a few females, but they shied away or pretended not to notice. He inhaled. Past the perfume, alcohol, sweat, and desperation, he could smell the fear. His smile faded. Riot sat down at the bar and ordered a beer. His shoulders hunched in an effort to make himself appear smaller, less intimidating.

At over six and a half feet tall, and pushing two hundred and eighty pounds of packed muscle, Riot wasn't exactly inconspicuous. He received more than a few curious glances, but everyone, including the females he'd come here to make contact with, kept their distance.

A few women approached the far end of the bar to order drinks. Riot tried to talk to them, but the words came out like he was issuing orders to new warrior recruits. He'd never been good at chatting up females. What little experience he had, had been utterly unpleasant. He could still hear the Phantom woman's cries of pain ringing in his ears from that fateful night. He'd been so excited by the opportunity of getting to couple that his beast had slipped its leash and nearly crushed the woman to death. Afterwards, Riot had been too embarrassed and horrified by the incident to ever try again.

He eyed the human women around him. They weren't nearly as strong as the Phantom and Atlantean women on his planet. How would he ever be able to touch them without injuring them? His insecurity must've showed because the women who'd been standing at the bar grabbed their drinks and disappeared into the crowd quickly, barely giving him a second glance.

Riot watched them go, a mixture of disappointment and relief coursing through him. He took a deep swallow of his beer and shook his head in disgust. *You can't find a mate by passively sitting here,* he chided. He slowly scanned the room and vowed to try harder with the next woman. It didn't take long for another to approach.

"Can I buy you a drink?" he asked as she bellied up to the bar.

The lovely redhead turned at the sound of his voice. Her gaze flicked to his, and her welcoming smile died on her face as she took in the scar on his cheek. Riot stood to move closer, so he didn't have to shout. The woman's eyes widened as she craned her neck to look at him, then she let out a scream that would've curled his hair had it not been so straight.

Flashbacks of the night he'd nearly crushed the woman rushed through his head. Riot stiffened. Afraid to move for fear it would scare her even more. She backed away, keeping a wary eye on him. Horrified and more than a little humiliated by the woman's reaction, Riot threw money down onto the bar and quickly left.

He knew he wasn't as appealing as his brethren. His face was handsome enough, if you could overlook the scars covering his cheek, arms, and hands. There was only so much a body could heal, when it was routinely shredded during battles. He glanced down at his hands and growled, curling them into fists.

Riot rushed out, only to find that it was raining. He let the cool wetness wash away his humiliation. He tilted his head up and closed his eyes, taking deep heaving breaths of sea air into his lungs. He could still picture the red-haired woman in his mind's eye, screaming at the sight of him. What would she have done, if he'd been in his bear form? Dropped dead?

He shuddered at the thought. Riot gazed at the people as they strolled down the wet streets. He needed to leave this place, needed to leave this planet. But he'd only just arrived and knew his commander on the ship wouldn't allow him back so soon. Riot had thought Washington State would be a good place to search given the history and the acceptance of the bears in the area, but he'd been wrong.

He pulled out a map and stared at the vast country before him. This search, *his search*, was useless. Riot knew that as sure as he knew his other half. Some warriors weren't meant to find a mate. And he was convinced that he was one of them. He only needed to hang on a few more days and then he would be able to return to Zaron and live out his remaining years fighting the planet's enemies. He growled in frustration and ripped the map up into tiny pieces, throwing it to the ground. When he was done, a small square section clung to his palm. Riot peeled the paper off and stared at it. What did he have to lose?

"The Great Smoky Mountains it is," he said, then took out his communications device.

* * * * *

Riot exhaled and scanned the small sign at the base of the strange mountains that appeared to exhale smoke. Was there a fire? Gatlinburg, Tennessee stared back at him cheerfully, welcoming him to the town. Riot scowled. He was in no mood for cheer. It had taken the ship most of a day to reach him in Seattle.

Not that it mattered how many days or hours that he'd lost. Unlike most Phantoms and Atlanteans, he'd been granted 'extra' time to seek his elusive mate. The Commander had told him as much when the ship picked him up. He'd barely made it onto the deck, when the orders came down directly from King Eros.

Once more, Riot had tried to argue that the 'extra time' was unjust to the others, but his words fell upon deaf ears. No way was he going to get out of this *punishment*. The King had spoken. He was to take a shuttle and return to Earth. He'd been instructed to stay for as long as it took.

The situation was made worse by the pity Riot had glimpsed in the Commander's aqua-colored eyes as he relayed the King's message. He still bristled when he thought about it. Riot didn't want, nor did he need, more days to prove that he'd failed. Two days were quite enough. But he was a good warrior. He followed orders, even ones he did not agree with. And he most certainly didn't agree with these. He'd stay the extra days or Goddess forbid—weeks, if only to return and tell them 'I told you so'.

He stared at the small but bustling town, taking in its quaint shops and souvenir T-shirts. The air here smelled different. Somehow better. Sweeter. His shoulders relaxed as an older woman walked by and smiled at him. In her wake, a younger woman followed.

As soon as the female saw him, she rushed to the elderly woman's side and hurried her along. He sighed and the tension he'd been holding returned in force. Despite its fragrant air and southern hospitality, this place would be like all the others.

Riot scanned the mountains as he strolled down the sidewalk. Several people crossed the road to avoid him. He pretended not to notice. He should be used to their response by now. He *was* used to it. He rubbed his chest, but it did little to alleviate the pain. "Just keep walking," he muttered to himself, but his feet had other ideas.

Within seconds, he was sprinting down the sidewalk, past alarmed faces in an effort to reach the woods up ahead. The second he entered the lush green canopy of trees, Riot exhaled. Really exhaled. His muscles flexed, then slowly loosened. The moisture from the forest clung to his skin, leaving a light sheen behind.

The cloying heat from the asphalt gave way to refreshing coolness. He took another deep, hardy breath, feeling at home for the first time since landing on this blue-green rock. Tonight, he'd go to his ship, fly it deeper into the mountains and hide it in these peaceful woods.

* * * * *

Nina arrived at the veterinary office she shared with one other doctor. The receptionist, Sarah Mouse, who also doubled as her assistant, looked up and smiled. "How is Harold doing today?" she asked.

She gave Sarah a sad smile. "I think he's worse, though he hides it well."

Sarah's smile faltered. "I'm sorry, Nina."

"Yeah, me too." She glanced at the clock on the wall. "Has Maggie Backwater phoned?"

Sarah looked at the notes in front of her. "No, not yet."

"Is she still scheduled to come in with Humpty and Dumpty?" The dogs were due for their rabies shots. Nina flipped through the phone messages on Sarah's desk to make sure there weren't any emergencies that needed immediate attention.

"Yes, she should be here anytime now." The phone rang and Sarah answered it. "Cherokee Pet Care Clinic."

Nina left her to it, and went to check on the few patients that were already receiving treatment. There weren't many. Liddy Whirlwind's cat, Speckles looked much better today. Her eye infection was clearing up nicely. She should be able to go home tomorrow. Robert Hummingbird had brought in his dog, Trixy to be spayed. With three litters of puppies under her furry belt, it was about time.

That left Ben, Max Dreadfulwater's Chow-Labrador mix. He'd managed to get himself quilled by a porcupine. His wounds were healing nicely and Ben wasn't in near the amount of pain he'd been in when Max dropped him off. Hopefully this had taught the dog a lesson like the skunk incident last year. If not, she'd be seeing him again soon.

Unless something changed, the recuperation kennel would be empty by the end of the week. Nina petted each animal and softly cooed to them. Most Cherokees didn't have much use for a vet. If an animal got sick and couldn't be healed by over-the-counter remedies, folks in the Qualla Boundary just shot them. In general, it was a pretty common occurrence in the south.

It hurt Nina to think about it, but a lot of folks in the area didn't have the money for such frivolous things as veterinary care. Not when the money was the difference between eating and not eating. The arrival of the casino helped, but it didn't eliminate all of the poverty.

She walked back into the front office and dropped phone messages back onto Sarah's desk. There was nothing there of any real importance. Not that she'd expected there to be. Work was slow. And quiet. The bell on the front door clanged in disagreement. Maggie Backwater struggled through the door with Humpty and Dumpty in tow. The two mastiffs had somehow managed to tangle their leashes and seemed to be determined to trip Maggie. Nina rushed forward to help.

"Come here, Humpty," Nina took one of the leashes from Maggie's hand.

"That's Dumpty," Maggie said.

"Of course." Nina guided the giant dog toward the examining room. He yanked her arm, nearly pulling it from its socket when he caught sight of Speckles. The cat's back arched and all the hair on her body rose as she hissed at the dog. Dumpty let out a loud *woof*. Humpty joined in, though he didn't appear to know what he was supposed to be barking at.

"Hush!" Maggie said.

Both dogs ignored her and continued to bark.

Nina dragged Dumpty away from the cage and into the examining room. "Sit," she said, waiting for Maggie to join her.

It didn't take long to give the dogs their rabies shots. While they were there, Nina took the time to examine them. They both appeared to be in good health. She helped Maggie take them out of the office and load them into the back of her pickup truck. Soon they were driving away and Nina was back to waiting for her next patient.

An emergency call came in from Lulu Ball. Sarah took the message and handed it to Nina. "Lulu says that you need to come right away. Daisy is bleeding from her nose and she can't tell what's wrong."

Nina walked back into her office and grabbed her 'Vet House Call Bag'. "Call if there are any other problems. You know where I'll be."

Sarah nodded.

It only took twenty minutes for Nina to reach Lulu's patch of ground. It wasn't large, only a few acres, most of which was wooded. Lulu had managed to clear a little over an acre and cram a lot into the space. Nina turned off the ignition and climbed out of her truck. She honked the horn once.

"I'm back here!" Lulu called out from behind the house.

Nina grabbed her bag and walked around the house to the backyard. There were a couple of cows fenced in on the north side of the property. Lulu had set up a chicken hutch in the middle and flanked it with a pigpen on the right. A small garden brimming with pumpkins and squash took up the rest of the yard, giving way only to a short clothesline.

"Where is she?" Nina asked.

Lulu pointed to her right. "I don't know what happened. She was fine yesterday."

"Let me check her out. It might be nothing." Nina walked over to the pigpen and gazed inside at the five piglets. Fresh blood covered one of their snouts. The rectangular pen stretched thirty feet and was ankle deep with mud. "I'm going to have to climb in there and catch her."

"Figured you would. I tried, but she was too fast for me," Lulu said.

Nina glanced at Lulu's boots. There wasn't a drop of mud on them. She arched a brow, but said nothing. Nina reached down and rolled up her pant legs, then grabbed a pair of gloves before stepping into the pen. Her boots sank down six inches. She took a step. Her boots made a sucking noise as mud and pig excrement covered her feet. She waded across the enclosure, slowly herding the pigs into a corner.

She let the first two piglets rush past her as she singled out Daisy. Nina reached for the piglet. She managed to get her hand on its back leg. Daisy let out an ear-piercing squeal, her little hooves spinning madly in the mud. Muck flew into Nina's face, splattering her cheek as she lifted the piglet into her arms.

* * * * *

Riot heard a high-pitched screech, echoing through the woods. The sound was loud, which meant it was coming from nearby. The squealing continued. What was it? And what was killing it?

Curious, he made his way through the woods toward the horrendous sound. A yard filled with livestock came into view. He stopped, keeping to the shadows. There were two women standing in the yard, discussing an object between them. One was wearing a long skirt with a flowery shirt.

She was a big woman, hearty and full of health. The other smaller female wore jeans and boots. She appeared to be holding something pale and squirming in her arms. There was another loud squeal. The object in her arms tried to escape and the smaller woman turned to catch it before it dropped to the ground.

Riot's breath seized, when he glimpsed the woman's mud smudged face. Her features were delicate and lightly browned. She had full lips, long lashes, and high cheekbones. Her long, dark hair had been pulled back and tied at her nape. She smiled, flashing a row of slightly crooked teeth, as she caught the squirming creature.

"Get back here, Daisy." She pulled the animal close once more and scratched it lovingly behind its ears. The squealing quieted and so did its struggles, giving her time to carefully examining its face.

Riot stared, mesmerized by her soft brown eyes and caring manner.

"Lulu, can you please hand me my bag?"

The woman wearing the skirt reached for something on the ground and handed it to her. "I'm going to give Daisy to you. Hold her close, so I can clean and disinfect her wound."

She handed the pale pink creature over to the woman and reached into her bag. She pulled out cloth, wetted it with a clear liquid, then carefully dabbed at the animal's nose. "It's just a scratch," she said. "Looks like one of the other pigs might've bit her."

Lulu glanced at the pen and frowned. "Will she be okay if we put her back inside?"

The woman nodded. "I've cleaned the wound and put some medicine on it. Pigs are pretty hardy, so you shouldn't have any problems with infection. If it looks like it's getting worse, give me a call."

"Thanks, Nina."

Nina…her name whispered on the air, bringing to mind cool breezes and sweet, fragrant wildflowers. Riot inhaled, but could only detect the odor of the livestock. He continued to stare, caressing her body with his eyes, longing to get closer. Something about the way she handled the animal drew his beast. It rose inside of him.

Nina's head shot up and she gazed into the woods, her brown eyes searching the shadows.

"What is it?" Lulu asked, doing the same.

A smile played on Riot's lips as he took a step back. She'd sensed him. For some reason, the idea thrilled him. She may not be able to see him, but she certainly knew he was there. He looked at the smudge on her cheek, longing to brush it off with his fingertips. The women continued to stare at the woods.

She shrugged. "I thought I…it's nothing." Nina shook her head and gave the creature in Lulu's arms one final scratch behind the ears.

Riot watched her gather her things and walk back to her vehicle. He looked at the truck, memorizing everything about it, so he'd be able to find it again. He wasn't going to get his hopes up. This woman may turn out to be like all the others. Even as the thought slipped through his mind, he dismissed it. There was something different about this woman. "Nina," he whispered her name aloud. "See you soon."

* * * * *

Nina couldn't shake the feeling that she was being watched. At first when she'd felt the sensation, she'd dismissed it. But when it grew stronger, she could no longer ignore what her body was telling her. She scanned the woods, searching the tree line.

Despite it being midday, the shadows were deep and could easily conceal someone who didn't want to be seen. Warmth scrolled down her body, pausing long enough on her beasts to make her nipples harden. Nina swallowed hard and rolled her shoulders. She didn't 'see' anything, but there was definitely someone there. She'd lay money on that someone being a male. She took a deep breath and shook her head. Maybe she was just tired, but that didn't explain her body's reaction. Nina could still feel the eyes on her as she drove back to the office.

The rest of the day was uneventful. Nina checked on her patients and finished the last of her paperwork. Numbers swam before her eyes as she stared at the balance sheet. If they didn't get more business, they'd have to close the office. There were clinics nearby, but none like theirs, in the heart of Cherokee. She rubbed her eyes and yawned.

"Hard at work I see." Kim Watt poked her head in Nina's office.

"What are you doing here?" Nina rose and came around her desk to hug her friend.

"I was out shopping for wedding decorations and thought I'd drop by. How are you doing?" Kim's sharp gaze took in the dark circles under Nina's eyes and her disheveled clothes. "You aren't sleeping, are you?"

Nina sighed.

"That good, eh?" Kim squeezed her hand. "What is that on your face?"

She laughed. "Pig crap most likely."

Kim's face scrunched. "Eww."

Nina grabbed a wet towel and dabbed her cheek. She met her best friend's caring gaze. "He's not getting better," she said. She didn't have to say who. Kim already knew.

"I'm sorry, hon. I really am," she said.

Nina scrubbed harder. The pain on her cheek distracted her from the pain burning inside of her. "I know. I've been praying for a miracle."

Kim hugged her again. "We all have."

She blinked back her tears. "Are we still on for tomorrow night?"

Kim's face brightened. "I wouldn't miss it." She grinned.

"Is Danny okay with you going into the woods with me?" Nina couldn't imagine Kim's fiancé, who also happened to be a deputy with the sheriff's department, being okay with his future bride traipsing through the woods destroying poachers' illegal bear traps.

Kim blushed and glanced away. "I didn't exactly tell him

that's what we were doing. I might've said that we were having a bachelorette night."

Which was the truth, and a lie. This was what they were doing *instead* of the bachelorette party. "What if he finds out?" Nina asked. She was happy for her best friend, but she couldn't help but feel a twinge of jealousy that Kim had someone to go home to. What would that be like? She couldn't imagine.

For the last two years, she had spent all of her time either working or taking her grandfather to doctor's visits. Dating and having a social life were foreign concepts and would remain so as long as Harold was in the hospital.

Kim shook her head. "Danny won't find out, unless you tell him." She winked.

Nina snorted. "You know that's never going to happen." Danny Alberty had never cared for her. Oh, he'd tolerated Nina because of her close friendship with Kim, but he didn't really *like* her. The feeling was mutual. One good thing she could say about Kim's fiancé was that he treated her best friend well. Nina knew Danny was counting the days until the wedding, since it meant that they'd be moving away. Fresh pain blossomed around Nina's heart. Soon everyone she cared about would be gone.

"I'll see you tomorrow." Kim nudged her out of her maudlin thoughts.

"See you then." Nina finished the day and dropped by the hospital once more before returning to her empty home. Without Harold there, the place seemed so quiet...so very lonely. There was nothing to do but go to bed and start all over again tomorrow.

* * * * *

CHAPTER THREE

Nina dressed in black, despite the dangers of traipsing through the woods near hunting season without reflective clothing on. It was safer to wear the orange reflectors, but if she did that, then the poachers might spot her. Or worse yet, a sheriff's deputy. She didn't want anyone catching her, or Kim, in the woods tonight. What they were doing was risky enough. She glanced at the clock. Her best friend would be here any minute.

She tugged on her boots and quickly laced them up. The hiking boots would allow her to move quicker, and hopefully protect her ankles on the uneven terrain. There was a full moon scheduled for tonight, but they wouldn't be able to tell beneath the canopy of trees. She'd pulled out a map of the Great Smoky Mountains and the Qualla Boundary earlier, circling spots that would be likely for poachers to set up traps.

Every year she went out hoping to not find them and every year she came back disappointed. Some people just couldn't abide by the hunting laws. She stood and stomped her feet to make sure her boots were secure. Nina heard the screen door creak. It was followed by a loud knock.

Kim opened the door without waiting for her to answer. "You ready to go?"

"Just about." Nina grabbed her hat and shoved it on her head, then took in her friend's outfit with an eye toward stealth. "If moonlight hits it, they might spot your silver necklace."

Kim's hands rose to her throat. "Oh, I forgot all about that. I had to dress up a little since this is supposed to be my bachelorette party. If I hadn't, Danny would've known something was up." She winked and flicked the latch on her necklace. Kim pulled the chain off, gently placing it on Nina's table. "How's that?"

"Better," Nina frowned at her friend's running shoes. "Where are your boots?"

"They're in the car. I couldn't exactly wear them out of the house without Danny getting suspicious," Kim said. "He was upset enough at the thought that you might've hired a male stripper."

Nina snorted. "Could you imagine?"

Kim shook her head. "No, I can't." She made a gyrating motion with her hips and burst into giggles.

Nina pointed to the necklace. "Remember to pick it up before you go home. Don't want to make Danny jealous for no reason."

Kim chuckled. "Danny doesn't get jealous. He just shows all the guys his big gun."

Nina laughed. "The last thing we need is him showing up tonight, waving his big gun around."

Her friend flushed. "No, that wouldn't be good." She glanced at her watch. "I can't stay out all night. He may not be the jealous type, but he is a cop and I don't want to worry him."

"We'll be back in plenty of time for your curfew," Nina said.

Kim swatted at her. "Very funny."

Nina pulled a face and Kim laughed harder.

"Have you given any more thought to that blind date I told you about last week?" Kim asked.

The humor fled from Nina's face. "You know I don't have time to date. What with Harold being so sick."

Kim looked at her. "You know I love you, so I don't want you to take this the wrong way, but I think you use Harold's illness as an excuse to keep your distance."

Nina blanched. "That's crazy."

"Is it, hon? Really?" Kim asked. "I thought so at first, but then I realized that you were like this before Harold got sick."

"I was not," Nina said defensively. She'd been busy building her veterinary practice. That took time away from everything, including her social life.

Kim sighed. "I know you're lonely, NiNi. I'm your best friend. I know you better than anyone and I'm worried about you. You can't keep your life on hold indefinitely."

"I'm not." She sighed. "I won't."

Kim stared at her. "What are you going to do after my wedding?"

Pain pinched Nina's chest. "Work, what else?"

"There's more to life than work."

Nina forced herself to meet Kim's knowing gaze. "I'm fine on my own. You know that."

She shook her head. "No, you're not. That's why I hate to see you pushing perfectly nice guys away."

Perfectly nice guys? When had she met a 'perfectly nice guy'? "Are you talking about Rick?"

"Yes," Kim said.

Nina fought the urge to roll her eyes. She'd met Rick through Kim. He'd 'accidentally' bumped into them when they were out to lunch. The man spent the entire hour discussing his guns. To be polite, Nina had feigned interest. Rick took it as encouragement. She'd been dodging him ever since. "I don't want to date a sheriff's deputy," Nina said diplomatically.

"Then don't!" Kim said. "But date someone. Anyone. It's not healthy to have more contact with animals than you do people."

"I don't—" Nina stopped mid-sentence as Kim arched a brow. It wasn't her fault that animals were more reliable and far better company than most of the people she'd met over the years. She rubbed the back of her neck. "Maybe I have been avoiding the dating pool," she grudgingly acknowledged.

"The first step is admitting that you have a problem." Kim grinned.

"Very funny."

"It's time to take off the water wings and get wet. Promise me that you'll at least talk to the next guy that captures your interest."

Nina sighed. "I promise, Mom." How long had it been since a man had caught her eye? She couldn't remember. Nina looked at her best friend. Thank goodness she hadn't given her a time limit. She had a feeling a set time would come and go before she encountered someone like that.

Kim stuck out her tongue and blew a raspberry at her, shattering the seriousness of the moment. She glanced at the map laid out on the table. "So where are we going to start?"

Nina jumped at the chance to change the subject. She walked over and pointed to one of the spots she'd circled in red. "I thought we'd check out the Qualla Boundary where it borders the park. We'll take the Blue Ridge Parkway to Heintooga Ridge Road and pull over somewhere along the side. The woods there are a good spot for poachers to set up their bear traps. Close enough to civilization to haul a four hundred pound bear carcass out, and yet far enough away to stay out of sight."

Kim's brow furrowed. "There are a few houses along there, before you reach the park and several hiking trails. I wouldn't think it would be smart to set up where a hiker may stumble across them. Too easy to get caught."

"Nobody said they were smart." Nina rolled her eyes. "Besides, given the money they can make by selling bear gallbladders to the Asian market, it's worth the risk."

"Good point." Kim nodded. "I'm going to grab my boots and backpack out of the car, then I'll be ready to go."

* * * *

It didn't take long to reach Heintooga Ridge Road. Black Camp Gap marked the entry to the Great Smoky Mountains National Park. If tonight wasn't successful, then Nina planned to check in the woods off Heintooga Round Bottom Road. At least there, their vehicle wouldn't stand out because they could park in Balsam Mountain campground. They wandered into the woods and quickly checked their bearings. The plan was to hike in a half a mile or so, and slowly circle back toward Nina's truck.

The woods were quiet this time of year. After the trees changed colors, most of the tourists left the area, giving the locals a chance to recover and get ready for next summer's arrivals. Nina preferred the fall. She liked the peace that descended upon the mountains. She just wished it didn't bring out the poachers. Daylight was fading fast. Soon the sun would drop behind the mountains and leave them in deep shadows. Darkness would descend an hour or two later.

"Ready?" She turned to Kim, who once again checked her watch.

Her face flushed with excitement. "Yep, let's do this."

They hiked deeper into the woods, leaving the road behind. Dead leaves covered the forest floor, crunching beneath their boots. Despite the dense, decaying foliage on the ground, the trees were far from bare. They walked for an hour in a grid pattern to make sure they covered the area thoroughly. Nina continuously scanned the ground for bear traps and obvious bait snares, while Kim kept her gaze glued to the tops of the trees, searching for camouflaged hunting blinds.

There shouldn't be any in the park or on Cherokee land. The People controlled who hunted on the Qualla Boundary. They kept chatter to a minimum as they slowly worked their way through the woods. The quiet became a living, breathing thing that surrounded them. Instead of feeling cocooned, it sharpened Nina's senses, making her hyperaware. Humans weren't the only things they had to watch out for in the woods. There were black bear and bobcats, though neither tended to bother people if they were left alone.

A twig snapped and the women froze, listening. The forest seemed to hold its breath. Kim pointed to a spot off to her right. Nina nodded in agreement. They waited until the regular sounds of the woods returned, then continued on. Nina caught a glint of something in the distance. She took a few steps forward, then held up her fist. Kim stopped instantly. Nina squinted and spotted the illegal snare. She pointed to the spot. Kim nodded and slid off her backpack. She reached inside and pulled out a pair of wire cutters, then handed them to Nina.

Nina looked around, scanning the woods for movement, then slowly approached the spot. She examined the ground carefully before she took each step. The last thing she needed was to get caught in one of the traps. The snare was strung across a tree branch and dropped onto the ground. Someone had covered most of it with leaves and placed a piece of deer shank in the center, along with smaller bits of flesh scattered around the area to draw in the creature.

She had two choices. She could either spring the trap, leaving it useless, but still reusable or she could destroy the trap so the poachers would have to buy another one. Nina decided to hit them in their wallets. It would hurt more that way and it just might save a bear or two in the process. She crouched down next to the snare and gently slid the wire cutters under one side. She'd have to cut fast or the snare might spring and they wouldn't be able to reach it. Nina took a deep breath and clamped down on the wire. The metal snapped a second before the snare whipped into the air, dangling uselessly from the tree branch.

"One down," she said to Kim.

Before Kim could answer, an angry voice shouted from a distance, "What are you doing?"

Nina jumped to her feet and saw a man coming toward them. She couldn't make out his features. He was too far away, but his tone was warning enough. She urged Kim to run.

"Get back here!" The man bellowed as the women took off. His heavy footfalls echoed through the trees as he raced toward them.

The man paused to look at his ruined trap. "Son-of-a-bitch!" His head jerked to the right.

That's when Nina heard stomping from a second pair of boots. He wasn't alone. Fear kicked her chest and she pumped her arms harder.

A shot rang out, shattering the tree trunk beside the women.

Kim screamed and stopped abruptly. "Oh my God, they're shooting at us."

"Just run!" Nina jerked her into motion. She didn't know which one of the men had shot at them and she didn't care. "Get back to the truck!" She urged. "I'll meet you later."

"What are you going to do? Where are you going?" Kim gasped. They ran side by side, keeping up their brisk pace.

Nina met her worried gaze. "I'm going to lead them away."

"No!" Kim cried.

"There's no time to argue. One of us needs to make it back to the truck." Nina pulled the keys out of her pocket and shoved them into Kim's hand.

"We can go together." Kim squealed as another shot rang out. "They're trying to kill us."

"I noticed. That's why we have to split up." Nina saw a

fallen tree up ahead. "I'm going to bank right at the tree. You go straight for the truck. I'll make sure they follow me."

Tears filled Kim's eyes. "What if they shoot you?"

Nina's side hurt. She wasn't used to sprinting for this long. She took a deep breath to answer, but it was difficult at this pace. Getting shot was a very real possibility. She prayed that she knew the woods better than these guys did. "The spirits won't let that happen," she said, hoping it was true. Kim didn't believe in the old ways and neither did Nina really, but her grandfather did.

"I'll get help," Kim said.

"No! Danny will kill us if he finds out," Nina said.

Kim hesitated for a moment, then nodded. "You better make it back in one piece," she said, then hurried through the woods toward Heintooga Ridge Road.

Nina watched her go, fear threatening to swamp her. Unlike Kim, she didn't have anyone besides her grandfather. There was no one waiting at home for her. That, more than anything, was the reason she'd urged her best friend to leave. She leapt over the fallen tree and banked right.

The light was fading fast, drowning the forest in shadows. All she had to do was stay alive long enough to lose them in the darkness. Nina ran harder than she'd ever run in her life. Already the men's voices were growing distant. The stitch in her side continued to stab her organs. She wouldn't be able to keep this up for much longer.

One of the poachers fired another shot. The sound echoed through the mountains, making it difficult to tell where it came from, but it seemed farther away. Nina slowed, even though she didn't want to. Her body was refusing to keep up the brutal pace. Besides, it was either that or trip and break her neck.

She kept moving, stopping every few minutes to listen. It was hard to hear past the intense pounding of her heart and the roaring of her blood. A branch cracked. It sounded like a cannon blast to her strung-out nerves. She froze. She didn't dare take out her flashlight for fear she'd be spotted. Instead, Nina scanned her surroundings. Nothing moved.

It's probably nothing, she told herself, but didn't really believe it.

* * * * *

"Did you hit her?" Hank squinted into the trees.

The red-haired man shook his head. "Didn't spot any blood, so I don't think so."

Hank stared at Markus in disgust. "I swear sometimes you couldn't hit the side of a barn, even if it was raised in front of you."

"I did find something." Markus pointed at a spot in the woods. "You need to see this."

Hank stomped after him, swearing under his breath. "What is it?"

Markus looked at the ground, studying a spot near his feet. "I think it's a bear track, but it can't be."

Hank shoved him aside. "Let me see."

He glanced at the ground, then did a double-take. What in the hell was it? Hank crouched down and dipped his hand in the track. It was at least five inches deep and the ground wasn't even muddy. He could distinctly make out the holes where the massive claws dug into the ground. The track had to be bigger than his head, which meant the bear was…

"What do you think it is?" Markus asked.

"A bear," Hank said.

Markus snorted. "There ain't no bear out here that's the size of that track. It would have to be huge. Nearly six feet at the shoulder."

Hank curled his lip in disgust. "If a bear didn't make the track, what did?"

Markus stared at the track and shook his head. "Don't know." His wary gaze scanned the trees. "Maybe it's one of those people who run around pretending to be Big Foot."

Hank scowled. "Does that look like a Big Foot track to you?"

Markus shrugged. "Ain't never seen one in person."

"Well it ain't! It's a bear, I'm tellin' you." Hank looked at the woods with renewed interest. If they could catch this bear, he'd easily bring in enough on the black market for him to save his house from foreclosure and have a little left over to retire on. He wouldn't have to put up with his boss demanding that he work extra hours, only to have those same hours slashed the following week. His gaze landed on their destroyed trapping equipment and he swore. "That bitch cost us a lot of money tonight. Not to mention a chance at a bear big enough for us to retire off of." He looked at Markus. "At least tell me that you got a good look at her. I don't want tonight to be a total loss."

Markus grinned, his front tooth missing due to an encounter with the wrong end of a beer bottle. "I sure did."

Hank smiled back. "Good enough to identify her?"

Markus nodded. "Oh yeah. She's one of The People all right. Most of the time they all look alike, but she was a pretty little thing. I'd know her if I saw her again."

"Did she see you?" Hank asked.

Markus's face scrunched. "I don't think so. She was too busy running away."

"Good, you take a ride into Cherokee tomorrow and to see if you can spot her. Maybe we'll get lucky," Hank said.

Markus looked at him. "What do I do if I find her? I can't just haul her out of town by her hair."

"Once you find her, we'll follow her until we can catch her alone," Hank said.

Markus's eyes sparked with excitement. "Then what?"

"We'll make her sorry she ever came into the woods. I'm not losing my house over some bitch out to *protect* the environment or whatever in the hell her reasons for being out here are. I'm tired of those people tromping all over our rights as Americans." He sneered. "Now let's pack up our stuff and get a move-on in case the bitch decides to call the authorities."

"Do you really think that bear is big enough for us to retire?" Markus asked, looking hopeful.

Hank nodded slowly. "If that track is any indication, then yes. I sure do."

"Whew wee! I could use myself a beer right about now. I'm in the mood to celebrate." Markus gathered up the destroyed equipment.

Hank watched him dispassionately. Markus was always in the mood to celebrate. If he wasn't so good at following orders, Hank would have dumped him long ago. Most of time, he was utterly useless. But Markus was a good shot, when he was sober. Unfortunately, that was becoming less often these days. Unlike his alcoholic friend, Hank had no intention of celebrating until they'd taken care of the woman, and the bear's vital organs were packed on ice in the back of his pickup truck. Then, and only then, would he raise a bottle and relax.

* * * * *

CHAPTER FOUR

Riot watched the woman. Her blue-black hair poked out from beneath her hat, slapping the pack on her back as she sprinted by. Her cheeks were flushed from exertion and she was holding her side. She slowed to a stop and gasped for air, bending at the waist. The move gave him a nice view of her round bottom. When she straightened, he saw that her face was dripping with sweat. She'd been running so fast that she hadn't even noticed he was there. Her slanted brown eyes warily looked around.

Even in the low light, he recognized her. It was the same woman he'd spotted with the squealing creature the day before. *Nina.* She took another loud gasping breath. His attention zeroed in on her full mouth. Her lips brought a plethora of fantasies to mind. Riot raised his snout to the air and inhaled the world around him. Her rich musky aroma filled his lungs and his whole body tensed. He knew she'd smell good. Better than good. Delicious. Her sweet feminine scent was followed by an acrid odor that Riot recognized instantly. Fear. She was afraid.

His hearts slammed in his chest. Had she seen him? Even as the thought brushed his mind, Riot knew that she hadn't.

She'd been running too fast and had kept glancing over her shoulder. If not him, then what had frightened her? Riot slowly scanned the woods, searching for the cause of Nina's distress. He caught the scent of sweat and grime emanating from east of their location.

Men.

His gaze swung back to Nina. Had she been hurt? He scanned her from head to foot, taking in her dark clothing. The cloth didn't look as if it had been disturbed. He inhaled deeper, but his sharp senses didn't detect blood. So Nina wasn't injured, but she was afraid. She walked deeper into the mountains. Riot followed at a distance. He didn't want to scare her anymore than she already had been, but he couldn't leave her here in the woods alone. Abandoning her went against every protective instinct in his body.

They walked for what seemed like an hour. Light had long since retreated to the other side of the world. The woods thickened and darkness closed in. With the full moon, Riot could see just fine, but Nina's human eyes could not. She kept cursing under her breath as she tripped over stones and fallen trees. Finally, she clicked on a light, keeping it flush against her body as she stared at something on her wrist. She shook her arm and cursed again, then scanned the trees. "Darn compass!"

Riot stayed in the shadows, listening for predators. He couldn't seem to take his eyes off her. She was even more beautiful up close. Slight in stature, delicate compared to him, he would've thought her weak had he not seen her true spirit yesterday. She'd proven her hidden strength again today by continuing on, when most people would've stopped moving.

The fear that had clung to her tinted skin was long gone, replaced by frustration. She sighed, then walked over to a fallen tree trunk and sat down. The temperature was dropping fast. Riot wasn't sure if she was dressed warm enough to withstand a night in the woods. As if in answer to his question, she shivered.

* * * * *

Nina couldn't believe that she was lost. She knew these woods. Knew them better than just about anyone, but the park rangers. How could she have gotten so turned around? She glared at her broken compass. Piece of junk. She knew better than to buy a cheap model, but between lack of customers and her grandfather's medical bills, she hadn't had much choice.

A breeze picked up, blowing cold air over her neck. Nina shivered and her teeth began to chatter. She hadn't intended to spend the night in the woods. She didn't think that she would freeze to death, but it wouldn't be comfortable. Nina wrapped her arms around her body. The little warmth it provided didn't do much to combat the cold.

It may have been fall, but the temperature in the mountains could drop substantially. Enough to where someone not prepared for the weather could find themselves suffering from hypothermia. She rolled her eyes. That would be just great. She'd never live this down. A twig snapped to her right. Nina shot to her feet and swung the flashlight around.

The beam flashed wildly, before landing on something with dark fur and red eyes. The animal ducked behind a clump of trees. Had she scared it away? Nina wasn't sure. She didn't want to wait to find out. She swallowed hard and slowly backed away. A bear could run thirty miles an hour. No way would she outrun one, if it were hungry and determined to get her.

Maybe it was a deer?

Even as the thought crossed her mind, Nina knew what she'd spotted had been far too big to be any kind of deer. She picked up her pace, wondering if there was any way she could shimmy up a tree in the dark. *Bears can climb, remember?* Something crashed behind her. Nina screamed and took off running, her flashlight bouncing as she tried to scan the ground in front of her. The sound grew louder—and closer.

Don't panic. Don't panic. It's as scared of you as you are of it. Wishful thinking on her part.

Whatever it was didn't sound frightened. It sounded like it was chasing her. Nina leapt over a log. The ground should've been there, but instead she dropped down an embankment. Her feet slipped out from under her and she fell with a loud '*oomph*', rolling end over end until she came to rest beside a shallow creek.

Nina shook her head to clear it and slowly sat up. Her arm hurt, but it didn't feel broken. Moisture from the creek seeped through her fingers. She reached for the flashlight and shined it on her body. Cuts and scrapes covered her hands. She was bleeding, but not too bad. She struggled to her feet. It took two tries before she made it. The trees swirled for a minute before righting themselves. Nina took a step. Her legs held. Thank goodness. No way would she make it out of the woods if something were broken.

She heard the crunch of footsteps as they slowly approached. *Oh god, the men had finally caught her.* With trembling hands, Nina turned the flashlight toward the sound. A giant bear stood twenty yards away. Its shoulders reached the bottom branches of the tree it stood beneath. Nina had never in all of her life seen a bear this size. It looked like a grizzly had mated with an elephant. Except, grizzlies weren't indigenous to the area.

She shined the flashlight into the creature's eyes, but it didn't flinch, didn't run away. So much for frightening it. Nina's heart leapt into her throat as the monster bear took a step forward. The irony that she was about to get eaten by a bear, when she'd been out trying to save them, was not lost on her.

Nina kept the flashlight trained on the animal. With her

veterinary practice, she knew every species in the area, along with many others. She should've been able to identify this species of bear, but its markings were all wrong. It was brown where it should've been black, its ears weren't shaped like a typical bear, and…

"Are you all right?" *It talked.*

The world spun again. This time Nina reached out to steady herself. She had to have hit her head in the fall. That was the only explanation. She was imaging its voice. She had to be. Bears didn't talk. That was animal kingdom rule number one. She stared at the trees around her.

The bear tilted its head. "What are you looking at?" it asked.

"The trees," she said calmly, like talking to a bear was an everyday affair for her.

Its furry brow rose. "Why?"

"I'm waiting to see if they're going to join in on our conversation," she said.

His mouth moved a few times without any words coming out, then he finally said, "Trees don't talk."

Her gaze met his squarely. "Neither do bears." She swayed as the gap in her reality widened.

"You don't look so well. Perhaps you should sit down." The voice was a deep rumble as the bear's jaw twisted to form their words.

Nina stared at its incisors, as the bear's mouth opened and closed. The teeth were longer than two of her middle fingers put together. "This can't be happening." She shook her head again and pain sliced through her skull.

"I think you need medical assistance," the bear said.

"I know I do," Nina said. "The fact that I can hear you is a dead giveaway."

"Good, I was worried for a minute that you couldn't understand me."

"I plan to schedule a psychological exam the second I get back to town." She'd finally lost it. Well and truly lost it.

Between the stress over her grandfather's failing health and trying to keep the business alive, she'd gone over the deep end. How else to explain talking bears? Nina swayed on her feet.

The bear gave her a look that on a person would've been interpreted as concern. "Please sit down. You need to catch your breath after a fall like that."

For some strange reason, Nina found herself following his suggestion. "I wouldn't have fallen had you not been chasing me," she muttered under her breath.

The bear pawed at the ground and ducked his head. "Sorry about that. I just wanted to make sure that you were okay. You were running like something was after you."

She blanched. "Men were following me."

His massive head rose and he scented the air. "I smelled them earlier, but they're gone now."

She exhaled. "Good!" Nina didn't think she could handle the poachers and a talking bear. Great Spirit, bless! She was talking to a bear. An honest to goodness bear.

"What's your name?" he asked.

She responded automatically. "Nina Whitetail." She hesitated, then added, "Do you have a name?"

"My name is Riot," he said groaned, which came out more like a roar.

"Riot?" *It's a bear, Nina. What did you expect him to be called? Yogi? Perhaps Bob?*

"Can I ask you something?" The bear shuffled his massive feet on the forest floor.

His gaping maul gave her the impression that he could swallow her whole if he desired.

"Sure, why not? None of this is real anyway," Nina said.

"You're not going crazy," he growled, then snorted as if to clear his throat.

"Sure, whatever you say." She wasn't about to take a bear's word for it that her sanity was still intact. Nina scooted further down the log, although it wouldn't do much good if he rushed her. A 'normal' bear could outrun a person. This one, given his massive size, could probably match a cheetah. "What do you want to know?"

He took a step closer and she stiffened. The bear stopped instantly.

"Why aren't you frightened of me?" he asked.

Nina frowned as she took inventory of her emotions. He was right. She hadn't been frightened since he began to speak. She was nervous, sure. Anyone would be when confronted by a bear the size of a draft horse. But she wasn't afraid. "How do you know that I'm not?"

"I can smell you." He sniffed. "You smell musky and sweet. You're rich, ripe, and full-bodied like a woman should be."

She blinked. "You make it sound like I'm a bottle of wine."

"In a way, you are. At least your essence is," he added.

Was the bear *flirting* with her?

Her face flushed. Nina didn't know why she was blushing, but it seemed odd to have a bear talking to her in the way that a man would. "Thanks," she murmured, then glanced away. She didn't want him to notice the affect he was having on her.

Flirting? What was she thinking? This was a bear, not a man. He wouldn't know embarrassment if it hit him upside his fuzzy head. And he darn sure wasn't flirting. Bears didn't flirt. But that didn't stop her from changing the subject.

"You asked why I'm not afraid of you. One reason is that I'm a vet. I treat all kinds of animals at my practice." It was a reason, but not the main one. Nina never fancied herself as a *Dolittle*. Her patients didn't routinely come in and talk to her. Nothing in her work life could have prepared her for this moment, but the same couldn't be said about her personal life. She thought about her grandfather. Nina couldn't believe she was about to admit this. She knew it would sound crazy, but did that really matter when one was talking to a bear? Nope, she didn't think so.

"And the other reason?" he asked, patiently.

"My grandfather, Harold Twofeathers," she said.

She was pretty sure that the bear's face crinkled in confusion, though it was hard to tell with all the fur. Maybe he just had fleas. "What does he have to do with your fearlessness?"

Good question. Without the bear meeting him, it was going to be hard to explain, but Nina did her best. "Ever since I was a little girl, he's filled my head with stories of The People. One of his favorite stories is that of the Great Bear."

"The Great Bear?" he sounded puzzled.

Nina laughed. For some reason, it struck her as funny that he wasn't familiar with The People's stories about him. "Sorry, I guess that concept would be weird to you. The Great Bear is a story that has been with the Cherokees for centuries."

The bear sat down. "What exactly does this bear do?"

She smiled. He looked so content to sit there and listen to the story it was almost comical. "He leads a band of brothers on a merry chase. See, the brothers are hunting the Great Bear. They are so determined to catch and kill him that they follow him into the sky, where they remain to this day." Nina glanced up, but could barely see the stars through the trees. When she looked back, she noticed the bear was staring at the sky too.

He didn't say anything for the longest time. He just continued to watch the stars. "Did they ever catch him?"

"Yes, and they killed him, but the Great Bear has powerful magic. He was able to put himself back together. When he does, the brothers chase him across the sky again," she said. "It happens every year."

His gaze lowered and he looked at her. "Hmm…Do you think I'm the Great Bear?"

For a bear, he seemed awfully serious. "What else can

you be?"

"Good question," he said, watching her closely. "Would you follow me to the stars?" The teasing lilt that had been in his voice all but disappeared.

Nina's brow furrowed. "Not to kill you. If that's what you're asking."

"It's not," he said.

She thought about it for a moment, then sighed longingly. "The answer really doesn't matter, since neither of us can run to the stars."

"But what if we could?" he asked.

She looked at him. "We can't, so it's a moot question."

"Someday, I might ask you again," he said softly, as if weighing each word.

Nina stared at him, wishing she could somehow read the strange bear's mind. She had a feeling that she was missing something vitally important in the conversation. Finally she said, "And when you do, I'll give you the same answer."

* * * * *

Riot's hearts raced. He couldn't believe that he'd finally found a woman who didn't fear him. He knew Nina would be the one, when he first spotted her splattered with mud. She was a woman who cared for beasts, and he was the biggest beast of them all. He may not be *the* Great Bear she was referring to, but he was a great bear.

He would be *her* great bear…if she'd have him.

Riot didn't want to rush her, or frighten her away, before he had a chance to test their compatibility, so he let her non-answer slide. She didn't understand the question. At least not yet. Or maybe she did, and didn't want to answer. Always possible. Females were far more complicated than their male counterparts—or so he'd been told repeatedly. He tended to agree. "Do you know the way back to town?"

She looked around warily, then slowly shook her head.

"My compass is broken."

"Climb on." He jerked his head to the side and stood.

"Excuse me?" Nina's eyes widened as she tilted her chin up. "Um, I don't think that's a good idea."

Riot growled, forcing his jaw to form words. "You are in no condition to walk. Besides, without that light, you can't see a thing. I can. So climb on." He gestured to his back.

Nina stood, but didn't move.

Riot stared at her. "What? Is there a problem?"

"You're too tall and…" She paused. "I've never ridden a bear before."

He snorted. It was the closest sound he could make to a laugh. "Well climb on and then you'll be able to say that you have."

Nina laughed, then slowly approached. "You're going to have to lie down or there's no way I'll be able to get on you."

Riot dropped to the ground on his belly. Even lying as flat as possible, Nina still had trouble scrambling onto his back. "Grab my fur."

"Are you sure?" She kicked her legs until she was high enough to swing one over his shoulder. Finally she was seated.

"It won't hurt me," he said.

"Okay, if you're sure." Nina grabbed a handful of thick fur at the back of his neck.

Riot slowly rose to his feet. She gasped and tightened her hold, pulling at his fur, but he hardly noticed. He was too busy enjoying the feel of her thighs clutching his sides. "Hang on. This might be a little bumpy."

* * * * *

CHAPTER FIVE

Bright sunlight splashed across her face, waking Nina, even though all she wanted to do was sleep in. She stretched and winced, feeling the soreness in her stiff muscles. Scratches still covered her hands from where she'd taken a fall. Dried blood was caked beneath her nails. She reached up and felt her head. It was tender, but there were no bumps. She wasn't nauseous and didn't have a headache, which probably ruled out a concussion.

Nina had called Kim last night after she found her truck parked in the driveway and her keys tucked under the mat on her porch. Her best friend had been about to send the sheriff's department to look for her. Fortunately, Nina was able to convince Kim not to, and claimed that she was fine.

Nina looked around the familiar room. A faded white dresser sat against the far wall, matching a small bedside table that had been covered with a blue crocheted throw. A dusty lamp stood on top of the small throw, next to a pile of paperbacks. She was in her bed, safe and sound. No talking bears in sight.

Had she imagined everything? Had it all been a bizarre dream brought on by stress? That made the most sense, but didn't explain her bruises. Nina threw back the covers and climbed out of bed. She knew she'd feel better once she'd had a shower. She'd grab a quick bite, then head to the hospital to visit her grandfather. He'd know what to do and just what to say. He was also the only person on the planet who wouldn't think she was crazy.

The hospital was obscenely quiet when she arrived. Only the sounds of machines beeping broke the foreboding silence. A few people waited in the Emergency Room, but they too sensed the odd quiet and kept their voices down. Nina made her way to the elevators and rode it to the third floor. Harold was sitting up, reading a newspaper, when she walked in. He put the paper aside and took a long assessing look at her.

"What happened, Little Deer?" His old eyes far too sharp for her peace of mind.

Nina ran a hand over her hair. "Nothing." She shook her head.

His bushy white brows arched, but he didn't contradict her. "Take a seat. The nurse said she would get me some coffee."

"You're not supposed to have caffeine. It's not good for you," she said.

"At my age, and in my condition, it doesn't matter." He patted her hand, staring at the fresh scratches. "You've been in the woods."

Nina thought about lying, but she'd never been able to get away with fibbing. Not when it came to her grandfather. He always knew when she'd told a lie. So she went with a partial truth. She didn't want Harold to worry, so she left out the part about being shot at by the poachers. "I was in the woods."

"Alone?" he asked.

"No, Kim was with me." At least for a while, until we had to run for our lives. "Grandpa, tell me what you know about the Great Bear. I mean, I know the story about the brothers chasing him into the sky, but is there anything else?"

He rubbed his chin. "Hmm…like what?"

"I don't know." She shrugged. "Does he talk?" The room suddenly felt too warm. Nina tugged at her collar.

Harold sat up straighter. "What happened in the woods, Little Deer?"

Nina looked around the room, noting that the door was open. She rose from her seat to shut it. She sat back down and looked down at her lap, unable to meet her grandfather's questioning gaze. Nina twisted her fingers and searched for words that wouldn't make her sound crazy.

"The truth will free your worries, Little Deer." Harold touched her hands, stopping her frantic wringing.

She glanced up at his kind face and felt her shoulders relax. "I think I met the Great Bear in the woods last night." Nina waited, holding her breath in anticipation of her grandfather's response.

He simply stared at her for what felt like an eternity, then slowly, with the utmost patience, Harold opened his mouth to speak. "Why would you think that?"

Nina looked at him. "I know this is going to sound crazy. If I was hearing it, I'd think I was crazy, but last night in the woods, I ran into a giant talking bear."

Harold's eyes lit up and he grinned. "What did he say?"

"Oh, you know, the usual kind of things," she joked.

"Come now, Little Deer. It's not every day that someone gets to speak with the Great Bear," he said.

Nina squirmed in her seat. "He apologized for scaring me, then asked if I was okay. I'd fallen down."

Harold's brow furrowed in concern and he gave her another once over. "Are you okay?"

She nodded. "I'm fine, Grandpa."

"Did the bear say anything else?" He looked like a five year old engrossed in his first good story.

Nina shook her head. "He asked me my name. He told

me he thought I should see a doctor, then asked about the Great Bear story. He seemed fascinated by it. Like he'd never heard it before, but how is that possible? He's the Great Bear." She hadn't forgotten how he'd also asked her if she'd follow him into the sky. For some reason, the innocuous question seemed too intimate to share just yet.

"You told him the story," Harold said. It wasn't a question.

"I saw no reason not to. It was so bizarre. The whole night was bizarre." Nina sighed. "Anyway, I got a little turned around in the dark, so he gave me a ride back into town."

Harold's eyebrows arched so high that they disappeared under his graying hairline. "How, may I ask, did he give you a ride?"

"He told me to climb on his back. I rode him like a horse all the way to town." Nina looked at her grandfather's mischievous expression. "What?" she asked.

"It sounds like the Great Bear has chosen you." Harold looked beyond pleased.

"Chosen me for what? He's a bear, Grandpa. I can't exactly go live with a bear." She shoved her hands under her thighs, so she'd stop fidgeting.

Harold's expression grew serious. "The Great Bear is not just a bear. He holds powerful magic." He waited.

Nina nodded to let him know that she understood.

"If the Great Bear has chosen to reveal himself to you, then that means at some point he will want to take you into the sky," Harold said. "It would be a great honor to be asked. And an even greater honor to accept."

"You told me the other day to stay out of the woods, that there was dangerous magic gunning for me," she said. Had he forgotten?

Harold nodded. "That I did, but I knew you wouldn't listen to me."

"So what's changed?"

He looked at her. "I wasn't sure where the magic was coming from. Magic is tricky. It can be good or bad. I was worried that if it was bad that you'd be in danger, but the appearance of the Great Bear is a good omen."

Nina wasn't convinced, but it was clear that her grandfather was. "Don't get your hopes up, Grandpa. I'll probably never see him again. It was a fluke that I ran into him in the first place."

"Chance doesn't exist, Little Deer. Not when we're talking about powerful magic," he said.

She sighed. "It doesn't matter what kind of magic it is. I'm not about to leave you to run off to visit the stars."

Harold shook his head. "Not visit. Live. The Great Bear would want you to *live* among the stars with him. It was a him, wasn't it?"

Nina blushed. "Yes, it was definitely a him. How many Great Bears are there?"

The sparkle in Harold's eyes returned. "There is only one."

"That doesn't change my answer," she said. "I'm not leaving you, so you can stop trying to get rid of me."

"I'd never do so." His smile softened. "Fortunately, you won't have to make that choice."

Nina frowned. What was he talking about? Of course, she'd have to make that choice. And she'd *always* choose her grandfather. No matter what. What was she saying? There was no such thing as a talking bear. She'd imagined it due to the stress of being shot at. She glanced at her watch. "I have an appointment this afternoon. I'll be back early in the evening. Can I get you anything?"

Harold shook his head. He was still smiling, but there was something in his eyes that worried her. "I'll see you tonight," he said.

"Get some rest, Grandpa." Nina kissed his forehead and walked to the door.

He waved goodbye.

* * * * *

Nina drove to the sheriff's station after dropping by her office to check on her furry patients. They were all doing well, so at least one thing was going right in her life. Too bad people weren't as accommodating as animals. Her mind flashed to the Great Bear. If only they made men like that. If they did, she'd be set. She hadn't wanted to report the incident from last night, but the fact that she and Kim had been shot at changed the situation.

She parked her truck and walked inside. Her plan was to leave Kim's name out of it. Her fiancé, Danny Alberty would be upset enough when he found out his future wife's best friend was out causing trouble again. He already didn't like how close the two women were. Some days, Nina couldn't exactly blame him. As soon as she walked inside, Nina spotted Rick Hensen, her unwanted suitor. Unfortunately, he saw her too. He waved and walked over.

"Hi, Rick," Nina said.

"You going to be at the wedding reception tomorrow?" he asked.

She kind of had to be, since she was the maid-of-honor. "I'll be there."

"Great. I'll be there, too." He smiled. His light brown face creased, showing off his beautiful white teeth.

Rick was a handsome man, but no matter how hard she tried, Nina just couldn't bring herself to be interested in him that way.

He continued to smile at her.

Nina's discomfort grew. What did he want her to say? He was a nice guy but she didn't want to lead him on. Over Rick's broad shoulders, she saw Danny's frowning face. He looked as if he'd been heading out on patrol, but changed directions when he saw her. His black cropped hair gave way to a square, uncompromising jawline. Like The People from old, his skin held a reddish tint beneath the brown. At five foot eight, he wasn't tall, but that didn't mean he wasn't intimidating.

"Excuse me," Nina said to Rick. "I have to speak to Danny for a minute."

Rick looked over his shoulder and frowned. "Okay. I'll see you later?" He made it a question.

To avoid any awkwardness, Nina nodded her assent. "Sure."

Rick wandered away.

Danny walked across the room and halted right in front of her. Nina could feel the waves of anger emanating from him. She opened her mouth to explain.

"Don't!" he snapped. "Do not say a word." Danny grabbed her elbow and ushered her into one of the few offices in the small station.

Nina waited until he shut the door behind them. "I came here—"

"Unless it was to apologize and promise never to do anything so stupid again, I don't want to hear it." He growled.

The sound reminded Nina of the Great Bear and a shiver raced down her spine. So much for leaving Kim out of the story. It was obvious that Danny already knew what had happened. "I'm not here to apologize because I didn't do anything wrong. I am here to report poaching within the Qualla Boundary."

"If it wasn't for my respect for your grandfather, I'd arrest you right now."

Nina crossed her arms over her chest. "On what charges?"

He hesitated, then said, "Disturbing my…peace of mind."

She pulled a face. "Those charges wouldn't stick and you know it."

"I'd make sure they did. At least until the wedding tomorrow," he said.

Danny had never had much of a sense of humor, so she

knew he wasn't kidding.

"Do you have any idea how long it took me to calm Kim down last night? Do you? Hours!" he answered before she could. "She was ready to call out the army until you phoned. I've never seen her so terrified. What in the hell were you thinking?"

"I—" He cut her off again with a sharp glance in her direction.

"You're a bad influence." Danny's lips pressed into a thin line. "The sooner we leave this place, the better Kim's life will be. The better *our* life will be." *Without you,* was left unsaid.

Nina didn't think she was a bad influence…Okay, so there was that one time in Raleigh, when she and Kim had been detained by the police for protesting factories for lax pollution controls because they were damaging the Smokies…and that other time when poachers had reported them for disabling their property.

The property in question had been illegal traps, but by the time deputies arrived on scene, the only broken equipment was the legal kind. They hadn't touched it, but the change made it difficult to convince the sheriff's department that they were telling the truth. Kim had gotten off scot-free— thanks to Danny's connections, but Nina had paid a steep fine.

It had been worth it though, since they'd managed to stop three sets of poachers from taking bears, and whatever else was unlucky enough to stumble across their snares. Not that it mattered now, as Danny had so tactfully reminded her. Tomorrow her best friend would leave Qualla—and her— behind.

He continued to glare at her. "You nearly got Kim killed last night." Danny's hands moved to his hips and his jaw clenched. "You may not have any concern for your own welfare, but you'd think that you'd care if something happened to your best friend days before her wedding.

Christ, Nina, we're getting married tomorrow!"

Nina deflated a little. It had been a close call last night. Closer than they'd ever experienced. As the poachers grew bolder, so did the dangers. "You know I would never knowingly place Kim into harm's way."

Danny shook his head. "But you did. You do. Every time you come up with one of these crazy schemes, you call Kim because she'll never say no to you."

"That's not true," Nina said. Her throat grew tight as she tried to swallow the lump that had suddenly formed.

He scowled at her. "I love her, Nina. I couldn't bear it if anything happened to her." Danny wasn't one to express himself, so the fact that he'd made such a declaration was huge, and Nina knew it. His dark brown eyes shimmered with emotion. He was laying his heart out there for her to see. He wanted her to understand just how much Kim meant to him.

Nina's eyes burned. "I'm sorry."

"I know you don't have anyone waiting at home for you, since Harold went into the hospital," he said.

The truth of his statement gutted her.

"But Kim does. She's my world, Nina," he said. "Remember that the next time you ask her to go traipsing in the woods with you."

Nina couldn't look at him. She knew if she did that she'd burst into tears. "Don't worry." Emotion choked her words. "There won't be a next time."

"Thank you," Danny said.

Nina started to leave.

"Why did you come in here anyway?" he asked, before she made it to the door.

She managed a painful laugh as she looked back at him. "I wanted to report the poachers we found."

"Consider them reported," he said.

Nina nodded and rushed out of the room. Danny wasn't going to do anything about the poachers. With his wedding tomorrow, they weren't a priority to him or anyone else. They only mattered to Nina. It had been a fluke that they'd encountered the traps at all. Poachers were always moving to avoid detection. If the sheriff's department didn't act now, the men would be long gone. If they weren't already.

She thought about her best friend. Nina had been telling Danny the truth, when she promised to leave Kim out of her own personal wars. Her friend should be worrying about last minute flower arrangements and catering, not bears and illegal trapping. She flashed to Danny's pained face. Fear had been there, along with the worry and anger. What if the poachers hadn't missed? Nina didn't want to think about it. Couldn't think about it. The thought was nearly too much to bear.

Kim was her best friend and would always be her best friend, but Nina knew that once Kim got married there would be no more wild exploits, even if they were for a good cause. She and Danny would be leaving the Qualla Boundary right after their reception. He had applied to be a Tennessee State Trooper and had been accepted, which meant that they had to move.

Though Nina hadn't realized it at the time, last night had been their last big adventure. An adventure she'd cherish, despite the unexpected danger. She finally let go of the tears she'd been holding in, as she stumbled to her car and headed home. Nina was so distraught that she didn't see the rusty pickup truck slowing as it passed by, or the red-haired man staring at her from its open window.

* * * * *

CHAPTER SIX

Nina arrived at Kim's house around noon. She had her maid-of-honor dress tossed over her arm, and a makeup kit in her hands.

Kim opened the door before she could knock, and smiled. She was wearing a pink robe and yellow fuzzy duck slippers.

"Don't just stand there. Help me." Nina juggled the items in her arms, threatening to drop some.

Kim snatched the dress from her. "You better not have wrinkled that dress," she said.

"Relax, I didn't." Nina walked inside and placed the makeup kit on the table, then went back out to her truck to retrieve the flowers. She placed the box full of blooms beside the make-up kit.

Kim opened the box and poked her head inside. "They're beautiful. And they smell glorious."

Nina stared at the bouquets. "They're what you wanted."

"They look expensive," Kim said, eyeing her suspiciously.

They *were* expensive. Nina had wanted to do something nice for her best friend, so she'd offered to pay for the exotic flowers. Kim had already over-extended herself paying for the wedding. She didn't need to add flowers to the bulging tab.

"They weren't too bad," she said. "Now let's get you ready. In a few hours, you're going to be a married woman."

Kim grinned. "I know. Can you believe it? I was the one who swore I'd never marry. You were always the one who wanted a husband and kids."

"Yeah." Nina looked away. Life had a funny way of changing all your plans. "Yet here you are."

"Here I am," Kim said. The humor fled her face. "Sorry that things didn't work out the way you wanted. And sorry about the other night."

Nina's stomach clenched, but she managed to keep her smile in place. "There's nothing to apologize for."

Kim shook her head. "I shouldn't have told Danny that we'd gone into the woods. It was wrong, but…I was so worried about you. I was scared that those men had caught you." She blinked rapidly as tears filled her eyes.

Nina squeezed her hands. "You did the right thing. It was dangerous," she said. "I'm just glad they were too far away to get a good look at us."

"Oh my God, me too."

Nina grabbed a tissue and handed it to Kim. "Now enough blubbering. You don't want to put makeup on over puffy red eyes, do you?"

Kim laughed and slowly let go of her fingers. "No, that wouldn't look good in the wedding photos."

Nina patted the chair in front of her. "Have a seat. We'd better get started. Do you know how you'd like to wear your hair?"

Kim looked over her shoulder. "Up for sure."

"Good choice," Nina said and went to work.

* * * * *

Kim looked radiant as she walked down the aisle. Nina

was convinced there'd never been a more beautiful bride. The hours spent getting ready had given the best friends time to relive old adventures and discuss future dreams. Those precious moments would stay with Nina for the rest of her life.

The ceremony went off without a hitch. By the time the minister declared Danny could kiss the bride, there wasn't a dry eye in the house. The guests filed over to the community center where the reception would be held, after the official wedding photos were taken. Kim and her family had transformed the space into a romantic country fairyland. Tables covered in delicate cream lace had been set up around the room. Each tabletop held three vanilla candles, and a Mason jar full of flowers. The twinkling candlelight illuminated the gold-rimmed, china place settings and the crystal wine glasses. A DJ played classical music as people found their seats. After dinner, the tables would be pushed aside for dancing.

Danny's friend and co-worker, Rick Hensen, went out of his way to catch her attention, but Nina steadfastly ignored him.

Kim hadn't stopped smiling since she'd said, "I do." Even stoic, stick-in-the-mud Danny kept grinning. Of course, he should be smiling. He'd just married the best girl in the world. He had better take care of Kim or he'd have to answer to Nina.

The dinner passed pleasantly and soon it was time to dance. Nina couldn't remember the last time that she'd been out dancing. She wondered if it was high school, then cringed at the thought. The night wore on and the party grew louder. Nina never realized she could feel so alone in a crowd of familiar faces. Several people stopped by to comment on different aspects of the wedding. Nina kept her answers polite, but short, especially when talk turned to Harold's health.

Nina glanced across the room. Kim had been dancing

with Danny's brother, who was now leading her off of the dance floor. Her gaze moved to her best friend's new husband. Danny kept looking at his watch, obviously anxious to leave. Nina wasn't sure that she could bear it when Kim drove away. She was already missing her and she hadn't even left yet.

Maybe she should go over and say her farewells now. Nina took a step toward the dance floor, but was stopped short by a gentle hand upon her shoulder. She turned expecting to see another familiar face and found a stranger. Her heart slammed into her ribs. Nina took a step back automatically as she registered the size of the man touching her.

She tilted her head way back, her gaze locking onto his face. Soft brown eyes met hers, as he gave her a crooked grin. The effect was devastating. The small action transformed his formidable face into a welcome refuge. Nina's mind raced, as she tried to recall if he'd been at the ceremony.

Was he one of Kim's cousins? She had a lot of them and Nina hadn't met them all. Surely she would've noticed a man standing head and shoulders above the crowd had he been there. Another thought came to her, if he was Kim's cousin, then why hadn't her friend introduced them? Talk about holding out on her! Nina decided that they'd have to have a chat before her best friend left.

The man glanced at the DJ. "Would you like to dance?" His voice rumbled despite the gentle tone.

Nina debated for all of a millisecond, then nodded.

He led her out onto the dance floor and took her into his arms. The moment his large hand settled on the small of her back, Nina's whole body began to tingle and warmth blossomed inside of her. He adjusted his grip and her breath caught. Had he noticed? She sure hoped not. If he did, the man didn't let on. Instead, he began to move with the rhythm. The song that was playing was very upbeat, but the man kept the tempo of their movements slow. Their bodies came together, brushing and swaying. His big hands flexed and his body tensed every time they touched. Nina's clothes suddenly felt too tight, as she flushed with the heat of arousal. The man's nostrils flared and she could've sworn that he growled under his breath.

"Have we met?" she asked. "There's something about you that seems familiar."

He hesitated, then said, "In a manner of speaking." His vague answer aroused her curiosity as he guided her expertly around the dance floor. For a big man, he was amazingly graceful, unlike Nina who'd managed to find his toes twice already. He brushed her clumsiness off with an easy smile and kept dancing.

By the time the song ended, Nina was breathless. From the looks of the man, she wasn't the only one affected by their close contact. He reluctantly let her go. The room came back into focus. Several people were staring at them, including her best friend, Kim, and Rick Hensen. The big man reached for her hand, drawing her attention back to him. Her vision narrowed as he brought her knuckles up to his sensuous mouth, and kissed the back of her hand. His lips lingered and Nina's eyelids drooped.

A fresh flush of desire roared through her, leaving her breasts aching and moisture pooling between her thighs. She slowly pulled her hand away. She didn't want to, but she had to, before she did something insane like throw him down on the floor and have her way with him. The loss of warmth was palpable and disconcerting. Nina pressed her feet into the floor to keep from rushing back into his arms.

"Thank you for the dance." His brown eyes twinkled as he spoke.

Anytime, Nina thought, but only nodded in response. She didn't trust herself to speak for fear her tongue would fall out of her mouth and onto the floor.

He brushed a lone finger over her cheek, branding her

with his touch. "I'll see you soon." He didn't wait for a response. He simply strode off, confidence oozing from every pore.

Nina stood there, her body twitching as if an electrical current had shot through her. "Wait!" she called out. "What's your name?" But it was too late. He was already gone.

Kim rushed onto the dance floor and spun Nina around to face her. "What was that?" She pointed in the direction the man had gone. "I can't believe you've been holding out on me like that."

Nina frowned. "What?" Her gaze strayed back to where the man had disappeared.

"Here I was worried about leaving you, only to find out that you've been hiding a massive hunk."

"I haven't been hiding anything. I thought he was your cousin."

"My cousin?" Kim reeled back. "I don't have any cousins that look like that. I would've introduced you," she said.

"Then who was he?" Nina asked.

Kim's brow furrowed. "You don't know?"

Nina shook her head. "No."

Kim took a deep breath. "I've never seen him before."

Nina's eyes widened as a horrifying thought crossed her mind. "He's not one of Danny's friends, is he?" She didn't have anything against Danny really, but she didn't want to date any of his friends.

Kim shook her head vehemently. "No way! I know all of Danny's friends. Besides, he asked me who he was. I just assumed that you knew him with all the dirty dancing taking place out on the dance floor."

Nina's face flushed. "I was not dirty dancing."

Kim giggled. "Sure looked like it to me...and everyone else watching."

"Wonderful," Nina deadpanned, which only made Kim laugh louder.

As if summoned by some internal warning system, Danny appeared beside his blushing bride. "So who's the new guy?" he asked.

"None of your business," Kim answered for her

Danny shook his head and kissed Kim on the nose, then glanced at Nina. "Thanks for being able to make it."

"I wouldn't miss it for the world. You take care of our girl," Nina said.

Danny pulled Kim into his arms and hugged her close. "You know I will."

"Yes, I know you will…or I'll kick your ass, badge or no badge." A lump formed in Nina's throat. This was it. This was goodbye.

"Are you going to be okay?" Danny asked.

"Be careful, Danny. Some folks might start to think that you like me," Nina said.

He laughed. "Wouldn't want that."

Nina turned away so they wouldn't see the tears in her eyes. When she regained her composure, she faced them once more. "You guys going to be leaving soon?"

Kim nodded. "Just as soon as we say goodbye to our folks."

"I'll give you guys a minute," Danny said, then wandered off, but he didn't go far.

"I guess this is it then." Nina met Kim's watery gaze. If they kept this up much longer they were going to both end up crying. "I'm going to miss you."

"Miss you too." Kim sniffled.

"You're going to ruin your makeup. What would your wedding guests think? "

Kim shook her head. "I don't care." She gave her a fierce hug. "Email me and call."

"I will," Nina promised.

Danny returned to Kim's side. "Time to go, hon."

Kim gave her one last look, then turned away.

A sob caught in Nina's throat as she watched her best

friend leave.

* * * * *

Riot stood in the shadows, watching the guests slowly file out of the building to wave the new couple off. Nina lingered toward the back of the crowd, wiping at her eyes. Her shoulders shook as she gave Kim a watery smile and a quick wave goodbye. Her pain seared him, scarring his two hearts, but there was nothing he could do to stop it. Riot recognized the emotion for what it was—loss. He fought the urge to return to her side. This wasn't the place or the right time for him to make his move.

His hands still tingled from where he'd held her in his arms. Despite their difference in size, Nina had fit against him like she'd been made for his body, and his body alone. At first, when he'd approached her and asked her to dance, Riot had feared she was like all the others. Especially when she'd taken a step back. Then Nina had done something that had surprised him. She'd held her ground. Just like the night she'd met his beast. That small gesture had cautiously renewed his hope that he had a chance with her.

Riot hadn't intended to drop into the reception, but he'd been unable to resist, when he caught a glimpse of Nina. She had looked so beautiful in her pale green dress with those flowers woven into her long, black hair. He opened his hand and stared down at a crushed bloom. He'd managed to pluck it without her noticing, needing to hold a piece of her until he could claim the real thing.

He brought the flower to his nose and inhaled. It was sweet like Nina. The scent brought to mind the moment he'd gathered her close. She'd melted against him. He could still feel her hard nipples brushing his chest. When the warm scent of her arousal had reached his nose, his beast had roared to life inside of him, urging Riot to claim her right on the dance floor.

He still trembled with the burning desire to touch her and taste her skin. Just the thought made his shaft pulse within his trousers. Riot shifted his heavy length to alleviate the pressure, then pressed a button on the band around his wrist. The dress clothes morphed into his flight suit. The change helped, but nothing would diminish his need. Not until he had Nina beneath him and he was buried balls deep inside of her.

Riot took one last look at the woman he wanted more than his next breath, then faded into the woods. His beast would not be denied for much longer, of that he had no doubt.

* * * * *

Chapter Seven

Riot stayed in the woods bordering the town. He'd told himself to keep away, at least until he'd put together a plan for how to approach Nina, but he hadn't been able to. He found himself returning to her home over and over, hoping to catch a glimpse of her again.

The man in him couldn't stop thinking about the feel of her in his arms, while his beast could still feel her small hands burrowing into his thick fur, holding him tight. He felt the warmth of her thighs as she gripped his sides. It wasn't hard to imagine those same thighs grasping his hips, especially after the dance last night. Riot closed his eyes and shivered, as his big body came to life.

He continued to skirt the trees, taking care to obscure his image from human eyes. Nina's delicious scent wafted from the small, well-kept house tucked against the woods at the edge of town. She had a small garden in the back and flowerpots that would be ready to bloom come spring. Her nearest neighbor was over a hundred yards away and obscured by trees.

Riot stared at the house, wondering what she was doing. Was she even awake yet? He'd hardly slept a wink. Had she thought about him after he left the reception? He hoped so because he hadn't stopped thinking about her. Riot liked everything about Nina, but it was her bravery that captured his hearts. Things were happening quickly, far quicker than a normal human mating pattern, but that's how it went when a Phantom Warrior encountered a potential mate.

A faded, paint-chipped blue pickup rattled down her driveway, bouncing as it hit a pothole. Riot's head perked up, hoping it was her, but the truck was the wrong color. His brow furrowed as the vehicle stopped, sputtering noisily as the engine died. Two lanky men climbed out of the cab of the truck. One had red unkept hair that could do with a wash, and the other had dark brown, which matched his misshapen beard.

Anger surged through Riot. It was followed by a swift wave of protectiveness, as the men walked up onto the front porch and knocked on the door. Nina was his. How dare these two men come into his territory!

Riot stepped deeper into the woods, no longer able to keep his form invisible. His emotions were running too high to concentrate, but he didn't go far. For some reason, he couldn't tear his eyes away. He had to know. He had to see for himself if Nina was attached to one of these males. No matter how much pain it inflicted upon him.

"You sure this is where she lives?" the man with the dark hair asked.

"Yep, she was at a vet place, when I first spotted her. I think she works there 'cause she had keys to the place. I wasn't sure it was her, until I saw her come out of the sheriff's station. I followed her from there to here," the red head said.

The dark haired man's expression turned cold, calculating. "What was she doing there?"

The man shrugged. "Don't know, but when she came out, looked like she was crying."

The dark haired man sneered. "Good! I'm going to give

her more to cry about. Let's get this over with."

"You sure, Hank?"

"Yes, and I think I know just how to get her to come with us," Hank said.

The conversation didn't make any sense. What were they talking about? If she knew them, then why had they needed to follow her home? Gooseflesh rose on Riot's arms as a wave of foreboding swept through him. He didn't know whether to interfere. His instincts were screaming at him, but he didn't fully understand Earth customs or behavior. There was too much room for error and misunderstanding. So he waited in the shadows of the trees, keeping his distance for now.

Hank raised his hand and knocked on the front door.

* * * * *

Nina was having the most delicious dream, when the first knock sounded on her door. The dark-haired giant of a man had his head buried between her thighs and he was making hungry noises in the back of his throat as he licked her into oblivion. The knock came again, this time louder. Nina opened her eyes and looked around, but her dream lover was nowhere to be seen.

The knocking sounded more insistent. She cursed under her breath, wondering who in the world could be stopping by. Harold was her only family. He had a key. And Kim knocked, but always walked straight in. Besides, she was already gone, off to start her new life with her new husband. Nina rolled out of bed, feeling decidedly disgruntled. The dream had been so vivid that she'd expected the man to be there beside her. She stumbled to the front door and pulled the curtain back.

Two men stood on her front porch. One had his fist raised, ready to knock on her door again. They looked vaguely familiar, but she knew she didn't know either of them. Were they lost? Dressed in jeans and work boots, they didn't look like tourists. They looked like locals, but they weren't one of The People. She knew all of them. Nina brushed a hand over her eyes and cracked the door open enough to quickly lock her screen-door.

"Can I help you?" she asked, eyeing the strangers.

The dark-haired man nodded. "We ran into a bit of trouble down the road." He hiked his thumb over his shoulder. "We clipped a bear with our truck. Someone told us that you might be able to help."

Nina's heart clenched as her mind flashed to the Great Bear. "Was it big?"

The dark-haired man's eyes narrowed. "Why do you ask?"

"I need to know. It'll determine the size of the tranquilizer I'll need." It was both the truth and a lie. She brought various amounts of tranquilizers with her when she made house calls. But this time, she needed to know for her own peace of mind.

The man shrugged. "It was about average I'd say. Isn't that right, Mark?"

The red-haired man ran a dirty hand over his scruffy jaw. "Yep, regular size. I reckon."

Nina stared at the men. Something wasn't right about their story, but could she really take a chance if there was a wounded bear out there that needed her help? "Are you sure it's still alive?"

The dark-haired man's face flushed and his nostrils flared. "I know the difference between a live bear and a dead one." His exasperation evident.

"Hank sure does," Mark said. "You might say he's an expert on the subject."

"Okay, wait right here. I need to get my bag." Nina rushed into her spare room and pulled out her medical kit. It was stocked with enough stuff to at least halt bleeding and allow her to assess the animal's injuries. She threw on yesterday's jeans and a long sleeved T-shirt, then hurried back into the living room. She grabbed her house keys and rushed out onto the porch.

The second Nina locked the door a large hand covered her lower face, clamping down on her mouth to keep her from screaming. Fear sliced through her. Who were they? What did they want? The possibilities were endless and terrifying.

"You cost us plenty the other night," the dark-haired man hissed in her ear. "We're hard working folks. We don't need the likes of you interfering in our business."

She swallowed hard. *The poachers*. Nina didn't think they'd gotten a good look at her. Apparently, she'd been wrong. And that mistake might very well cost her, her life.

He manhandled her over to the truck and tossed her inside. The man he'd called Mark shoved a dirty rag into her mouth and held her down so she wouldn't be seen in the cab. They drove out of Cherokee, heading toward the Smoky Mountains. It was easy to tell the direction since there weren't many roads running through town. They let her sit up once they left the paved roads. There weren't many cars on the rural roads. No one to spot her. And no one to hear her scream. Cliché horror movie fodder. Too bad it was really happening to her.

Nina glanced into the bed of the pickup, grateful that her best friend had left town and wasn't lying in the back. Sooner or later, they'd stop. Once they did, she'd do her best to get away. Nina didn't want to think about her odds. If she did, she knew the fear would stop her. They drove off the Qualla Boundary toward the park.

The men turned down a fire road and drove until they reached a locked gate. Mark jumped out of the truck and pulled a pair of bolt cutters out from behind the seat. He walked up to the chain on the gate and snapped it in two. He pushed the gate open and waited for Hank to drive through, then shut it behind them, laying the chain over the top.

From a distance, it would look like the gate was still locked. It would only be upon closer inspection that someone would notice it had been broken. They drove on. Signs appeared on a few trees stating that they were trespassing on private property. Where were they taking her? She didn't know and that scared Nina even more.

They drove until the road ended.

Hank shut off the truck and turned to his partner. "Grab the guns, traps, and the rope," he said, then gripped her arm and dragged her out of the truck. "Start walking." He shoved her into the woods.

* * * * *

The men were taking Nina. His Nina. Riot stared at the truck in disbelief. By the time he rushed out of the woods, the truck was pulling onto the road and driving away, smoke billowing from its exhaust pipe. He was fast, but he wasn't quick enough to catch a speeding vehicle. He watched the truck begin to fade into the distance.

Riot raced back into the woods, trying to keep an eye on the truck as it made its way toward town. The traffic was light, giving him no chance to catch up to the men. He couldn't see Nina anymore, but he knew she was in there. Shoved between the two men. Why wasn't she screaming? Trying to fight her way out of the vehicle? Had they struck her? Was she even conscious?

Rage boiled through him and he was forced to move deeper into the woods. By the time he came out on the other side, the men's vehicle was fading into the distance. Riot bellowed, the sound echoing through the hills.

He pushed on, running as fast as he could. Trees fell in his wake as he shoved through the brush. The truck turned off onto an unpaved road and continued on. Riot fell further behind. His hearts slammed in his chest. He couldn't lose her. Not now that he'd finally found her.

Deer scattered to get away from the raging beast terrorizing the forest. The smaller creatures huddled, trying to remain out of sight. Riot didn't care. He raised his head into the air and took a deep breath. All he could scent was the truck's noxious exhaust. It would be enough. It had to be enough.

The smell of the truck faded on the wind. Had they slipped off the road? It seemed unlikely since traffic only moved in one direction, but he circled back nonetheless in order to catch all the scents floating on the wind. Riot couldn't afford to miss anything. Nina's fear soaked scent was but a wisp of memory. Riot stood on his hind legs and bellowed. His roar shook the ground beneath his clawed feet. It was a warning to the men who'd taken Nina, and a promise of things to come.

* * * * *

Nina's head shot up as a monstrous sound battered the woods. She couldn't tell where it had come from, but it had sounded *close*. Birds instantly stopped chirping and the forest shivered, then grew unnaturally quiet. Hank and Mark looked around nervously.

"What was that, Hank?" Mark ran a shaky hand through his red hair, then clutched his pistol.

Hank's grip on Nina's arm tightened and he checked the safety on his shotgun. "Don't know. Don't care," he said, but she felt his hands tremble.

He yanked her forward and she stumbled, falling onto the ground. Hank didn't give her a chance to get up. Instead, he pulled her to her feet, dragging her over twigs and rough stones.

"Where are we going?" Nina asked.

"We're going to scare you. Scare you bad," Mark said in a taunting voice. "You won't ever come back in these woods again. Right, Hank?"

Hank nodded, but the look on his face said he had more in mind than just frightening her. The stark hatred burning in his eyes scared Nina more than any verbal threat.

"Why are you doing this?" she asked.

"You know why," he spat.

Nina shook her head. "I'll pay for the traps. Just let me go."

He squeezed harder. "I don't take handouts from red trash. You people with your casinos and government checks go around flaunting your status as a sovereign nation, while hardworking folks like us lose everything. We don't get a land grant from the government. We have to buy our own. It ain't right." Hank shook her so hard that her teeth rattled.

"Yeah," Mark said. "The least you can do is give up a few bears."

"Oh, she'll do more than that," Hank said. "She's going to bring the bears to us. Aren't you, sweetheart?"

How did they expect her to do that?

They marched her deeper into the woods. Nothing looked familiar. Nina spotted a small clearing up ahead, then a drop off where the land sloped down. She could hear water running, but it didn't sound deep. A creek? Maybe if she could twist out of his hold, she could get to the creek and follow it downstream. It would have to lead back to the Qualla Boundary...eventually.

"Don't even think about it," Hank said. "I'll fill your backside full of buckshot before you make it ten steps."

Nina shivered as her body broke out in a cold sweat.

"Tie her to that trunk." Hank pointed to the nearest tree.

Mark grabbed her arm and wrapped one end of the rope around her wrist. He pulled her over to the tree that Hank had indicated, and looped the rope around the trunk before tying her other wrist. Nina twisted her hands. If she kept twisting, she might be able to work herself free. Even as the thought crossed her mind, Mark wrapped the rope around her body until she was trussed like a Thanksgiving turkey.

He tied the ends behind the tree, way out of her reach.

Unless a hiker stumbled upon them, she wasn't going anywhere until they released her. Which from the looks of things, wouldn't be anytime soon. No one knew where she was or who she was with. With Harold in the hospital and her shifts at the clinic over for the week, no one would even think to look. Oh, Harold would notice when she didn't show up for her daily visits, but he wouldn't be able to do anything about it, but worry. Her eyes started to burn, but she blinked back the tears. She wouldn't give these men the satisfaction of seeing her cry.

The men proceeded to set up snares and bear traps around the perimeter. They even placed one by her feet. Nina pulled at the ropes, while they were distracted. No matter which way she twisted the ropes wouldn't budge. Mark may be stupid, but it was obvious he knew how to tie a good knot. By the time they'd finished laying out all the bear traps, all she'd managed to do was scrape her wrists raw and tighten the rope. Each breath cut into her chest, compressing her lungs.

"Could you please loosen the rope a little? I can't breathe."

Mark took a step in her direction, but was stopped short by Hank.

"You should've thought about that before you tried to wiggle out of it," Hank said. "Take shallow breaths. You'll be fine. Least until the bears get here." Hank walked up to Nina and pulled a knife out of his pocket. He flicked the blade open and stared at her. The knife wasn't long, but the curved blade looked well cared for and sharp.

Nina straightened against the tree trunk. "What do you plan to do with that?"

"You need bait in order to catch bear." His gaze scrolled down the front of her long-sleeved T-shirt, but there was nothing sexual about the look he gave her. "We forgot ours, so you'll do." Hank's hand shot out. The blade sliced through her shirtsleeve and opened the skin on her arm. Blood welled, then began to run along the cut before dropping onto the leaves at her feet.

It took the pain a second to register. When it did, Nina screamed.

He cut her again, tearing through her other arm. She thought he might stop then, but he didn't. Instead, Hank moved onto her abdomen, crisscrossing over her stomach. Blood made her shirt stick to her body. The cuts weren't fatal, but they were deep enough to bleed for a while. Happy with his handy work, he stepped back.

Mark's face was green and his eyes were wide with fright. He obviously hadn't anticipated this part of Hank's plan. He stumbled over to a nearby tree and ducked his head behind it. Retching followed. Nina listened to him empty his stomach. Her mouth watered and she barely kept her breakfast down. Her skin burned. Every breath hurt.

"Get yourself together!" Hank shouted. "It won't take long for the bears to smell her."

Mark staggered out from behind the tree, his face pale and his hands shaky. He wiped his mouth with the back of his sleeve, then carefully made his way to the creek. Nina heard splashing and gargling. When he returned, his color looked better, but he appeared wary of Hank. He should be. If things went the direction she imagined, neither she nor Mark would be leaving these woods today.

* * * * *

Chapter Eight

Riot ran through the woods frantically, stopping every so often to sniff the air. Where was she? What had they done with her? He snarled and switched directions, nearly missing the sweet aroma wafting on the breeze. His ears perked as he jerked his head toward the scent. He inhaled again and froze as the coppery perfume registered with his beast. Blood. And lots of it. Riot filled his lungs, his head swimming as the delicate fragrance washed over him again.

Nina.

Fear enveloped him, locking every muscle, while causing his hearts to hammer in his chest. Never in his long life had he ever experienced this level of bone shattering fear. Not in the midst of battle. Not when he'd fallen under an enemy's sword. Never. Nina had scrapped her hands the night they'd met, when she'd fallen into the shallow ravine. Riot had gotten a good whiff of her blood then. He'd recognize her scent anywhere. He was moving before the thought filtered through his mind. Nina was hurt—or worse.

She had to be alive.

He couldn't think of any other possibility. Refused to. Riot barreled through the woods, shattering small trees into kindling and crushing the underbrush beneath his massive paws. His anger quickly morphed into despair, as the scent grew stronger. Riot was so focused on reaching her that he didn't see the first trap. For once, his massive size worked in his favor. The trap bent under his considerable weight.

Riot bellowed in rage. He couldn't see Nina yet, but the smell of her blood was so thick that it practically dripped from the sky. He caught movement out of the corner of his eye. The sun glimmered on something silver a second before there was a loud crack. Pain seared Riot's side. A crimson blossom appeared along with a hole where his flesh used to be.

Riot roared again and changed directions mid-stride, bearing down on the man holding the pistol. He caught sight of Nina bound to a tree. Tears streamed down her cheeks and blood covered her shirt.

"Get out of here. It's a trap!" she screamed.

Riot switched directions again and ran toward her.

"Watch out for the snares!" she shouted.

He stepped on one and it sprang up toward the treetops. It yanked Riot's right foot out from under him and toppled him onto the ground.

"We got him, Hank!" The man who'd shot him shouted. "We got the big one."

"He's not down yet. Finish him off." Another man stepped out from behind a tree and raised the barrel of a longer weapon and pointed it at Riot's head.

Nina jerked at the ropes binding her. "No! Don't shoot him! He's the Great Bear. You can't kill him."

The man snorted in disbelief and took careful aim. "He's just a bear."

Riot jumped to his feet. He raised his free paw, spreading his massive claws wide, then sliced through the metal holding his right leg like it was fine lace.

"What the hell?" the red-haired man said, as he took a step back. "How'd he do that Hank? He shouldn't have been able to do that."

"Damn it, Mark! Shoot him! Shoot him now!"

Both men took aim. Riot's image wavered and he disappeared.

* * * * *

Nina shook her head to clear it. Her brain refused to believe what her eyes were telling it. The bear had disappeared. One minute, he'd been in front of her. The next he was gone. But bears couldn't just disappear, she reasoned. *They could if they were the Great Bear,* the little voice inside her head chided. She glanced around the clearing, but there was no sign of Riot.

"Where'd he go?" Mark scoured the clearing, and then looked down the slopped hill. "Hank?"

"Shut up!" Hank shouted. "I'm trying to think." He walked over to where Nina was tied, to examine the ground.

Nina followed his gaze and noted the smeared bear tracks and fresh blood. Her heart slammed against her ribs painfully. The Great Bear was hurt.

"He couldn't have gone far. You shot him." Hank sounded far more reasonable than the situation called for.

"But he disappeared." Mark's brow furrowed, making it look like two red caterpillars were inching their way across his forehead. "Bears can't disappear."

Hank rounded on him. "Don't you think I know that? Shut up and let me think." After a few more minutes of silence, Hank approached her. "Why were you talking to it?"

"What?" Nina asked.

He backhanded her before she saw him raise his hand. "I'm going to ask you again. Why were you talking to that bear like it could understand you?"

Nina clenched her jaw, then turned her head to spit blood out. "I talk to all the animals. I'm a vet. It's what I do."

Hank smacked her again. "You were warning this one to

stay away. Are you somehow controlling it? Is that why it disappeared?"

"Are you listening to yourself?" she asked.

He raised his hand.

Nina flinched.

"I'm going to give you one more chance to answer. If you don't say the right thing, then I'll start to think that you've outlived your usefulness." He glared at her, but his gaze kept shifting to the woods around them.

"I didn't make the bear disappear. I have no idea how he did that."

Hank brought his face next to hers until Nina choked on his rancid breath. "But you do know more than you're telling us."

She started to shake her head no, but stopped short when she got a good look at his expression.

"Now here's what's going to happen. You're going to call out to the bear. Get it to come back from wherever it went. And when it does, I'm going to blow its head clean off its shoulders," Hank said.

"And if I refuse?" Nina asked.

"Then you'll be joining the bear in the afterlife," he spat. "Now call him!"

* * * * *

Riot's side burned, but the pain was nothing compared to the anger churning inside of him. How dare this puny male threaten Nina's life! He moved around the perimeter of the clearing, examining each trap that they'd set for him. It was easy enough to disable them, but he did so with care to make sure the men wouldn't immediately notice until it was too late.

He watched them take their positions on opposite sides of the small clearing. This would give them a clear shot at anything unfortunate enough to wander in. With any luck, they'd end up killing each other. Riot glanced at Nina. Tears still shimmered in her eyes, but her fear had been replaced by rage. He needed to get her clear before the men started firing. It would be all too easy for her to be killed in the crossfire.

He finished with the last trap, then made his way to Nina's tree. Riot needed to let her know that he was still there, but he didn't want to startle her. The men would notice and want to know why. He moved as close as he dared, then leaned in next to her ear. "Nina, can you hear me?"

She jerked to attention and slowly looked around.

"You're not hearing things," Riot said.

"How?" she whispered.

"How isn't important right now. What is important is that I get you out of here. Nod if you understand."

Nina gave him a slight, almost imperceptible, nod.

"Good. Now I'm going to slice through the ropes holding you. I want you to keep your hands in place until I tell you to move," Riot said.

Another slight head jerk.

"Call to him!" Hank shouted.

"Do as he says," Riot said.

She inhaled deeply and said, "Bear. Here, bear. Where are you?"

Hank scowled. "What in the hell are you doing?"

"I'm calling the bear like you asked me to," Nina said.

"That's not how you call a bear," Hank said.

"Well then how do you call one?" she asked. "I've never done it before."

Hank's mouth opened and closed as he searched for the words to reply. In the end, he said, "Just call him again."

Riot moved to the back of the tree and sliced through the ropes. He caught them before they could drop to the ground and gently laid them against the trunk. All he had to do now was get Nina out of the way and move her behind the tree. They'd fire the second they realized that she was loose. He'd have to put himself between her and the men, until she was clear of the gunfire. Riot's head swam. He reached down and clutched his side. Despite his current invisible form, crimson covered his fingers. He needed to get himself and Nina out of here before he lost consciousness.

"When I say go, I want you to shrug off these ropes and run. Don't stop. Don't look back. Just get out of here," he said.

"What about you?" she murmured.

"I'll be fine." And if he wasn't, at least Riot would have died honorably.

She turned her head toward the sound of his voice. "I'm not going to leave you. These men may not be bright, but they do know how to hunt."

"Who are you talking to?" Mark asked. "She's talking to someone, Hank. I heard her."

Hank stepped forward and looked around. "There ain't no one here."

"I'm telling you. I heard her," Mark insisted. "She's whispering to someone or something."

"Who are you talking to?" Hank asked.

Nina shook her head. "No one."

"Only crazy people talk to themselves," Mark said.

"Call the bear again," Hank ground out between clenched teeth.

"Go! Now!" Riot shouted and shoved Nina to the side.

* * * * *

The ropes dropped from her wrists a second before Riot pushed her. Nina stumbled out of her bindings, and scrambled on her hands and knees to get away. She still couldn't see Riot, but she knew that he was there.

"Get her!" Hank shouted.

A roar shattered the silence. Something shimmered like sunlight on water and Riot appeared.

"Shoot him!"

Shots rang out. Bullets struck the trees around her. Nina ducked her head and kept moving. She stopped when she reached a dip in the woods and dropped to her belly, waiting.

Cries, grunts, and screams filled the air. She thought she recognized Mark's voice at one point, but the warble was cut short. Fear gripped her as shot after shot punched the air, deafening her. Gunpowder clogged the small clearing until she could no longer see the truck. There was a loud crash, then Riot stumbled out of the putrid cloud, his fur covered in blood.

Nina screamed and jumped to her feet, racing toward him. She didn't see the other men.

His eyes were glazed and it seemed to take him a moment to recognize her.

"I have to get you back to my office. I have…" Her vet go bag. They'd tossed her kit and her purse into the back of the truck, when they'd abducted her. Nina ran in the direction of the vehicle.

Fear slowed her limbs, when she finally spotted the beat up truck. What if Hank and Mark weren't as hurt as they seemed? What if they caught her again? What if they shot her? She heard a loud animalistic moan. None of that mattered. Riot had saved her life. And right now, he needed her.

Nina quickly scanned the area, then rushed forward. She grabbed her bag and purse out of the back of the truck and raced to where she'd left Riot. He was sitting now, his head sagging toward the ground. She glanced in the direction of the tree she'd been tied to. The cloud of gunpowder was beginning to clear. "We have to go. It's not safe. Can you move?"

Riot grunted and stumbled to his feet.

"Come on. This way." Nina guided him back toward the private property signs. They had to get off this land. It would be safer once they reached the Qualla Boundary or the park.

"Get on my back," Riot said. Each word took effort to speak.

Nina glanced at the blood dripping down him. "I can't get on you. You're bleeding too badly."

He looked at her. "We don't have time to argue. The gunshots will have drawn attention. There were too many to go unnoticed. I don't want us to be here when the bodies are found."

Her eyes widened. "You killed them?"

Riot shook his massive head and swayed. Nina reached out a hand to steady him. "I only wounded them. They shot each other."

She nodded in understanding. "I still need to get you back to the clinic. I have more medicine there and better equipment."

"My health and safety isn't important. Yours is." He took a shuddering gasp.

Nina crossed her arms over her chest. "Says who?" She didn't know a bear could look exasperated until that moment.

"Just get on," he grit out. "I won't be able to stand for much longer.

Against her better judgment, Nina slung her purse over her shoulder and climbed onto his back. Riot staggered, then seemed to get his balance.

"Hang on," he said.

His fur was wet with blood, making it slick to the touch, but Nina did her best to cling to him. She leaned over her bag and held on to his sides. Despite his many injuries, Riot took off, leaving the carnage behind.

* * * * *

CHAPTER NINE

Riot took her deep into the forest.

"The trees look different here. Familiar…yet, I've never been here before," she said.

His big body staggered. Riot couldn't seem to focus. The trees swam before his eyes. He could smell the lake up ahead. All he had to do was make it to the water. "Hang on." He groaned.

Nina sat up. "How far have we traveled? I've lost track, but I know it's been quite a distance." She squeezed his fur. "I don't see anyone following us and I can't hear anyone. You need to stop. You are bleeding too much. I have to take a look at your wounds."

"We're almost there." His garbled voice ended with a moan. He'd lost more blood than he realized. He needed to shift, but he couldn't—wouldn't do that, with Nina on his back.

The trees parted up ahead. A small lake lay beyond, mist rising from its placid surface. Nina slid off his back. Riot kept walking. If he stopped, he'd collapse.

"Where are you going?" she asked. "Wait! I have the medical kit right here."

He didn't answer. Couldn't. Riot stepped to the edge of the lake, leaned forward, and let gravity take over. His big body fell into the water, disappearing below the surface. The splash sent ripples cascading outward.

Riot swam for the other side of the lake, switching forms multiple times as he did so. The cool water burned his skin as the bullets made their way out of his flesh, slowly sinking down to the murky bottom. He stroked harder. His wounds were already closing. He was no longer bleeding. In another day, his injuries would disappear, except for the scars.

He glanced down and saw his small shuttle resting beneath him on the lake floor. Riot debated whether to climb inside. Hiding in his craft would be taking the coward's way out. He knew that, but what if Nina wasn't there when he surfaced? What if she was so frightened by everything that had happened that she'd abandoned him? Then another thought occurred to him, what if she was there? What if when she saw his human form she was frightened?

Sure, they'd danced the previous night, but he hadn't exactly been honest with her…about anything. Riot didn't think he could handle seeing rejection on Nina's face. Not after everything they'd been through. He hesitated underwater, knowing he'd have to surface soon.

* * * * *

Nina stood on the shoreline staring at the placid surface. She didn't recognize this lake and she knew *all* of the lakes in the area. Where were they? Where was Riot? He should've surfaced by now. She scanned the lake looking for a hint of bubbles. Was he drowning due to his injuries? Pain sliced her at the thought of losing him. Nina didn't think, if she had, she would have realized how ridiculous her actions were. Instead, she stripped off her clothes and prepared to jump into the lake to save him.

The second her toes touched the frigid water there was

another loud splash. This one on the other side of the lake. Nina looked up, expecting to see the Great Bear.

A dark head surfaced. Broad shoulders and a muscled back followed it. Water dripped down the man in rivulets. As he walked forward out of the lake, it became apparent that he was naked.

Nina's mouth dropped open. "Riot?" She stepped back from the water and stared. She couldn't help it. She'd never seen anyone quite so beautiful. So perfect. He walked onto the shore and turned toward her. If her jaw could've gone any lower, Nina was sure it would've been dragging on the ground.

She'd been wrong about his beauty, but not about the perfection. He was massive. Her gaze traveled from his feet to his head. She did a double-take, when she reached his waist. *Who wouldn't?* It wasn't everyday a woman encountered that kind of endowment. Their eyes met and in an instant, Nina knew who he was.

"It's you." The man from the wedding reception. The man she'd danced with. The man she'd dreamed about. The Great Bear. But how?

"It's me." He hesitated but a moment, then continued walking toward her, closing the distance between them. His gaze took in her swollen face before moving on to the cuts on her arms and across her abdomen. "I am so sorry that I didn't reach you in time," he murmured. A distance of only three feet separated them. It might as well have been a continent.

"How?" she asked, even though her brain registered that it was a stupid question. He was the Great Bear. The Great Bear had powerful magic and he'd just proven it again.

Riot gave her a sad smile. "I'll explain everything, but first let me tend to your wounds."

A nervous laugh bubbled out of her throat. "I'm the one supposed to be helping you." She looked at him. His face had a vicious scar running down the side of it. She hadn't noticed it in the candlelight or perhaps she'd just been too mesmerized by his soft brown eyes. Smaller scars crisscrossed his hands like he'd been in so many fights that they'd given up hope of trying to heal properly. Fresh pink skin covered the spots where the bullet holes had been. The scratches and scraps had scabbed over. She couldn't see any blood anywhere on him.

He glanced down at her. "Why did you take your clothes off?" he asked.

Nina crossed her arms over her chest, covering her underwear, and looked around for her clothes. She'd forgotten for a moment that she was nearly as naked as him. "I was about to jump in and save you. I didn't want my clothes weighing me down."

Riot arched a brow and a smile played at the corners of his sensual lips. "In my *Other* form?"

Nina felt her face heat. "I know it wasn't my brightest moment, but I couldn't just let you drown. You saved my life."

White lines bracketed his mouth. "I allowed them to touch you. In that regard, I failed."

She picked up her shirt, but he stopped her before she could put it on. Nina looked at him questioningly.

"You're still bleeding. It has slowed, but I can get it to stop. I can make sure that there are no scars," he said.

She glanced at his hands.

His smile widened. "It's too late for me."

"How can you heal me? I only brought medicine for animals." She pointed to her bag.

Riot shook his head. "I won't need your medicine. I have medicine of my own. But I will need you to close your eyes."

Nina hesitated, but then complied. She realized that even though she'd only known Riot a couple of days that she trusted him. He would not harm her. He'd been injured trying to save her life. He'd earned her trust and more. She heard him take a step closer and she swallowed hard. A warm hand brushed her hair out of her face. Nina sucked in a surprised breath.

"Don't move." His breath brushed across her lips, making them tingle.

"I won't."

* * * * *

She hadn't run. She wasn't scared. Something inside of Riot burst, leaving his two hearts strangely tender. Absently, he rubbed a hand over his chest. He'd known Nina was special when they'd met. He just hadn't known how special until now. Was she the one? He thought so. He hoped so. What he was about to do wasn't solely for altruistic reasons. Yes, he wanted to heal her wounds. It was his fault that she had them. Had he been faster, those men would've never been allowed to touch her.

He winced as he looked down at the cuts covering her smooth skin and the bruise on her cheek. Riot would heal her. But he also wanted—needed—to see if Nina was a compatible mate for him. There was only one way to do that. Riot's conscience warred with his need, and lost. If she was compatible, then what he was about to do would start the bonding process. He closed his eyes and allowed his body to dissolve. The second his form disappeared, Riot stepped forward and passed through Nina, leaving bits of his essence, his very being, behind.

Gooseflesh rose on her arms. "Whatever you're doing tingles."

"Stay still." Riot reversed direction. More of his essence filled her, healing her body, while attempting to bond to her. If the bond didn't take, then Nina wasn't his mate and his time here would be over. But if it did…soon Nina would start to change and he wouldn't be the only Great Bear wandering these woods. Riot looked at her face. Her eyes were still closed, but her lids trembled. "You can open your eyes now."

Nina's eyelids fluttered. The lovely brown looked the same as it had upon their first meeting. There wasn't even a hint of a red ring that came with a Phantom bond. It was still early. These things didn't happen instantly. Riot forced himself to be patient though it pained him to do so.

She stared at him, then glanced down at her body. Her hand rose to skim the now healing wounds. Her mouth opened and closed as she gave him a questioning look. "There's no pain."

"No, but you'll be tender for another day. What I've done should take care of the damage and leave no scars." Riot couldn't seem to tear his gaze away from her lush mouth. She looked so bewildered and confused, yet somehow remained utterly enticing. How did she do that? No other human female had managed it.

As if feeling the heat of his stare, her tongue darted, wetting her bottom lip.

"Forgive me," he said.

"For what?" she asked.

"For this." Riot pulled her into his arms and took her mouth in a searing kiss.

* * * * *

CHAPTER TEN

Heat exploded the second his mouth touched hers. Nina couldn't seem to catch her breath as she was swept up in a whirlwind of sensation. As a bear, he was fascinating. As a man, Riot was lethal. More lethal than any man had a right to be. She'd gotten a taste of it at Kim's reception, but this was like being on the receiving end of a cannon blast. His mouth fed from hers, nibbling on her lips, begging for entrance.

Everything tingled from the top of her head to the bottoms of her feet. Riot ran his tongue along the seam of her mouth. Nina opened on a moan. Flames leapt inside her as their tongues touched and explored. Her hands fluttered to his chest. The second she made contact, Riot flinched, his hard body going even more rigid.

The world around them dimmed as Nina sank into the kiss, giving back all the passion that he was imbuing. Her body temperature rose until it felt as if her skin would crack. She stepped closer, burrowing into his chest. Nina needed the contact. Wanted it more than her next breath. Her nipples beaded against the hard muscled slab of his abdomen, leaving her breasts aching.

How long had it been since a man held her like this? Nina couldn't remember. She'd been so busy taking care of everyone but herself. Oh how she'd missed the simple pleasures of touch, the sharing of one's breath.

Riot's hand gently grasped the back of her head, turning it slightly so he could deepen the embrace. It was as if he feared that she'd break. She was stronger than that. Nina vowed to show him just how strong she was, starting now. She returned his passion with the flame of her own, igniting them both. He growled. The sound rumbled down her throat, settling between her thighs.

Need burst inside of her. Nina hooked a calf around his thick, muscled leg. She wasn't tall enough to get it any higher, but she was prepared to climb him if necessary. Riot groaned, then reached down to scoop her up, saving her the effort. The second her core made contact with his rigid length, Nina's eyes rolled back in her head. She would've ripped at his clothes had he not been naked already. She ground her small body against his hard shaft, rotating her hips in order to reach her clit. Sensation rocked her and she shuddered.

Nina threw her head back and gasped. "I need more," she said.

Riot grunted, then moved toward the trees. When they reached one that had its trunk hollowed out, she noticed a small pack sitting inside of it. He didn't put her down. Instead, he grabbed the pack and shoved one hand inside it. He came out holding a blanket. It didn't look like much, but Nina was too far gone to care. She didn't think she'd feel the ground right now, even if he laid her on sharp rocks. She needed release. She needed *this* release. It had been far too long, since she'd allowed a man inside of her body.

He laid the blanket onto the ground and fiddled with something on the side of it. The blanket inflated. "Now," he said, carefully placing her onto the makeshift bed.

Nina sank into the 'blanket', its thinness deceptive. She

couldn't feel the ground below her.

Riot followed her down, covering her with his large body. "Am I hurting you?"

She frowned. "No, why would you think that?"

Red blossomed in his cheeks. It was followed swiftly by a wave of insecurity.

She wouldn't have believed it if she hadn't seen for herself. What had caused this magnificent man to feel so unsure?

"If you hadn't noticed, I'm rather large," he said.

Nina's lips quirked. "Yes, you are." She glanced down at his erect shaft. "You won't hear me complaining."

He snorted, but there was no mistaking the relief in his red-ringed brown eyes. Riot's hands shook as he slowly stripped away her bra. His breath caught as he stared down at her erect nipples. His gaze moved to her face, his expression full of wonder. "You are beautiful."

Nina released a breath she hadn't known she'd been holding. She had never been ashamed of her body, but she was well aware that she was average. Nina had always been okay with that. She'd long ago accepted that she'd never be one of the pretty people. But for some reason, it was important that Riot not think so.

His head lowered, but he never took his eyes off her face. Riot latched onto one nipple and sucked it between his teeth. His eyes fluttered shut for a second and he gave a pleasure-filled moan. His gaze flashed back to her face, gauging her reaction. Nina bit her lip and smiled.

Bolstered by her response, he reached up and kneaded her other breast, while he feasted on the first one. His clever tongue swirled around and around, flicking and lapping the pebbled flesh until Nina writhed beneath him. Riot released her nipple and blew a hot breath across the puckered skin, before switching to the other breast. His free hand pinched and played until her breasts grew heavy.

Nina rocked her hips, brushing his shaft encouragingly.

She still had her underwear on and desperately needed to feel flesh upon flesh. The second time she nudged him, Riot must've gotten the hint because he reached down and ripped her underwear off her body, quickly tossing them aside. Her sex brushed his testicles and Riot shuddered. His erect shaft seemed to grow even larger, thickening and lengthening like a Leviathan rising from a sea of dark curls. He sat up suddenly and took her mouth in another savage kiss.

"Not yet." He groaned against her lips. "First I want to taste every inch of you." With that said, he slid down her body and buried his face between her thighs.

* * * * *

Riot couldn't seem to get enough of Nina's unique aroma or the taste of her. She was tart and honeyed all at once. He kept glancing at her face to make sure what he was doing was pleasing to her. Fear still rested firmly in the back of his head that with one wrong move he could injure her like he'd done to the only other person he'd ever been with.

He quieted the nagging voice with a vow to take care, then stared at the dark curls covering her sex. They were soft beneath his large fingertips. He carefully spread her, then slid his tongue along her moist seam, taking in her juices. Flavor that could only come from the Goddess burst inside of his mouth. He ran his thick fingers over her, spreading her wider, revealing the hidden bud that held so much pleasure for Earth women. He sucked on it, worrying the bundle of nerves with his teeth, while swirling his tongue around it.

Nina's hips rocked and her thighs shuddered.

The beast inside him roared. It wanted its own taste. It wanted to mark the female with its pheromones. Riot kept it in check. He couldn't afford to let his *Other* side out. Not until he knew that a bond had been created. Not until he could claim her completely.

He plunged his tongue into her scorching channel and

flicked it from side to side. Thanks to his *Other* side, his tongue was longer than usual, able to reach places that no human male could.

Nina cried out as he curled his tongue and found the patch of sensitive nerves inside of her.

Riot pinched her clit and continued to tongue her until she quivered on the edge of release. He doubled his efforts.

A second later, Nina cried out and her juices flooded his mouth. Riot lapped up every drop as he savored what he'd done. When the last twitch stopped, he gave her sex one last long lick, then rose above her body and positioned himself at her entrance. He waited until their eyes met, then he leaned down and gently kissed her lips.

"Thank you for trusting me," he murmured, then rocked back with his hips and plunged inside of her.

Despite the moisture easing his entrance, Riot still had to work his way into her body. Nina was a small woman by Zaronian standards and he was a *huge* man. For one fearful moment, he thought he might not fit. Sweat broke out across his forehead. The Goddess wouldn't give him such a precious gift only to take it away. Would she?

His fears were eased when Nina tilted her hips and relaxed her body. She ran her hands over his shoulders and pulled him close, clutching him like she'd never let him go. Something inside Riot exploded. Something he'd fiercely guarded. His eyes burned. He quickly looked away, not wanting her to see the turbulent emotions she'd churned up.

"It's okay," she whispered. "I'm fine. This feels wonderful."

Riot closed his eyes and began to move.

* * * * *

Nina felt every last inch of Riot's long, thick shaft as he drove in and out of her body. For a moment, she'd feared that he'd stop. He'd looked so scared, so insecure that it nearly broke her heart. Someday she'd ask him what had happened. It had to be a woman. Of that there was no doubt. But what kind of woman had wounded him so badly that he doubted himself?

Whoever she was, Nina had the overwhelming urge to strangle her. How dare she destroy such a sensitive, caring man! She'd just have to show him that the woman was wrong, starting now. Unchecked emotion flowed through her, surprising Nina with its intensity. Their eyes met and held. The brown had faded until all that remained was softly glowing red. It was a swift reminder that she wasn't dealing with a man. Riot was something *other*. It would do well for her to remember that fact.

He rolled his hips, sending himself even deeper inside of her. Nina's breath caught as the heat inside her began to build once more. Her fingers dug into his back, tearing at the skin.

Riot growled and thrust harder.

She felt another orgasm building inside of her, tightening her skin, sharpening her senses. Her womb clenched as her nipples scrapped along his muscled chest. The over-stimulated flesh was so sensitized that the pleasure bordered on pain. "I'm…I'm." Nina gasped, then locked her legs around his tight bottom and held on as the world shifted around her. Her body spasmed and she cried out, a second before she bit him on the shoulder.

The moment her teeth sank into his flesh, Riot grunted and went wild above her, driving in harder and faster, all sense of rhythm lost. Nina released his shoulder and hung on. He thrust and thrust, his powerful hips rolling madly as he locked himself deep within her fluttering channel. Riot grunted. His big body strained, then shuddered, as a wave of moisture flooded Nina.

Nina lay in Riot's arms, her body still twitching from the amazing orgasms he'd wrung from her only moments ago. She'd never felt the kind of connection she'd had with him.

It was like they were one and the same. Yet, that was impossible. He was pure 'magic'. Next to him, Nina was painfully aware of her fragile humanity.

She stroked his biceps, following the nicks and healed cuts with her fingertips, amazed again at how quickly he'd recovered from the bullet wounds. She reached his massive hand and interlaced her fingers with his. Riot gave her a gentle squeeze. He felt so strong, so content beneath her that she hated breeching the tranquility, but there was something she desperately needed to know.

"How did you heal me?" she asked.

He took a deep breath, and for a moment Nina thought that he might not answer. "I shared my essence with you."

She shifted her head higher onto his chest, listening to his heart beat. It was strong, steady…and doubled. She jerked her head up to look at him.

"What's wrong?" Riot asked. His dark eyes were slumberous and filled with satisfaction.

"Your heart…"

"What about them?" He hoisted himself up onto one elbow.

Nina's brow arched. "Them?"

Understanding dawned on his face. "I forgot that humans only have one heart."

"I didn't know that the Great Bear had two," she said.

Riot grew concerned. "About that…we need to talk."

"Sure, but first I need to know more about your ability to heal."

His face flushed.

Nina studied his expression. At first glimpse, she'd thought that she had somehow embarrassed him, but upon closer inspection she recognized the color shift for what it was—guilt. What did he have to feel guilty about? She pushed the thought aside. There was plenty of time to find out later. What she needed to know couldn't wait. "Can you heal anybody?"

Riot sat up, his dark eyes growing wary. "Why do you want to know?"

"Someone I care deeply about is ill. Doctors can't do anything more for him. I thought maybe you could..." her voice trailed off.

Pain shredded Riot's two hearts. She cared for another. Why hadn't she said something before she gave herself to him? *You didn't give her the chance,* a gruff voice admonished in his head. They'd shared such passion that he couldn't imagine her experiencing the same with another.

Perhaps that was ego on his part or more likely wishful thinking, but he hadn't imagined her wild abandon or her passionate cries. They still rang in his ears. He swallowed hard, choking down the rock that had suddenly formed in his throat. It took him two tries to speak, but he finally got out what he needed to say. "It doesn't work that way."

"What do you mean? You were able to heal me." She glanced down to her chest and abdomen. "Why can't you heal my grandfather?" Desperation filled her voice.

Shame drowned him as he realized his earlier mistake. How could he believe that she'd betray another? Nina had shown him nothing but loyalty, and at the first chance to return the favor he'd failed. She wasn't talking about a man. She was referring to her blood. Even with the new circumstances, it didn't change his answer.

Riot rose, unable to bear looking upon her pain-ridden face. "I cannot."

"Cannot or will not?" Bitterness disbursed some of the desperation in her question. He'd seen that look on other faces. It was the look one got when a loved one was facing death.

Riot didn't think the pain could get any worse, but he'd been wrong. He was about to destroy their fragile connection and there wasn't anything he could do to stop it. He took a deep breath. "Cannot. I am a great bear, but I am not 'the' Great Bear."

Nina's chin dropped. "I see," she said, though he knew she did not. She wanted a miracle, but there was no bargaining with death. Sometimes you could escape it, but there was no avoiding forever. Every warrior knew that in his bones. Phantoms lived far longer than Earthlings, but still they died. Such was the way of the universe.

"Then why did your ability to heal work on me?" she asked, ignoring his confession about not being the Great Bear.

"You are different," he said. "Special." She just didn't realize how much. And he had no idea how to explain.

Her lips tightened. "Just not special enough to help. Is that it?"

"You know it is not." Riot reached for her, but she stepped out of reach and went in search of her clothes.

"Why did you let me believe that you were the Great Bear?"

"At first, I was too shocked by the fact that you weren't frightened of me. Later, I didn't know how to bring the subject up. You were invested in me being the Great Bear," he said.

"Didn't know how, or didn't want to?" she asked.

Riot opened his mouth, then closed it again. The truth was he hadn't wanted to tell her for fear she would leave. He knew now that had been a mistake. "Come with me," he whispered, laying his soul bare to her, though he knew the answer before she replied. He could see rejection floating in her dark brown eyes.

"I can't." She sobbed. "I can't just leave him alone. He needs me."

He looked at her. "I need you, too." It was the truth. She was his only hope. All he really wanted. Riot couldn't imagine anyone ever taking her place. He knew everything he needed to know about Nina. She was brave, fearless, and strong. Her mind was quick, and she stood up for what she believed in. That was important to him. It was also why he would have to let her go.

Tears swam in her eyes. "He needs me more."

Riot gave her a slow nod. "I understand." And he did, but that didn't stop the pain from ripping him apart. He'd done his best to find a mate. He glanced at Nina. She was everything he could hope for. And everything he'd never have.

"I better get you back home. Climb on," he said, then shifted to his *Other* form.

* * * * *

Chapter Eleven

They didn't speak on the long walk home. What was there to say? Riot had lied to her. And when she'd needed him and his abilities the most, he'd let her down. Nina knew she wasn't being fair, but the painful disappointment left no room for rational thought. She left Riot standing at the edge of the trees, his big body quaking with emotion.

She could feel his hot gaze burning a hole in her back, but Nina couldn't bring herself to turn around. She was afraid if she did, she'd cave in and go running back to him. Even though he'd lied about who he was, part of her still wanted him. It didn't make sense. And neither did his explanation about his abilities.

How could he possess so much magic and still not be able to help her grandfather? It didn't seem right. And it damn sure wasn't fair. Like a flash fire, her anger erupted to life, then quickly burned itself out. She might be healed, but she still felt bloody and raw. She rubbed a hand over her chest to ease the pain. It would never truly go away.

Nina wasn't really mad at Riot. He was just an easy target, a gentle giant who wore his hearts on his fur-covered sleeve. No, the anger came from the sense of helplessness that she'd been feeling since her grandfather had taken ill. No matter what she did or who she prayed to, her grandfather was still going to die. And when Harold passed, she would be the last of her bloodline. The last of her family. Truly alone.

Her heart clenched as she pictured Riot's face. He'd been so disappointed. So hurt. But she had to say no. What choice did she have?

She scrubbed a hand over her face. Death sucked!

Nina pushed her way inside her house and closed the door. Tears stung the back of her eyes, blurring her vision so much that she almost missed the blinking light on her answering machine. Like most modern women, she had a cell phone, but it rarely worked since her house was tucked between the mountains. She walked across the room and pressed the button.

"Ms. Whitetail, we need you to come to the hospital immediately. It's about your grandfather, Harold Twofeathers—" The message cutoff abruptly.

Nina's heart dropped. She rushed into her bedroom and quickly changed her clothes, then grabbed her purse and keys.

* * * * *

Riot had failed her when she'd needed him most. And worst of all, he'd lied to her by omission. What kind of warrior lies to a potential mate? Not one with any kind of honor to be sure.

He slowly turned and walked into the woods. There was nothing left to do now but return to the ship. With Nina's rejection, he'd finally given up on finding a mate. His commander would just have to understand. He wasn't going to return to Earth again. He'd taken a shot and had failed. Nina's face flashed in front of him. Okay, maybe he hadn't totally failed. He had after all found the woman he wanted for a mate and lost her.

The thought of being ordered to seek another didn't sit well with him. It would be Nina or no one. And since she didn't want him—at least not enough to come with him—it was an easy decision. Besides, as far as he could tell, the bond hadn't taken. One more sign that they weren't meant to be. The truth only made the pain worse.

Riot made his way through the forest and returned to the lake he'd created to keep his ship hidden. He grabbed his backpack and pulled out his wristband. He slid his finger across the surface, finding the invisible button with ease. He pressed it, and the water surrounding his ship evaporator into the air, forming a thick white cloud, emptying the lake in seconds.

He dropped the wristband back into the pack, and climbed down the slope. He opened the hatch to his ship and crawled inside. The metal creaked then settled under his weight. Riot sat at the control panel staring at the instruments as if he'd never seen them before, his mind once again betraying him with thoughts of Nina.

He growled in frustration. It wouldn't do him any good to sit here and sulk. He'd lost. There was no going back. She'd made her decision. "Get on with it," he muttered under his breath.

Riot concentrated on making his flight suit materialize. Thin fabric rolled over his body, cocooning his skin until he was covered from neck to toe. His pressed his large palm to his chest to check the seal. It was secure. Riot started his preflight checklist. Flipping switches and sliding his fingers over panels, he checked all the instruments.

Lights dimmed and panels chirped as the shuttle pulsed with power. He was almost finished when he glanced out the window and noticed his pack sitting next to a tree. Riot cursed loudly and powered down, stopping the checklist just short of liftoff. He climbed back out of the craft, dropping down into the muddy 'lake' bed, then slogged back up the hill.

He gathered his backpack and started to close it. As he reached for the sealer he noticed the blanket he'd made love on with Nina, sticking out of the top. Riot clenched the material and brought it to his nose and inhaled. Nina's sweet scent filled his lungs. His whole body stiffened as need threatened to buckle his knees.

He glanced back at his ship, suddenly torn. It was ready. All he had to do was complete his checklist and the shuttle would liftoff and return to his ship. His hands automatically clenched the blanket tighter. He was a warrior. A Phantom Warrior. Was he really going to give up this easily? What if the bond was just taking extra time to form?

The beast inside of him roared to life. Riot tried to calm it down, but there was no soothing it. The beast wanted its mate. It wanted Nina. And so did Riot. But how could he get her to leave with him? She'd made it perfectly clear that she wouldn't and couldn't abandon her family. Riot understood loyalty, probably better than she did. But that still didn't help the problem at hand.

Nina wanted him. Riot was sure of that. She wouldn't have surrendered to him so fully had some part of her not known they were meant for each other. But how could he get her to see the truth, when she was so blinded by pain? He would never and could never force her. She'd never forgive him and he wouldn't be able to forgive himself. She had to come to him willingly. There was no other way.

Riot stared at his ship for a minute longer, then reached inside the backpack once more for the wristband. He pressed a button and the door to the shuttle closed with a clank. Once it had sealed, he pressed another. The air above the shuttle began to swirl and churn, growing thicker and darker with each pass. The cyclone hummed, picking up loose debris as it grew in size. It built and built until there was nowhere for it to go but down. When the cloud thickened to the point that he could no longer see through it, Riot slid his finger across the wristband. With a splash, the churning mass dropped into the dip in terrain, filling the space. Gone was the shuttle. In its place stood a tranquil lake once more.

* * * * *

Nina made it to the hospital in record time, but could barely remember the drive. Her heart pounded until she could hear nothing else. She ran into the hospital, ignoring the startled stares. She pounded the elevator button as if that would somehow make it come faster. The chime rang and the doors slid open. Nina rushed inside, earning a scowl from the people trying to exit. The second the last one made it out the door, she pressed three and hit the 'close' button. Every floor the elevator passed felt like an eternity.

The doors finally opened and Nina jumped out. She bypassed the nurse's station, ignoring their shouts for her to wait. Instead, she sprinted to her grandfather's room. She was running so fast that she had to grab the doorway to slow herself down. Nina slid into the room and came to an abrupt halt. A neatly made bed sat next to the window, waiting for its next patient. The uncomfortable cream chair she'd spent hours in had been pushed over to the side. Her gaze swung to the adjoining bathroom.

"Grandpa?" she called out, moving toward the closed door.

Soft footsteps stopped behind her and a gentle hand touched her shoulder.

Nina shrugged her off. She didn't want to know what the nurse was going to say. "Grandpa!"

The nurse waited patiently as she searched the empty room again. "I'm sorry, but he died a few hours ago."

"No! You're wrong," Nina said, hearing the desperation in her voice. He had to be here. He couldn't have died when she and Riot were...

Oh God! Her eyes closed and she sank to the floor. "I'm

so sorry. I'm so sorry. I should've been here, so you weren't alone." Nina rocked back and forth, as the tears spilled from her eyes. Why hadn't she been here? Because she was being selfish, that's why. Instead of sitting with Harold during his last minutes on Earth, she'd been making love to the Great Bear. No! Not the Great Bear—an impostor.

The nurse grabbed a tissue box and handed it to her.

Nina barely noticed as guilt ravaged her. She didn't want comfort. She didn't deserve comfort. She should've been here so that Harold didn't have to die alone. The pain in her chest exploded, winding her. Nina's head spun.

"Breathe, you need to breathe," the nurse said.

"It hurts too much," Nina gasped.

She gave Nina a sad smile. "I know, and I'm sorry." She reached into her pocket and pulled out a folded envelope. "He left you this," the nurse said. She handed Nina the envelope.

Nina recognized her grandfather's rough scratchy penmanship on the outside. "Where is Harold's body?"

"As per his instructions, we have sent his remains to the crematorium," the nurse said. "He was very exact in his instructions. He didn't want you to see him once he died."

A fresh wave of pain struck, stronger than the first. Even in the throes of death, her grandfather thought of her. Too bad Nina couldn't say the same. "Can you give me a minute?" she asked.

The nurse nodded in understanding. "Take all the time that you need," she said, then slipped out of the room, closing the door behind her.

Nina rose from the floor and placed the envelope on the small side table, and walked over to the bed. She ran her trembling hand over the crisp sheets, then crawled on top. The room had already been sanitized. It no longer smelled like her grandfather. She gripped the thin pillow to her chest and squeezed it tight. Tears came again. This time harder. Nina didn't bother to hold back. Her whole body shook as she sobbed out her grief. How did any human survive this kind of pain? She didn't know. Didn't want to.

An hour passed before Nina could bring herself to get up. How was she going to live without Harold? Her grandfather was her world. Her everything. And now he was gone. She crossed the room and picked up the envelope. Nina held it to her nose and inhaled deeply, as if doing so would somehow bring him inside of her. She tore the envelope open and peered inside. There was a letter. Her fingers shook as she slid the paper out and carefully opened it.

Dear Little Deer,

I knew the time was near for me to join our ancestors. I didn't tell you because I did not want you to wait by my side. This is one journey we all have to take alone. Do not be sad for me, for soon I shall see my precious daughter and your father. I cannot wait to tell them all about your adventures with the Great Bear. They will not believe it. Though they'll immediately know why he has chosen you. You are truly special. Your life was magical before, but now you've been given the greatest honor of them all. If you choose to follow the Great Bear into the sky, know that your ancestors will be waiting for you when it is your time to come home.

Love,

Grandpa

Fresh tears dropped onto the paper. Nina gently rubbed the teardrops in, then folded the letter and put it back inside the envelope. There wouldn't be any more adventures for her. She'd given Riot her answer. By now, he was probably on his way home. Wherever that may be. She glanced out the window at the sky as the sun dropped below the horizon. She didn't see Riot. She didn't see anything, but her dreams fading before her eyes.

* * * * *

Chapter Twelve

It took a week for the funeral home to get Harold's ashes prepared. During that time, Nina buried herself in work, avoiding home as much as possible. She was at the clinic, when Sheriff's Deputy Rick Hensen stopped by in the afternoon, to ask her if she knew anything about the deaths of two hunters.

Nina told him about the kidnapping and promised to fill out a formal report. Rick was shocked and asked her why she hadn't come to him for help. She was honest and said after the last time she didn't think reports from her would be welcome. Rick assured her that wasn't the case and hinted about them going out on a date once she was feeling up to it.

Nina had only nodded, though she had no intention of taking him up on his offer. How could she, when her heart belonged to another?

She left the clinic and headed to the funeral home. Her grandfather's ashes had been placed in a plain wooden box with a screw top lid. It looked like something she might've put spices in, which for some reason made Nina smile. The box definitely fit Harold to a tee. She thanked the funeral home director and tucked the small box under her arm. Nina climbed into her truck and started the emotional journey to *Kuwah' hi*, the sacred mountain known to outsiders as Clingman's Dome. There among the highest reaches of the Smokies, Harold would find his rest.

Nina drove the winding road, climbing higher and higher into the mountains to reach the spot where the Great White Bear ruled the spirit world. She couldn't help but think of Riot as she neared the top. "I wish that you could've met him, Grandpa. You would've really liked him," she said. "He was huge, but such a gentle soul." She downshifted with a thunk, as her truck protested the climb.

She glanced at the plain box, hoping for a response, but none came. So Nina continued. "I think I made a big mistake," she said. "Riot asked me to go with him and I sent him away." Pain blossomed and it took two tries to clear her throat. "I wish you were here, Grandpa. I don't know what to do."

Have faith, Little Deer.

"That's easy for you to say. You're not here. You don't have to wait on anything, anymore."

Believe in the Great Bear. Trust in the stories.

"I do believe in him, but I did reject him, Grandpa. For most guys, once is enough," she said, carrying on both sides of the conversation. Nina knew what she was doing was crazy, but it did bring her comfort, if only for a little while. Despite what her *'Grandfather'* had told her, Nina didn't really think that the Great Bear would return.

He's not the Great Bear, she reminded herself. He's just *a* great bear.

Nina snorted. Like there were dozens and dozens of them wandering through the woods. She made the final turn to reach Clingman's Dome. The Smokies were living up to their name today. Earlier it had been sunny, but now low clouds hung in the sky, crossing over the road in front of her. She slowed her speed and continued on until she reached a safe spot to pull over. She chose one of the many lookout locations, then shut off her engine.

"This is it, Grandpa. The end of the line." She brushed loving fingers over the smooth surface of the box and glanced out the window. The air seemed sweeter up here, somehow fresher. "You always loved this place for mystical reasons and for its beauty. I hope you can find peace here. I have no doubt that you will." Nina swallowed hard past the lump in her throat. "I will visit as often as I can. You know that I love you. I'll always love you…no matter where I am." She took off her seatbelt and gently lifted the box off the seat.

The truck door groaned as Nina opened it. No one was around thanks to it being low season. Nina walked around the front of her truck, carrying Harold's remains with her. The wind caught her hair, lifting it away from her face. She stared out over the mountains, drinking in their beauty. "You were right to pick this place, Grandpa. It's perfect."

Nina took a deep breath and slowly unscrewed the top of the box. She held it up to the sky offering Harold's remains to the Great Spirit. "Take care of me, please," she murmured, then slowly turned the box over. The ashes were immediately caught by the wind and carried away. Nina watched them go, her emotions churning with a mixture of happiness and sorrow. "Bye Grandpa. Godspeed."

When the ashes were well and truly scattered, she closed the box and turned to walk back to her truck. It was then that Nina caught a flash of brown fur, hovering near the tree line. Her heart raced with excitement. The brown bear ambled out of the woods, dashing her spirits once more. It was just a normal bear. Nina stared at it in disappointment. *What did you expect? Riot is gone.*

The second it caught sight of her, it took off in the other direction, crashing through the trees. Nina had no idea how long she stood there, staring after it or why she bothered, but for some reason she couldn't bring herself to leave. It was only when the sun dropped below the mountains that Nina knew she had to go home.

She placed the box in a litter receptacle and drove back down the mountain. There was no use keeping it. Harold wasn't in it. And she didn't need it as a reminder that he was gone. She felt the loss in her bones. Just like she felt the loss of Riot, though in his case it was a different kind of loss, a different kind of heartache. Nina had no illusions about both taking a long time to heal.

It was dark by the time Nina arrived home. She'd stopped for some fast food to kill time, but it had only bought her forty-five minutes. She pulled into her driveway and turned off the key. Nina crawled out of her truck and walked toward her front door. At first, she didn't see anything, then the shadows shifted and she jumped back. Her eyes hadn't adjusted to the dark well enough to tell who it was, but she could tell the mass was male.

"Rick, is that you?" she asked. Nina really wasn't up to entertaining anyone tonight, especially not Rick.

"No," the voice growled as anger seeped into it.

Nina's heart kicked in her chest. She'd know that voice anywhere. Was it really possible? Had he come back? "Riot?" All her hopes and dreams of the future were riding on the answer to that simple question.

He stepped forward cautiously, almost as if he were afraid that she'd send him away.

"I was hoping it was you," she gasped and rushed up onto the porch.

Riot automatically opened his arms and caught her.

"I didn't think I'd ever see you again," Nina said.

"Does that mean you wanted to?" he asked.

She looked up into his face and grinned. "Silly, silly man. How could I not?"

His brow furrowed. "But you sent me away."

Nina stepped back and her chin dropped. "I know. So much was going on. I just couldn't handle anything else, including you. You came into my life like a storm, sweeping me up, making me forget about everything…at least for a little while."

"I am sorry about your grandfather," he said.

"How did you know?" she asked.

"I wanted to leave. Started to. But something kept me from going. It was you," he said softly. "I just couldn't imagine my life without you." Riot took a deep breath. "So I stuck around. Waiting. Watching. Listening to you cry, when all I wanted to do was rush over and hold you."

Nina shook her head. "But you didn't."

"No, I couldn't. You needed time to grieve," he said. "I know you still need time, but my time is short. I had to take one more chance before I left for good."

Nina opened the door to her house and turned on the light. "Please come in."

* * * * *

Riot's hearts were hammering in his chest. What if she rejected him again? What if he'd made a mistake by coming here? He watched Nina put her purse down on the table. She played with a stack of mail on the table, straightening an already neat pile. Was she stalling because she didn't know what to say to him? Blood roared in Riot's ears as something akin to panic struck.

"I know I am not much to look at," he said. "But I vow that I will always take care of you and treat you well. My fealty normally lies with my King, but I'd gladly transfer it to you, if you'd find it in your heart to give me another chance and come with me."

Nina turned to look at him. She seemed to search his face. Looking for what, he did not know. It was only when the light struck her brown eyes that Riot noticed the ring of red around the outer part of her iris. Elation filled him, but he quickly stomped on it. She hadn't given him her answer yet. Until that happened, he would assume nothing.

Time seemed to run backwards as Riot waited. Torture, pure torture. He dropped to his knees before her. "Please Nina, I must have your answer. I do not think I can last another moment without it."

Her lips twitched, then spread into a smile. "Yes!" she said.

"Yes?" he asked, fearing he'd heard her wrong.

Nina nodded her head. "I said, yes."

Riot jumped to his feet and pulled her into his arms. His lips brushed hers, then deepened into a passionate kiss. His muscles locked as her body softened against him. Riot wanted to throw her down right here, right now, but there wasn't time. He forced himself to let her go.

"Thank you." Nina had slipped beneath his defenses, easily dismantling them until all that remained was love. Their bond would continue to grow and soon there would be two Great Bears roaming the wilds of Planet Zaron. He couldn't wait to show Nina his world and the mountains that existed there.

Nina wasn't sure why he was thanking her, but she knew she'd made the right decision. There was no doubt in her mind. Her grandfather would approve. She looked toward her ceiling and thought of Harold. *Thank you, Grandpa, for bringing him back to me,* she thought as she squeezed her eyes shut.

"We need to gather your things and go." Riot brushed her cheek.

Her eyes opened. "Right now?"

"Yes," he said.

In the end, it didn't take long to get her things together. Nina didn't want or need much that was left in the house. She wrote a note to the clinic. The sheriff's department would eventually find it. Rick would only stay away for so long before he came looking for her. She wanted to make sure that no one worried, especially her best friend, Kim. She placed her things by the door and turned to look at Riot.

"Where are we going?" she asked.

He grinned. "Where else? The sky."

Four hunters had chased the Great Bear into the sky, but they hadn't managed to permanently bring him down. Yet one woman with soft brown eyes and a big heart had slayed him with a smile.

Riot planned to work hard every day to keep that smile on Nina's face. If he was able to do that, then he'd die a happy warrior. Until then, he planned to live with his new mate, love without restriction, and enjoy every moment they shared together.

* * * * *

Riot held the summons in his hand as he pushed open the stone doors to enter the Great Hall. He couldn't keep the smile from his face, as he strode down the long aisle toward the man seated on the crystal throne.

King Eros looked up when he entered, his aqua blue eyes watching him closely as he approached. A pale brow arched as he took in Riot's grin. "I heard your search was successful. I wanted to see for myself, now that you've had time to settle in."

Riot dropped down onto one knee. "That it was, Your Majesty."

"She must be quite a woman to put up with you," he said.

Riot's grin widened. "That she is."

"I look forward to meeting her," the King said. "Did you have any trouble this time around?"

Riot thought about mashed potatoes. "Not at all, Sire. Everything went smoothly."

Eros' lips twitched. "Is that so?"

Riot met his gaze. "As good as I could hope," he said.

The King stared at him for what felt like an eternity.

Riot fidgeted under his unwavering regard. Already he

longed to return to Nina's side. He'd left her lying in bed, sated and sleeping. Riot had promised to take his new mate to the mountains today. No way would he disappoint her. Not even for his King.

The silence stretched between them, thickening the air.

Riot thought about deep fried shrimp Po Boy sandwiches with remoulade sauce and fries. His stomach growled loudly, shattering the tense silence.

King Eros laughed. "I see that you did not take my advice."

"What advice was that, Sire?" Riot asked, genuinely confused.

"You didn't eat before you came to see me." The King chuckled.

Riot's face flushed. "Won't happen again, Sire." But they both knew that it would.

"Go enjoy your new mate, Phantom Riot. Take good care of her," the King said, dismissing him.

He rose from his kneeling position. "I will, Your Majesty. That's a promise." One promise Riot could keep.

* * * * *

The forest rose like a Leviathan around Nina, blotting out the light green sky and dual orange moons. If not for the trees' anise-colored bark and dark purple leaves, she'd swear Redwoods surrounded her. Except this wasn't Earth. It wasn't even the same solar system. This was planet Zaron.

"What do you think?" Riot asked, indicating to the mountains ahead. His expression remained open, hopeful. It was one of the many reasons that she loved him. He rarely tried to hide his emotions.

Nina stared at the jagged range. It reminded her of the Grand Tetons...if they'd been injected with steroids. "Impressive." And they were. The whole place was amazing. Very different from Earth, but not in a bad way. It was just going to take a while to retrain her brain to accept all the new sights, sounds, colors, and aromas.

"Do you like it?" he asked. The same insecurity she'd seen in his eyes the first time they'd made love appeared in a flash. Her answer meant a lot to him.

Nina nudged Riot with her fur-covered shoulder. The tension left him, replaced by relief. Nina was still getting used to shape-shifting into a bear. It had taken what felt like forever to learn how to walk on all fours without falling over. Her speech still wasn't clear, but somehow Riot understood her. "I love it," she said. Her voice was garbled like she had a mouthful of gumballs. "And I love you."

His muzzle dropped open in a distorted smile, then Riot rumbled. "Let's get going."

Nina nipped at his flank and took off running. Her big paws slapped the ground as she raced through the trees. The sweet scented air filled her lungs, making her euphoric. She couldn't outrun Riot and really didn't want to, but it was always fun to try, since he had an *enjoyable* way of punishing her, when he finally caught up. These woods weren't like the ones in the Smoky Mountains, but with Riot by her side, it was home.

Other Books by Jordan Summers

Phantom Warriors 1:
Bacchus
Phantom Warriors 2:
Saber-tooth
Phantom Warriors 3:
Talon
Phantom Warriors 4:
Arctos
Phantom Warriors 5: Linx
Phantom Warriors 6: Riot
Hawk's Slave
Phantom Warriors
Anthology Volume 1
Phantom Warriors
Anthology Volume 2

Atlantean's Quest 1:
The Arrival
Atlantean's Quest 2:
Exodus
Atlantean's Quest 3:
Redemption
Atlantean Heat 3.5
Atlantean's Quest 4:
The Return
Atlantean's Quest 5:
The Dark King
Atlantean's Quest Bundle
Volume 1
Atlantean's Quest Bundle
Volume 2

Dead World Prequel:
Raphael
Dead World Prequel:
Kane
Dead World 1: Red
Dead World 2: Scarlet
Dead World 3: Crimson

Moonlight Kin 1:
A Wolf's Tale
Moonlight Kin 2: Aidan's
Mate
Moonlight Kin 3: Nic
Moonlight Kin 4:
Tristan - Coming Soon

Tears of Amun
Heat of the Night
Gothic Passions
Rose's Rapture
Paris After Dark

Ghost Hunter:
Solomon's Seals

Private Investigations
Mesmerized
Hot Shot
Ride Em' Cowboy
Off Limits

About the Author

Jordan Summers has thirty-one published books to her credit and has sold over 145,000 ebooks. She's a member of The Horror Writer's Association, International Thriller Writers, the Author's Guild, and Novelist Inc.

Connect with her online:
Twitter.com/jordanwriter
www.facebook.com/authorjordansummers
www.JordanSummers.com
Join the Endless Summers Newsletter to find out about upcoming releases and author signings.
http://www.jordansummers.com/contact/